PRAISE FOR *THE W...*

"In prose elegant and sensuous, Rosanna Staffa brings robustly to life Renata, an acupuncturist in Minneapolis, who returns home to Milan to see her dying father. As this novel richly unfolds, her journey also becomes one of memory and matters of the heart. Sensitive, yearning, and hopeful, Renata is caught between 'venturing into the wilderness' and 'driven by a longing to belong.' As a vibrant Milan opens before us, with family tales and love stories, we see a woman daring to be joyful and, traveling through her past, finding a way to become new."

—Roy Hoffman, author of *The Promise of the Pelican*

"In her first novel, *The War Ends at Four*, Rosanna Staffa writes with elegance and conviction of the darker sides of life—the pain of loss and regret, the finality of death and of roads not taken—but her true gift as a writer shines in the warmth and agility of her prose, the desire and passions of her characters, and the hope that exudes from these fluid and nimble pages. This is a novel that grabs your heart in unexpected ways—one that can take your breath away like a strong shot of grappa, yet demands to be savored like a fine Brunello di Montalcino. Escaping into this story was, like a longed-for trip to Italy, a once in a lifetime experience that will challenge your expectations of how far a novel can transport you and illuminate your understanding of what another person's story can teach you about your own. *Magnifica!*"

— Rachel M. Harper, author of *The Other Mother* and *This Side of Providence*

"It's hard to say which comes more to sparkling life in Rosanna Staffa's magnificent debut: the rich cast of characters, or the city of Milan they inhabit. Papoozi, Tito, Renata, you'll feel you've lived and lost with them, and been found again. Their lives are beautiful, heartbreaking, unforgettable. The entire novel is. You won't be able to put it down once you pick it up, so plan accordingly. And look for more brightness from this rising star. I'm already impatient."

—Peter Geye, author of *The Ski Jumpers*

"This is an extraordinary novel of glance and gesture—one of the finest I've ever read. How to know your essential self? How to know that of another? If you're a galloping reader, Horseman, pass by. Here, a warm eye is cast on the mille-seconds of feeling and meaning—the real stuff of life. Stay, read on: All your senses, attention itself, will be enriched."

—Sena Jeter Naslund, author of *Ahab's Wife, Four Spirits, The Fountain of St. James Court*, or *Portrait of the Artist as an Old Woman*

"There is a burnished glow to Rosanna Staffa's gorgeous first novel, *The War Ends at Four*, which has the singularity of a fingerprint: no one else could have written it. But like Elizabeth Hardwick in her great novel *Sleepless Nights* (first published in 1979), Staffa's writing has the luminous quality of a sensibility forged by time and experience, thought and feeling. Witness these two passages: 'Like the abstract art she would grow fond of, Chinese medicine was a representation of the world the way she experienced it and was unable to define, so fluid in its design that a new vocabulary was needed.' 'Her solitude in the house so fully absorbed her that once she started to sense her presence fading, like photosensitive paper exposed to light.' Staffa's prose is so packed with insight, delight, and—dare I say it?—wisdom, her metaphors, syntax, and word choices are so right, that one almost holds one's breath as one reads, waiting for a wrong move. Exhale, reader; it never happens. This is a bravura performance."

—Robin Lippincott, author of *Blue Territory: A Meditation on the Life and Art of Joan Mitchell*

"Rosanna Staffa's captivating novel, *The War Ends at Four*, is so fine, the language so startlingly fresh, bursting as it is with such dead-on accuracy and humor. The joy—and suspense—of turning these pages is to encounter life at its most spirited and unexpected. The enticement, too, is in the deeper, quieter folds of the story, where time flickers seamlessly between past and present. The book is powered by an intelligence deep and brave enough to face the full range of what life delivers. *The War Ends at Four* will make you glad to be alive, thankful to notice human quirks, small tendernesses, to feel the heat of longing and desire between lovers, to wonder at the vivacity and richness of memory."

—Eleanor Morse, author of *White Dog Fell from the Sky* and *Margreete's Harbor Playwright*

"Rosanna Staffa has written a luminous novel in *The War Ends at Four*. Acupuncturist Renata leaves behind her Minneapolis clinic and a faltering marriage when her brother, Tito, calls from Milan to say that their father, Papoozi, is dying. Memories of childhood unfold for Renata as the airplane hits the tarmac in Italy. Staffa writes about children, memory, love, and the words not spoken in a family in a magical way. She is an extraordinary writer."

—Maureen Millea Smith, author of *The Enigma of Iris Murphy* and *When Charlotte Comes Home*

"What's that they say about going home again? In *The War Ends at Four*, Rosanna Staffa raises the question afresh, with an intriguing Italian lilt. Over a few jet-lagged and feeling-full days in Milan, the protagonist Renata feels roots coming loose from San Francisco to Napoli. This starts as soon as the Old Country calls her back— a family crisis— and before long she confronts similar identity shifts in everyone close to her. At dinner, the meal may be sumptuous, but the table seems to tremble. Yet amid all the turmoil, Renata finds ways to keep her feet, a plucky new heroine of the Italian diaspora."

—John Domini, author of *The Color Inside a Melon*

"What a beautifully complex novel about reaching out and

letting go, about the blurry borders between past and present. In Staffa's generous voice, Milan becomes the reader's home, Renata our closest friend."

—James Tate Hill, author of *Blind Man's Bluff*

THE WAR ENDS AT FOUR

Rosanna Staffa

Regal House Publishing

Published by
Regal House Publishing, LLC
Raleigh, NC 27605
All rights reserved

ISBN -13 (paperback): 9781646033317
ISBN -13 (epub): 9781646033324
Library of Congress Control Number: 2022943761

Cover images and design by © C. B. Royal

Regal House Publishing, LLC
https://regalhousepublishing.com

Printed in the United States of America

For my family

1

Renata secretly lusted for other people's lives. She liked to guess what was missing between the lines she overheard at bus stops, in cafes. At the end of her second year in Minneapolis, spoken English was still a bit difficult for her, and when she was tired, the words bit with tiny teeth. Just a few months before, she'd occasionally stopped mid-sentence, trapped in a blur of English and Italian. She loved that fear, like when she pedaled faster and faster on her bike at night in Milan until the wind closed her ears to any sound but her breathing.

She delighted in visiting thrift stores, a marvel that did not exist in Italy. The names themselves—Goodwill, Arc Value Village, Steeple People—sounded like discarded marquees of dubious establishments. Her father would have called them the ruin of the spirit, deadly traps of memories and relics. He'd thought that longing was an illness, not understood in all its gravity by the afflicted. By her.

The Goodwill near the College of Alternative Medicine she'd attended was Renata's favorite. It gave her comfort, the way entering a church did for others. In the eyes of the customers, the merchandise seemed magically altered into a thing of beauty: no longer chipped cups and crude postcards, but seashells to be picked up on a beach. She'd learned in acupuncture classes that things were not what they seemed. Her breathing quickened each time this point came up. During clinic practice, she still marveled that she could visualize precisely but not see the pathways of energy vibrating at the insertion of the needles, nudging the patient's body to heal itself.

Even more extraordinary to her, during the breaks between classes Dr. Chen Yi Min, the master of acupuncture from Shanghai, went to splash water over his pale face, then smoked a cigarette. He ate greasy pork from a tin lunch box. No incense sticks, no grim diets; acupuncture was science to him, and the energy of the *qi* a kind of electricity to tap.

The final exam to obtain the acupuncture license was a practical test, the diagnosis of patients, and a detailed written treatment plan. Dr. Chen observed in attentive silence. Some of the patients, rumor had it, were actors and some Dr. Chen's cousins. They were paid a nominal fee and given lunch.

For the occasion Renata bought a white shirt for $3.99, labeled Anne something or other. End of my student visa, she told herself while putting it on. End of life in America, unless she pressed her instructors about a possible future at the clinic. Standing in her professional outfit, she felt as weightless as a paper boat. She'd slept badly—the jitters, lack of faith. Her father always suggested the need for a ruthlessness of desire, a kind of arrogance successful people had.

She thought of the old Italian school primer she was so fond of: little Maria had three apples, her dog had four legs, her bird two wings, and there were five steps to her front door. Renata always wanted to be Maria and live in a house with one window per room, where nothing ever happened but math. Nothing at all was desired, and never would be.

She'd arrived early at the clinic and picked up her lab coat. In the designated treatment room, a warm breeze wafted through the open window, and a young man in a light shirt stood looking outside with his back to her, hands in his pockets.

He turned when she walked in.

"Oh, I'm early. I'm your ten o'clock patient." he said. "The doctor, right?" His hair was light brown, thick and unruly. His eyes conveyed a hint of teasing, a suggestion that he knew more about her than he should.

"Oh, well. It's me," she said.

"I'm a doctor too." He grinned. "On stage."

She smiled. At twenty-five, the term *doctor* seemed somehow untrue. "Not yet. This is my final exam." She regretted her words almost immediately; her voice sounded as thin as a child's caught sneaking candy.

"By the way, I'm Steve."

"Renata."

"I feel a bit on edge too," he said. "We have something in common, see? Performance anxiety."

"Oh, I could not be an actress," she said.

"You never know," he said.

"I do. An actor, hmm? Interesting."

"Interesting? It's like nothing else."

"They say that about everything." She gave a light shrug, but any desire fascinated her, the more passionate the better, whether for something totally impossible or for merely a cigarette.

"Well, doc, frankly, acting is my drug of choice." His laugh was soft. "But I'm not here for a detox treatment. The problem is when I'm not on stage. I'm sitting at home a few days, and even coffee seems different, weird. And everything else does too." He opened his arms. "You don't know."

But she did. Her last day off, she'd run a bath, pouring water over her chest and belly, feeling the warmth. She'd eaten toast with butter and jam, licking the jam from the spoon. Life had seemed to recede, with only a sputtering of sounds trickling in—phones ringing, cars screeching. And something floated up—a buzz of cicadas, and herself as a child, standing at a gate, with roses for her mother's grave, her father giving her a little push, pointing the way, and she, not moving, as if this refusal kept her mother from truly being dead.

"I made you sad? Nah," the actor said. "I talk big, but on stage, I'm just a parrot repeating the words of others. And there are better parrots." He made a dismissive gesture. "I'm just nervous, and I'm talking nonsense."

"No, no. And no reason to be nervous, you'll be fine, whatever made you come here."

"Curiosity, mostly. And a free lunch." He shrugged. "The reasons that typically get you in trouble."

"They didn't tell you? Today is like a rehearsal. I don't needle you, but I am going to ask you a few questions, press the tip of my fingers on your wrists, look at your tongue. That's all. Then my supervisor will do the same. Today is diagnosis only."

"That's a bit of a letdown. All the fuss and I'm an understudy."

"Oh no. Not in my script. You are *the* patient for me, the one who can tip the balance," she said.

"Now that's something, but you must hate this test, and me," he said. "It's all right. I get my strongest emotions when I inspire dislike in an attractive woman. Look, I'll be cool, I promise."

She liked men uncool, rough around the edges, with a scratch of bitterness late at night or after one glass too many. The last one had left her, then returned again and again like a jazz refrain.

Dr. Chen walked in, nodded, then stood by the wall.

"Let's do it," Steve said. "Shall I tell you I'm afraid of gaining weight, losing hair, getting wrinkles?"

"You can tell me anything." She smiled, taking notes. "In fact, you should." She asked him the usual questions about food and sleep, but their exchange somehow felt more exhilarating than usual. She sensed in Steve a flutter of apprehension, which transformed him into a real patient. Vulnerabilities, imaginary or real, always touched her and inspired her to use every tool at her disposal to ensure her patients' wellbeing. In those moments, she felt her warmheartedness as a strength rather than a trait her father deplored.

She'd encountered traditional Chinese medicine for the first time in Milan as an entry in an encyclopedia. She had felt as if she were venturing into the wilderness, catching only a flutter, a flickering of what lay ahead. She hounded librarians, seeking more books on the subject. Like the abstract art she would grow fond of, Chinese medicine seemed a representation of the world the way she experienced it and was unable to define, so fluid in its design that a new vocabulary was needed. She relished the qi's symmetry in the cosmos and under her skin as a promise of harmony.

She glanced at Dr. Chen and started writing notes. Steve's Five Elements were in good harmony but suggested an agitation of the Wood meridians that, if unattended, might lead to back pain and a wandering, uprooted spirit. Interestingly, it was a pattern she shared. Did he also have dreams of rain? she wondered. Wood meridian dreams. At the end of the examination, she wrote a treatment plan, added an herb formula, and handed it to Dr. Chen, who carried out his own exam. Afterward, she walked Steve out of the room and to the exit.

"So," he asked, "am I prey to some terrible destiny? My financial condition aside."

"Not at all," she said. "Nothing out of the ordinary."

"Just as I feared." She liked his focus on her; it suggested the thrill of impending disorder.

Large acupuncture charts hung in the hallway with male figures drawn in hieroglyphic-like poses, meridian pathways tracing their way across their bodies.

"You look at naked men all day?" he said with a twinkle in his eyes.

"Yup. It's part of the training."

"Well, I undress women on stage, and kill men," he said.

"And move on?"

"My best quality. I'm always someone else. Somewhere else," he said.

There was a short silence.

"Expats are always somewhere else. Someone else," she said.

A rush passed between them. She noticed the monochrome of the hallway, the blinking neon lights, and the clicking of heels. There seemed an artificiality to everything but the two of them together, looking at each other.

He jotted something down on a piece of paper and handed it to her.

"Here is the address of the theater. Come see me tonight. Just don't fall in love with the doctor on stage; he is nothing but a shadow. But feel free to fall in love with me," he said. "It's a small theater right in Minneapolis. I only work in town, playing musical chairs with the same venues. I'll get you in free of charge, of course."

"Oh, I'm not sure I can make it." Renata's voice was barely audible, so that her watchful self, the one who would respond *no, I absolutely can't* in a panic, was not stirred.

"Suspense is fine, keeps it all fresh. I'll just be wondering, hoping," he said. "I'd like to know what you did with the tips of your fingers on my wrists, what was speaking to you. All the secrets. The show is at seven p.m., the innocent hour, too early for anything interesting in life. Come, then you can tell me if I'm a good doctor. All right?"

"All right, I'll try." She smiled.

"Aahl-right. I like your accent. And everything else about you so far. Do you like beer?"

"Yes."

"We'll have some afterward. Italian?"

"The beer, no. Me, yes."

"I read once that in Rome there is a crypt adorned with the bones of monks," he said. "Talk to me over a beer about things I know nothing about. I love it. The beer is on me, to celebrate your becoming a doc. I'm sure you aced the test. Will I see you? Yes?"

"I'll try to make it, but I do have other plans." She saw her room in a shared apartment, with a large Law of the Five Elements poster pinned to the wall with thumbtacks, a bed, a small bookcase, and not much else. She liked the unadorned efficiency, which Dr. Chen highly recommended, as it allowed the mind to roam freely, but her roommates hinted that it evoked a feral loneliness rather than the harmony of feng shui.

"I might have to take a rain check," she said.

"'Lord, what fools these mortals be!' Shakespeare," he said, in a playful tone. "Take me instead."

2

It was a difficult weekend in Minneapolis, with wind, snow, then rain. Steve had promised to call from California but did not. Renata hadn't been able to reach him; his cell phone was off, as usual. The receptionist at the theater in LA where he was in rehearsal, told Renata that she'd give Steve the message—her voice sluggish with late-night socializing. So who knew what would happen.

Renata stayed up late watching cartoons: mice and birds chasing each other, tap-dancing, going up in smoke. She felt restless, missing her cigarettes. In a fragment of a dream, Steve came in through the window like a burglar and told her that he'd fallen in love with a street musician on the Third Street Promenade and would not return home.

"Why stay awake waiting for me?" he'd always asked, when coming home late. Her answer contained a deeper question she did not want to put into words. He'd told her he'd been at the house of a fellow performer after rehearsal, and he maintained that the entire cast was there.

They talked again of traveling to Milan in the summer to see her father and brother; perhaps this year they would have the money. Dizzy from wine, Renata agreed. Her family rattled around in her brain like restless ghosts. *What are you doing there in America? Doing something good? What?*

Steve knew a few words in Italian but no verbs. He could not eat, sleep, or love in Italian. *Mangiare, dormire, amare.* He could not lie—*mentire.* She remembered his fling, years before, with a woman in Colorado crazy for horses. One time only in the five years they'd been together, he swore. His phone was still off. She could only wait. *Aspettare.*

❦

Weeks before Steve left for California, he sat at their kitchen table, highlighting a script he had just downloaded. Reading over his shoulder, Renata's eyes fell on the line at the bottom of page fifteen. *I feel I am—a creature of darkness.* Oh Lord.

"New play," he said, in a firm tone that made her look away. "A big theater in Los Angeles. It's a unique opportunity."

California. And what about me? Renata melted inside.

"Oh, well, let's hear it. Steve, go to page fifteen," she said, in a buzz of panic at the prospect of him taking a job across the country. *A unique opportunity, my ass.* That idiotic line she had caught a glimpse of would surely make him rethink accepting the role.

"Hmm. Let's see," he said. There was a little silence, the flutter of pages, his breathing.

"I feel I am—a creature of darkness," Steve whispered, with the softness of a private thought brimming to the surface for the first time, startling and innocent.

"Oh, Steve," she said, overwhelmed by emotion. Sensing it, he looked up and smiled. His delivery was astonishing, despite such asinine writing. Hollywood would snatch him up, or should.

"You can join me later," he'd tell her, whenever LA came up. "When things are clear." Things never were clear with Steve. Like a man with a chronic eye problem, he'd become comfortable with blurry vision. The truth was undefined, as were the gates between himself and the characters he inhabited. While Renata was driven by a longing to belong, he felt the lure of levitating. These were, in fact, the traits that had most fascinated her. Still did.

On Monday, she arrived at the clinic Wellness Within Acupuncture and Herbs right before Tessa, her colleague. Rain beat on the windows and Renata and Tessa worried about making rent. They'd plastered notices everywhere, advertising the clinic at local stores and the corner co-op. Renata could see shreds of the discolored flyers fluttering in the breeze like tiny flags of surrender. A brand-new poster was hovering over the flyers, in red-and-blue-crayon intensity, featuring Barack Obama's pensive face and the word *Hope*. A "Hillary Clinton for President" poster communicated a steely determination at the bus stop a few steps away. *Hillary should run Wellness Within*, Renata thought. *It could do with some Hillary efficiency.*

❧

Tito called from Milan while Renata was ripping the disposable paper from the treatment bed of the last patient, a dancer. A regular, he had come in, fussy and unshaven, for back pain.

"A twenty-dollar bill and two comps to see my show at The Pantages. Is that okay?" he'd asked. "It's not La Scala but—"

He was one of their many pay-as-you-can patients. One client had given her new sneakers, another read her Tarot cards. A few lawyers, a couple of financial advisors, and a butcher were keeping the clinic afloat. *A Fellini scenario*, Steve mused.

"You might not see me again, *Dottore*," the dancer said. "My back is doing great; you are too good."

"You did it yourself," Renata told him. "I just guide the flow of your energy. It's a bit like directing traffic."

"You do it well." He grinned. "Don't miss me too much, okay?"

She would miss him very much, just as she did all her other patients who had left their unfinished stories behind: a young woman who was going to cut off her hair in the spring; a painter set to ride a night train to his exhibit in Chicago; and a timid man who had moved to Atlanta to follow his new love.

"Let's grab a bite tonight," Tessa said, after the dancer had left. "We need to talk. We just got two new referrals, but we need to do some thinking and look hard at the numbers."

Accounting was Tessa's job. For Renata, numbers froze into a meaningless mass of dead insects when she gazed at them for too long. "What good is math in life?" her mother had asked a distraught little Renata, unable to comprehend the arithmetic lessons at school. Math would be, in fact, no good at all.

When the phone rang, Tessa picked it up. When one was busy, the other acted as the receptionist, which gave prospective clients the sense of a front desk, despite the fact that the waiting area consisted of two chairs lined up in the narrow hallway between the signs "Wellness Within" and "Cholodenko Violin Repair."

Tessa and Renata had agreed to always use the term *clientele* for the patients who came to Wellness Within, each seeking relief from either rheumatism, back pain, or migraines. Few of their patients could afford health insurance, and deals on payments were made and broken daily in a whirl of listless negotiations.

"A guy with an accent is on the phone. Says he's your brother," Tessa announced, loud enough that Renata could hear her through the half-open door of the treatment room. Tito only called at Christmas, if she didn't call first. Their exchanges were invariably short, breezy, and casual, by habit as well as the expense of long-distance rates. His voice always startled her—he sounded different without the visual of his pensive eyes and gesturing hands.

"Tito. Tell me," she said.

"Reni? Oh. Reni. Yeah, it's, uh, about Papoozi." Papoozi was their nickname for their father, a blunt man with frizzy white hair and an excess of cheeriness. "The doctor says—Doc-tor Erici, the one at the hospice—the Ospedale Sant'Erasmo, right?" He fumbled with language as if he were learning each time to speak anew.

"Tito! What are you saying?" But she knew, despite Tito's eccentric sequence of non sequiturs. God, it seemed, at last wanted to take Papoozi to Him.

Her father had lived so long that Renata had assumed God had forgotten about him, in his tiny Milan apartment overlooking the Centrale train station. She'd called him at Christmas, barely a month before, and listened to the ringing of the phone while he, as usual, looked around for his crutches. Then, his sudden energetic "*Pronto?*" as if he was ready for the excitement of all sorts of calls. Tito had tried to give him a cell phone, but Papoozi had found it too chaotic to manage.

"Tito. Tell me."

Papoozi's kidneys had given out, and he'd been taken overnight to the Sant'Erasmo Hospice, the only facility with an available bed. Renata was rattled by the vision of Papoozi being taken from his bed in the middle of the night. Surely he'd protested, rearing and threatening in his pajamas.

Doctor Erici requested that all relatives be summoned immediately, Tito told her. Neither Renata nor Tito could recollect the name, much less the address, of Papoozi's second cousin who lived in Naples. They remembered her from their childhood, bulky and sentimental, with a birthmark by her breast they had examined at length while she napped on the couch.

"And Flavia?" Renata asked.

"Ah. Called her already," Tito said. Flavia was Papoozi's long-time cleaning lady and lover. For twenty years, Flavia had been a presence in his life—every day but Sunday—with an air of cool detachment that reminded Renata of fallen nobility. Flavia came from Abruzzi, a barren part of Italy known for its ninety-nine fountains that dignitaries from Rome visited whenever an earthquake struck.

"Reni—" Tito said.

"I'm coming," she said.

"Immediately?"

Tito had frightened easily as a child. Birds, wind—all conspired to alarm him. He stammered while asking directions. He had been their mother's favorite.

"Don't worry. There is no use in worrying," she said, repeating the words that Papoozi had often told them while their mother was dying and too tired to see her children. They'd stood against the wall, just outside her sickroom. After she died, she left behind the memory of a Brâncuşi-like shape in the doorway, and a shopping list in her pretty handwriting—*cipolle, patate novelle, piselli*. Renata stored the shopping list in a box; she liked to keep track of things that never happened.

"Papoozi is very strong," she told Tito.

"I don't think so, Reni."

"I'm taking the first plane," she said, after a moment of

silence. It sounded like a phrase from some movie. Renata had left Milan seven years before, and the city always seemed both too close and very far. Her life in Minneapolis felt like a narrow escape from something dangerous but hard to define. As in her childhood war games, everything seemed both mysterious and terrifying. "I'll be there as soon as I can."

Renata expected Tito to ask her to stay at his place, but he did not. Maybe, she thought, he was confused and exhausted. Or perhaps it was something else. Her chest tightened at the thought of staying in the old house alone—she could not bear it. "You have a timid nature," Papoozi had told her once, raising a glass of wine in her direction as if the damning pronouncement was a toast.

"See you soon," Tito said.

Once in Milan, Tito would ask everything about her life. In the meantime, she hoped to come up with something that would make her look good.

O'Hare Airport was crowded, and Renata had little time to catch her final connection. She hurried to gate G-21 with half-laced boots and an unzipped backpack, her only luggage. Lines formed and broke in front of her. *Presto. Vai vai. Sbrigati.* Words in her head appeared and disappeared—there was no English for them. The maze of hallways went on and on. She was always almost there. She pushed her way through a group of travelers milling in front of a large-screen TV.

"Sorry, I'm a little bit late." Renata fumbled her way through shoulders and elbows. She heard herself say, "*Ima liddle bileat*," and her accent made her cringe.

Over the loudspeaker she learned that her flight had been delayed due to bad weather. She caught a glimpse of her reflection in a large window streaked with rain. Her features seemed held together by a tense singular thought: *I need to be home now* and then, before she could stop it: *it might be too late anyway.*

"There is still time," Papoozi had told her when, as a child, she'd burst into tears at being unable to swim underwater like a mermaid or memorize a poem. "There is time," he'd say, holding her hand.

Fairy tales, Papoozi would say, were foolish. So every evening during her childhood, Papoozi used to open the *Enciclopedia dei Ragazzi Mondadori* and read an entry in his gravelly voice. Renata had learned that songbirds lived for two years and mosquitoes for less than a month. She'd learned that air had memory, that every word ever uttered remained in the ether forever.

Hillary stared at her from the big-screen TV in a replay of the South Carolina debate from the night before. Obama refuted her accusations with precise charm, and Hillary's gaze turned toward the camera, piercing Renata with a fierce look. Renata admired how Hillary was buoyed by antagonism. I'll be back in time to vote for her, she thought, fortified by a sense of purpose.

Renata looked around the airport lounge for a quiet spot to call Tessa. She'd tried to reach Steve before she left home, but his phone was dead as usual. She'd told him innumerable times how important it was to keep it charged. Her anxiety intensified when she was unable to contact him. Her cheap cell phone produced static in most locations, and she felt a raw joy in finally acquiring good reception by the glass windows, her eyes fixed on the storm that lashed against the panes of the departure lounge.

"Hi, Tessa. Got a pen?" Her unmistakable accent made it superfluous to announce herself.

"Um, yeah. Go ahead." It sounded as if Tessa was munching on popcorn. They'd agreed not to eat popcorn while answering the clinic phone in the interests of professionalism, but this time it felt oddly comforting to Renata.

"This is really important. My cell phone doesn't work in Europe. If Steve calls, give him my hotel phone number," Renata said. "I'm staying at the Albergo Am-bro-gi-no, if he wants the name."

"Got it." For once, Tessa's wretched brevity felt efficient.

"And tell him I'll be back in one week."

☞

On the plane Renata sat by an elegant woman wearing a Hillary button on the lapel of her designer jacket. Renata felt discomfort at the idea of sharing a candidate with her, suspecting the woman had never walked on her tiptoes to preserve the heels of her good shoes.

An older man, with hair ruffled like the feathers of a sparrow, sat on her other side, his blue eyes framed by wire-rimmed glasses. He emanated the ineffable aura of a lifetime of solid values and honest labor.

"Going home?" he asked.

Renata sank deeper in her seat, deflated by the fatigue of the inevitable conversation to come. Whenever it was revealed that she was Italian, she was regaled by long-winded anecdotes about Venice, Florence, and Rome.

But the man only smiled when she nodded.

"Nice," he said simply. The hum of the plane swarmed around them.

For a moment Renata could maintain the fragile delusion that she, too, was traveling to Milan for a simple visit.

He also lived in Minneapolis, the man revealed, and while he found the winters hard, they were ideal for his love of cross-country skiing. In the warmth of his smile, Renata felt a surge of affection for skiing, forgetting that she had tried it only once at Cortina d'Ampezzo at the age of eleven and hated it.

Her seatmate was old enough to have been one of the American soldiers who'd liberated Mauthausen during World War II, saving Papoozi's life—he'd just finished digging his grave at Mauthausen and was about to be shot when *gli Americani* arrived to save him. "At the very last moment," Papoozi declared. No details, ever. Her father maintained a strong belief in the game of chance and the necessity to forge ahead in life without looking back. Of his time in the army, he said only that he had been captured by the Germans and was lucky to be alive. That was it.

In their childhood war games, Renata and Tito had impro-
vised.

"C'mon," Renata used to say to Tito. "Hit me." Tito would
give her a little jab. "Harder. Fight me. I'm a Nazi. You want to
die? Fight hard. The Americans might not come this time, no?"
If she could block him, again and again, he was declared dead
and couldn't eat the bread and Nutella Flavia had given them
for their four-o'clock snack.

"But it's four! It's snack time!" he'd protest. "The war is
over."

Renata had wanted to know where the prisoners washed,
where they ate and defecated. Who broke the rules and how
had they been punished?

"Did it snow sometimes?" she'd ask Papoozi, trying to elicit
more information with an innocuous intro.

Papoozi did not fall for it.

"Why talk about it? It's over," he would reply.

He refused to be the taxidermist of his own life. "An over-
burdened plane cannot fly," he told Renata, for she kept every
little thing, including broken pencils and rusty bottle caps.

After his wife's death, Papoozi gave her things away and for-
bade any mention of her. "Onward," he'd warned, as if guiding
them through minefields in a march to safety. Tito and Renata
scavenged for anything left of her. They found hairpins on the
floor and a small rosary between the pillows of the couch. They
could not remember the night she'd died, only that afterward
Papoozi had opened all the windows to let the wind inside.

It was now dark. The flight went through turbulent air pockets that kept Renata awake. Everybody went quiet on the plane
and put a great deal of effort into reading the duty-free catalog.

3

On the train from Malpensa's International Airport into Milan, Renata fingered the dead cell phone in her pocket; she found the gesture comforting. She felt a shot of anxiety as another traveler wondered aloud as to the good restaurants in Milan. She hoped nobody would discover her to be a local and ask for suggestions, for she knew only sketchy dives with no appetizers, just an occasional woman selling roses.

The train was almost empty by the time they arrived at Stazione Centrale, and Renata felt happy getting off alone in the milky light of a foggy afternoon. It was quiet under the high-vaulted ceiling of the station, until she walked out into the bustle of Via Ferrante Aporti. *Milano*, she thought with a surge of recognition. *Home.* She breathed deeply the damp smell of ancient tramways and wet cobblestones, mixed with a soupy effluvium that seemed to emanate from the walls of the city. Milan was the grandmother's attic she'd never had.

Despite the late-afternoon crowds, a hush seemed to hang in the air, a quiet that anticipated thick white moths of snow falling. She remembered a photo of herself as a child of six or so, standing stiff, chin up, with a tight grin. She'd always felt observed by an irascible audience when in front of a camera. In the photo her back was to the Duomo, a graying iceberg of marble, topped by a golden Madonna floating against the sky.

Pulling her coat tightly about herself, Renata turned down Via Ferrante Aporti. Young women, stylish in knee-length coats, walked with the surly, determined pace of models on a runway. She felt the old pang of being unfashionable, straining for nonchalance in her old black coat, fists clenched in her pockets. Her clothing, she knew, had rendered her nearly androgynous, devoid of the fashionable feminine allure so important in Milan. That old fear rose within her—that all passersby knew of her family's crappy underwear dripping dry over shower rods. Flustered, Renata hurried onward. She was indeed back.

The bearded, heavy-lidded man at the newspaper kiosk gave a cursory assessment to her legs when she stopped to ask for a newspaper. "*Il Corriere della Sera*," she breezily requested in her perfectly Milanese-accented Italian. Quickly, though, his attention turned to the coins she dropped in his plastic bowl.

"*Signorina!* This is change for what? Chewing gum?" he demanded.

The price listed in the upper corner of *Il Corriere della Sera*, she then realized, was almost three hundred lire—which seemed an exorbitant amount.

"Hey. All right, all right. I've been away a long time," she muttered, fumbling in her wallet. "It cost a few lire then. Okay? Yeah?" Her feisty Milanese attitude was as perfectly intact as her Italian.

"That long? You still have a Milanese accent."

Calculating that a cab at that hour would take too long, she bought a ticket to the subway in addition to her paper. The man passed it over to her with stubby fingers stained by nicotine.

"Germany? Switzerland?" he asked with genuine interest. They had reached closeness by attrition, the Milanese way.

"Nah. America," she replied.

"Oh dear, all the way there." He smoothed his sparse hair under his beret with a low whistle. "But you are home now. Nice, no?"

Renata gave him a distracted nod and hurried off. Living in Milan had not been easy either. She and Tito had been teased by bullies at school, called *terroni*, dirt-eaters, filthy southerners, just for having been born in Naples.

Terroni were deemed foreign to many Milanese, and their customs suspect. Little Tito used to walk close to her as they passed through the schoolyard, humming a tune to show that he was not afraid. "Stop that," she'd say, picking up stones just in case.

In Minneapolis she'd felt a lightness, as if the memory of childhood hostilities could be shed together with her native language, one word at a time.

"So, what's the big deal about being a Neapolitan in Milan?" an acupuncture patient had once asked her.

"We are considered of inferior status by many idiots," Renata had replied. "As a Neapolitan, you are often treated differently, offered lower-level jobs. And you are a bit grateful. Angry and grateful." She'd heard that things had improved, but her recollections of past slights were still sharp and cut deep.

"Well, I'm glad you're in America now," the patient had said. "Aren't you?"

"Sure, yes," Renata had replied; but she had missed the gruff Milanese manners that signaled familiarity, the cheap MS cigarettes—nicknamed *Morte Sicura*, which translated as "ensured death"—and the ancient *osterias* along the Navigli Canals, where after midnight a stranger would sing or play the guitar and daylight arrived reluctantly.

"And what else about Milan?" the patient had asked.

"Not much," she had said with a chuckle.

It was a lie. There had been a young man in Milan that Renata had fallen hard for, but he was not interested. She was too shy—the quiet type, she knew, the kind of private person that friends playfully chided to watch her blush. One evening at a party, she'd been alone in the kitchen when the young man, Cosimo, sought her out. They smoked together in a comfortable silence, as if they knew each other inside out. She'd returned to that memory sparingly over the years, as if reluctant to contaminate it. Cosimo was darkly handsome and possessed a quick urgency to his movements. Women were crazy for him. That evening, in the kitchen over cigarettes, Cosimo's casual glance had made her knees weak.

The light of the day was receding, leaving a familiar chill in the air. A soft gust of wind lifted dry leaves and sent Renata's long hair dancing upward in playful slaps. She wished Papoozi could be amused too, walking by her side.

The subway map showed a route to Ospedale Sant'Erasmo, where Papoozi was in hospice. The subway MMRossa, Linea 1, took her to the Gambara stop, with almost alarming speed. She was totally unprepared to see Piazzale De Angeli. So here Papoozi was waiting to die, she thought, in this treeless, gray-brown little square.

The massive Ospedale Sant'Erasmo was painted in ochre with an ornate archway leading to a spread of buildings beyond. Inside, in the foyer nobody sat at the switchboard. She hurried through the glass doors and into a windowless hallway, crowded with old people pushing walkers under flickering fluorescent lights.

"Excuse me, excuse me," Renata found herself saying in English, hurrying around old women in wheelchairs holding paper cups of juice, a biscuit and paper napkin in their laps. They seemed oddly self-righteous, refusing to make way for her. Perhaps this narrow hallway was their recreation area, she thought.

The fourth-floor hospice was an austere setting in pale blue. A male nurse approached her with a smile and a toss of his head that sent his long hair over one shoulder.

"Domenico," he said, offering his hand. "I'm the evening shift." He had a detectable southern accent, brilliant eyes, delicate features, and the perfectly designed lips of a Masaniello portrait.

Renata felt drained at the idea of having arrived with no clue about what to do, only a sense that she had to be here.

"I'm Renata. Nice to meet you," she said. "I am here to see—" *Papoozi*. She tapped the air with her fingers, searching for words. "Uh, my father—Cesare. "

"Oh, Cesare? Cesare is right here!" Domenico interrupted with a luminous smile, pointing to a half-open door to the right. A small rectangular tag hung on the wall with *Cesare* printed on it. Just his first name, as if it designated a child's coat hanger in nursery school. Renata felt a tight, strangled knot grip her chest.

Tito came to the door. There was a wild look to him, his eyes bright. He put his glasses on, then took them off, waving a hand in the air. "Reni, you are here," he said.

"Tito."

They stood at a small distance, like two potted plants marking the opposite sides of a doorway.

Renata hungered for a hug, but her family had always considered displays of affection excessive.

"Cesare!" Domenico called softly into Papoozi's room. "You have a visitor!"

Renata hurried in, then stopped, bewildered. Papoozi looked small, as if he were a child cowering under the bedsheets in a strange room. His expression was tense as if disturbed by Domenico's announcement. He opened one eye slowly, with much effort, and fixed it upon her with fierce mistrust. There would be no last words, she realized. His arms were lying limp on the bedsheets, covered with purple bruises from IV pricks. His skin was paper thin, the color of stagnant water. In Papoozi's one fluttering eye, she recognized a consciousness fighting to live on. His cracked lips bubbled with a sound that could have been anything.

"It's me," Renata said. "I made it." She touched his hand, brushing her fingertips over swollen veins and broken capillaries. He had no reaction to her touch.

On the nightstand she saw Papoozi's prized watch, the one reckless acquisition he relished. His watch, he'd claimed, was guaranteed not to miss one second in 100 years. He used to hold it up to her ear when she was a child. The whirring had felt like a tickle, and her giggling had delighted him.

"Your daughter is here. All the way from America," Domenico said, turning his attention to the IVs. "You just arrived, dear American lady, but I need to do something here. Could you leave Cesare and me alone for a moment?"

Stepping out, Tito led Renata to the end of the hall where

a small waiting area was dimly lit for the night. A thin man in slippers occupied one chair, smoking a cigarette as he thumbed through a worn *Oggi* magazine. The Marlboro in his fingers seemed jarring to Renata, until she realized that health restrictions made little sense in hospice.

"*Dear American lady?*" Renata muttered. "What the hell."

"Well, it's been years."

They stood, then, in awkward silence, shifting now and then on the edge of words.

"This is Signor Giovanni," said Tito at last with desperate cordiality, waving in the direction of the man in slippers. "He played the flute with Toscanini." The man glanced up from his magazine with the timid smile of an elf. "This is my sister, from America." *Buonasera.* Giovanni waved. *Buonasera.* She returned his wave.

"What time is it for you?" asked Tito.

"Who knows? Late."

"Yes, late is late. If you're tired, who cares what time it is," Tito agreed, with a nuance of challenge in his tone. Perhaps, she thought, this was something he had pondered behind his sales desk at the Mobili Garbatti furniture store, where he had followed in Papoozi's footsteps.

"Let's go back to Papoozi," she said. "He's dying. What the hell are we doing here?"

"Didn't you hear? We have to wait. Domenico *said—*" Law-abiding-Tito.

But Renata found comfort in standing next to someone who looked like her. Tito had the same small frame; they were both pale, with dark frizzy hair. Papoozi had kept a black-and-white photo of the two of them on his desk, taken after their mother had died, when she was ten and Tito six. They looked like two boys after a blunt haircut executed in the kitchen. They had the luminous beauty of Neapolitan street punks, or *scugnizzi*, as Papoozi had once been.

Signor Giovanni rose to his feet, glancing at her with a timid smile. "They serve dinner early here," he finally said.

This simple statement stirred anxiety in her—it seemed an odd observation.

"Ah, dinner."

"Early, like in America," Signor Giovanni added, his cheeks flushed. "I saw it in the movies."

Renata realized he was trying to be encouraging, letting her know she could look forward to something familiar.

"Why do we see so many American movies?" Tito said, with excitement in his voice for the animated discussion sure to follow. But Signor Giovanni had already turned to go, shuffling down the hall in his slippers. Renata wondered if it was appropriate to bum a cigarette at Ospedale Sant'Erasmo if one was in vibrant good health. Signor Giovanni's pack, she'd noticed, was full. She hadn't smoked in years because Steve hated it, but suddenly she craved the familiar unrolling of pungent smoke filling her mouth.

"I thought you gave up smoking," Tito said, catching her surreptitious glance.

"I did. Steve hates the smell," she said.

"Ah."

"And with my job, you know—" she added. But Tito did not ask about Steve, or her job.

A small TV was turned to the RAI 2 channel at a low volume; they could see a female announcer with a Modigliani gravity. Then the broadcast switched to footage of Barack Obama gesturing in rolled-up sleeves at an outdoor rally. His voice was dubbed and sounded sweetly off-kilter. The word *cambiamento*—change—crisp in English, rang with surprising harmony in the sequence of Italian vowels. Papoozi's magic word: *change*. His nemesis: *war*. Renata recalled that it had been Obama alone who had voted against the war in Iraq.

"War? A disaster," Papoozi used to thunder. "When cowards in charge play dress-up with uniforms and send others to die." Obama, this young intellectual from Hawaii, knew this truth. For a moment Renata wanted not to make a sensible choice and felt a rush of desire to give Obama her vote. A spontaneous, glorious act.

"Who is your candidate? Obama?"

Renata hesitated slightly before replying. "Hillary."

"Ah, well."

"Well, what?"

"Nothing." He shrugged. "Papoozi was wondering."

"If I like Hillary or Obama? That's what came to him, think-ing of me in America?"

"Well, I don't know," Tito said. "He also worried about the food."

"The food?"

"In America."

"You talked about what I eat? That's it?" She had fantasized about Tito and Papoozi peppering their conversations with questions about her life. *Does she think in English? Does she dream in English? What does she miss most about Italy?*

"Reni, we were having dinner together or something. It was just small talk. You left a long time ago."

"I did. It was supposed to be just two years, no? I met Steve and got a job. What's there to say?"

"There is nothing to say."

The windows in the hallway were closed shut, and the space felt suddenly tight.

"Papoozi wondered if you would have kids," Tito said.

"Oh no. I'm not the mothering kind."

"You were *bravissima* with me."

"I was a kid. I was terrible," she said. "*Un disastro.*"

"No," he said firmly. "You were not."

His conviction moved her. The little kid who had loved her so much was still there. Renata experienced a fleeting, delicate hope.

"Look, I'm sorry I left you," she said.

"It's okay."

The only sound in the hallway was now the hurried staccato of game shows. The hospice ward was eerily deserted in a way that reminded Renata of Edina's Southdale Mall at night, after the shops went dark and the last walkers in sweats shuffled out to their cars.

Tito nudged her. Domenico was gesturing from the door-way of Papoozi's room.

"Papoozi would want us to take him home," Renata said.

Tito gave her an incredulous look, then turned away. Just imagining the epic lunacy of kidnapping Papoozi from Ospedale Sant'Erasmo felt good to Renata anyway.

Papoozi, she knew, had always wanted to die in his apartment.

"*A casa,*" he'd insisted, banging his palms on the armrests of his armchair, sending the doilies aflutter. "Right here." He used to wander through the rooms at night, the town crier of the house. Little Tito and Renata stirred in their sleep, and all was well.

Tito and Renata returned to their father's room without another word. Papoozi wasn't the only one to find the idea of death at Ospedale Sant'Erasmo intolerable.

4

Papoozi was now alone with a young female doctor, who was standing at the foot of the bed with the quiet resignation of the last passenger on a subway platform at night. Her features were delicate, her light hair gathered in a loose chignon.

"Here is my sister," said Tito.

"Ah, you made it." The doctor smiled at Renata, offering her hand. Renata held the doctor's hand in hers a little longer than necessary, as this seemed to blur the truth that Papoozi was dying. "I am Doctor Erici. You are the American daughter?" *A-me-ri-can-a.* The word stretched in Italian.

"I just live there."

Now Renata detected a repeated gasp in Papozzi's breathing; she sensed a wedge trapped between one breath and the next.

"New York?" the doctor asked.

"Minneapolis." *Small talk, really? Was Papoozi breathing normally, then?* Perhaps Dr. Erici was deliberately casual so Renata would remain calm. *On the contrary,* Renata wanted to say, *you are absolutely totally freaking me out with your cool.*

"Ah. Minnesota. The Mall of America."

Renata glimpsed a veiled dismissal in the eyes of the young doctor—Renata was from an *America minore.* America, to Italians, consisted of New York or San Francisco. The rest of the country rang a somewhat sinister bell in their ears, evoking a mindless sprawl intent on self-destruction, complete with shootouts, riots, and natural disasters.

"I am sure your father liked visiting you there," said Dr. Erici.

Renata did not want to tell her that Papoozi had never visited Minneapolis or expressed the desire to do so. Their exchanges had become tentative after Papoozi had gotten wind of Steve's affair. His unfaithfulness had been difficult to mention and equally hard to ignore, much like a terminal illness.

"Where is the bathroom?" Renata asked

"There," Tito said, gesturing to the door behind her.

There was no mirror over the bathroom sink. Renata looked up from washing her hands to face a bare wall. Her surprise was compounded by the impression that, for an instant, she saw a ripple of her reflection in the pale-green paint. She knew that Steve would have loved this story of the imaginary mirror.

"Cool," Steve would say, locking eyes with her. "Tell me more." She imagined telling Steve about her awkwardness with her brother, about Papoozi's frail state; then her thoughts, with splintered anxiety, turned to all she had left behind: the rent due at Wellness Within; the deranged homeless man who would camp out in the waiting room; the money she owed Tessa for her plane ticket to Milan.

She came out of the bathroom to find Tito alone, pacing at the foot of Papoozi's bed, the soles of his shoes making whispering sounds across the linoleum floor.

"Did you call Flavia?" Renata asked softly, unnerved by their abrupt intimacy in the brightly lit room. "Yes? Did you?"

"Of course I called her," Tito said.

"Where is she?" Renata wished to have the reassuring presence of Flavia with them.

"Flavia's at home. She was here last night and all morning, while I was at work."

A *Donna Moderna* magazine had been left on the night cot in the corner, Renata noticed, open to a page of illustrated recipes. The sight filled her with a warm lassitude, as if this was the Milan she had missed for so long, when she had found little to comfort her in America.

"So, is Flavia coming?" Renata pressed. "Soon?"

"Eh no," Tito replied. "*Che dici?* What are you saying? Flavia taking two buses at this hour? At her age?"

"Flavia! What age?"

"Reni, she's eighty now, and in bad shape. I'm going to pick her up by car, now that you are here."

A ferocious vision tore at her—Tito leaving and Papoozi dying while she was alone with him.

"Don't go. Tell her to call a taxi!"

Tito looked at her, bewildered. *"Che Americana,* Flavia calling a taxi?"

Renata fantasized for a brief moment being the one able to drive away, to be swallowed by the sluggish Milan traffic. But of course it was Tito who took off, after pausing at the door for a quick *"ciao,* Papoozi."

With Tito gone the room was as airless as a crypt. Renata gave a desperate look at the *Donna Moderna* magazine for possible support, pausing at a recipe for *zuppa invernale leggera.* The ingredients were comforting and familiar: *zucchine, cipolla, porro.* Papoozi loved soups, tilting his bowl to scrape the last drops with his spoon. Renata loved that her father went for what he wanted. When hungry, he ate; when upset, he railed. He didn't have much of a singing voice, but when Renata started a Neapolitan song, he joined in, vigorously off-key.

For a time, there was only the sound of the wheels from the morphine cart rolling down the hallway. The noise would stop, then resume. This didn't seem to break the silence, just made it feel bigger.

Papoozi made an oddly childish gesture, his fingers fluttering like the wings of a butterfly. His arms lay limply on the bedsheets, as if they weighed too much. When he saw that she was frowning, paying close attention, the movement morphed into a dismal attempt at grasping upward.

"Are you thirsty?" Renata asked. His fingers fluttered in an increasingly frenzied fashion.

"Water?" Again, the brisk movement. With a burst of pride, Renata realized she had nailed it.

Renata remembered an occasion when she'd figured out how to operate Papoozi's first TV remote. "Perhaps your head is not all bad," Papoozi had acknowledged, with a playful grin. *My firstborn,* the spark in his eyes seemed to say, *the one to fulfill the father's wishes.* She wasn't a son, as the first-born was supposed to be, but Papoozi had made do.

Renata poured water from a bottle on the nightstand into a plastic spoon and tried to insert it into her father's mouth, but he gagged, water trickling down his chin and wetting his pajama top. *Idiota.*

He emitted an urgent rasping sound.

Finding a wad of gauze on the nightstand, Renata wet it under the bathroom faucet, then squeezed it on Papoozi's tongue. They went through several gauze pads. Then he bit one. She felt his teeth tear at the fabric, sucking hard. She tried to pull the gauze away, panicked that he might choke. They struggled and finally she pushed the red alarm button on the wall.

A moment later Domenico arrived.

"*Buonasera,* Cesare. Any pain?" He shot an inquisitive look at Renata, who shook her head no, then yes.

"He was thirsty," she said. "I tried—"

Domenico nodded, averting his eyes. His pity blew her off balance. "Why don't you wait outside?" he said.

Stepping out, Renata glanced hopefully toward the elevator. It was too soon for Tito and Flavia to be back, but she hoped to see them nonetheless.

After several minutes Domenico appeared in the doorway, signaling that she could return to her father's bedside. With a deep breath Renata walked briskly, with a crazy conviction that her attitude could alter the situation.

Standing by her father's side, she watched him breathe with a fierce concentration. She resisted reaching out to touch him, reluctant to disturb his focused inhalations and exhalations. She imagined she was looking at this moment in retrospect, imagined some distant time when this powerlessness and uncertainty was behind her. *Calm, calm, calm,* she told herself. After a time, she sensed a slight change in Papoozi's breathing, a choppy gasping that struggled to find a rhythm. His chest rose, floated, fell imperceptibly, then rose again. Papoozi's lips tightened in a combative manner.

"Breathe, Papoozi, breathe!" Renata would not give up

either. She, too, refused to admit defeat. "More oxygen!" she yelled.

Domenico adjusted the mask over Papoozi's nose, but the increased oxygen did little to help; it only agitated Papoozi to pointlessly fight harder.

"Perhaps," Domenico said, in a quiet, soothing voice, "perhaps you let him go."

Guiding Papoozi toward death seemed unthinkable. He always used up everything to the very last: bread or toothpaste, with a poor kid's panic. "Oh yeah?" he used to ask. "You call this finished?"

"Tito and Flavia are almost here!" Renata said to encourage him to keep fighting. "Any minute now." Her voice echoed strangely throughout the room with what seemed an underwater sluggishness. She shot a glance at Domenico, wondering what to do as Papoozi's open eye was asking her to do *something*. His eye then drifted closed, and his chin dropped to his chest as he did when he sang "Fenesta ca Lucive," his favorite Neapolitan song, with the thread-thin voice of nostalgia.

Domenico's expression seemed to say, *Let him go*. And for a moment she did.

"Let yourself go. You are loved," Renata whispered.

The muscles of his neck tightened and his lips contorted. Renata realized it was a massive effort for one more breath.

"*Forza*, Papoozi!" She fought alongside him. Papoozi would make it. He would astonish everyone. He emitted a sound between a gasp and a sigh. The emptiness that followed built with a powerful intensity. Papoozi's chest stilled, and his head dropped to his shoulder. A tear made its way down one cheek and came to rest just below his cheekbone.

Renata caressed Papoozi's forehead, wanting to feel the whisper of his soul leaving, but she felt nothing under her palm.

The body, lying immobile beneath white bedsheets, seemed a shrunken version of Papoozi, one he himself would have had difficulty recognizing as his own.

❧

"*Il traffico*," said Tito behind her.

Turning around, Renata saw that Tito had arrived, followed by Flavia, dressed in a camel coat. She was clasping a scarf to her neck, a frail wisp of a woman with carefully brushed white hair, thin and fluffy like a chick's. Her coat glistened with rain, the crisply pungent Milanese rain Papoozi used to rage at with gusto but had loved so much.

"*Il traffico*," Flavia said, opening her arms with a fatalistic resignation that gave Renata a wave of unexpected comfort. *Il traffico*. Fate.

Flavia walked to the side of the bed, wobbly from a slight limp, and simply stood there looking at Papoozi. Domenico left discreetly, after whispering something to Tito, who went to stand by Flavia biting his lip.

Flavia leaned over Papoozi, clasping her hands. Tito took her elbow gently, as he must have done many times before. She absently patted his hand, a gesture that spoke of the intimacy of shared family life over the years. Flavia glanced at Renata with the uneasy solemnity one assumes with a stranger. Tito brushed Flavia's shoulders delicately with his palm, whispering encouragement. Flavia agreed with gentle nods.

"I'm sorry," Renata murmured. She found nothing else to say.

She turned away and stepped out of the room.

In the hallway she was touched by the sight of a young doctor speaking softly to a charmingly awkward man in an elegant suit. The doctor offered his hand to shake, but the man kept gesturing, distraught, trapped in the chaos of bad news and intimacy with an unfamiliar person.

The daylight had gone, and Doctor Erici's white coat floated in the gray dusk amid skittish shadows.

5

W̶ant a ride?" Tito said.

Domenico filled out the necessary papers. Tito gave Renata the same look they used to exchange over the dinner table as kids, when they'd promised one another that neither would die before the other. Papoozi, she recalled, had been rinsing glasses at the sink. Outside, someone had been scraping snow with a shovel. Tito and Renata, enveloped in a circle of lamplight, had struck their bargain with locked eyes.

"I'll take a taxi," she said.

Tito looked up, stunned, a flicker of combativeness in his eyes.

Renata knew that there would be no mention of their father's death, now or later. Onward, as Papoozi had prescribed. Their mute intensity during the ensuing car ride would be intolerable.

"It's best, so you can give a ride to Flavia," she said.

"I can give a ride to both of you."

She studied him in silence—a private young man with the melancholy aspect of a troubadour. His aggressive use of hair gel and the punctilious way he dressed felt touching; they suggested the awkwardness of a kid who had grown up without a mother to tuck in his careless shirt or fix a loose button.

"No, it's fine," she said. "Just take Flavia. Come closer so I can see you." He did.

"I thought I heard Papoozi breathing," Tito said.

"He wasn't," she said.

"I heard it," Tito insisted.

They leaned against the wall, shoulders touching, like when they'd watched their mother sit up in bed darning an imaginary sock with an imaginary needle.

Tito whispered something that could have been *oh, fuck me*.

"You want me to go back in with you and check?" she asked.

"No."

"You are going to be fine if we don't?"

"Yes."

Domenico called Radiotaxi for her, then turned to her and said, "Firenze 32 in three."

"Firenze? What?" she asked, perplexed. When she'd lived in Milan, cabs had numbers.

"It's what's written on the side of the cab," Tito told her. "You need a phone that works here, no?" He handed her a cell phone "I have an extra one I don't use much."

"Sure, thanks." She took it. "*Ci vediamo*, Tito."

"*Ci vediamo.*"

He looked away, shifting uneasily in the sharp light of the hall.

"Look, Reni. I cannot host you at my place."

It felt like a kick in the gut. She'd wondered why he hadn't offered. Such an arrangement was considered a sign of affection, and, after all, simply polite.

"No problem. I booked a hotel room."

"Sorry."

"I understand." Renata didn't, but it felt like the right thing to say. Maybe Tito was still furious that she had left him alone so many years ago.

Tito's face was suffused with a light flush, his eyes downcast. His frail timidity now seemed less endearing to her.

"I'd like to pay for the taxi," he said.

"Oh, no problem." Tito's attempt at monetary compensation made her miserable. "Nah."

They both shifted in place. The three minutes for Firenze 32, whatever that meant, were up.

"*A domani*, Tito," she said, feeling the need to fill the silence that always seemed to fall between them.

"*A domani*, Reni."

Once, as a child, Tito had been terrified by high waves in Sestri Levante. In the late afternoon, when the beach was deserted, Papoozi had swum out too far and could not be seen for a long time. He had never done that before. Renata had

held Tito tightly, feeling his tears on her cheek. She had been
frightened too, but her brother's closeness had comforted her,
even if she'd been the one saying "Don't cry."

Now, Renata made her way to the entrance of Ospedale
Sant'Erasmo, without, thankfully, meeting a soul. She could not
bear the thought of being stuck in an elevator with strangers.

The gray mist slowly rising in the courtyard was just as she'd
remembered; it was a distinct memory of Milan she'd cherished,
and the mist that evening felt like a personal nod from the city.
The bright beam of car headlights occasionally filtered through
the gate. Milan now was still and quiet, long done with the bedtime rituals Papoozi had pursued with ferocious precision.

"You must draw blood," he'd instructed Tito and Renata as
they brushed their teeth.

In Chinese medicine, the rise of Yang energy was visualized
as a man, a dragon, or a mighty crane. Over the years Renata had
playfully identified this symbol with Papoozi. Practitioners of
Chinese medicine believed that after death, the body dispersed
in particles of energy. While this notion appealed to Renata, she
hoped that Papoozi might resist this metamorphosis as long
as possible. Papoozi was still Papoozi. Bread was bread, but
crumbs were something else entirely.

A compact white taxi with Firenze 32 painted across its side
drove into the gate, followed by another car marked Torino 35.
Both drivers looked at her with tentative hope.

An old man hurried out of the doors behind her to claim Torino 35. Renata got into the back of Firenze 32 with a nod and
a *"Buonasera"* to the driver, a greeting so low and hoarse that it
sounded conspiratorial. Strictly speaking, she should have said
"Buonanotte," but goodnight seemed too intimate. Discretion,
she knew, was expected in tight spaces. It was late, and for the
duration of the ride Renata and the driver shared a bone-tired
silence. They drove through gusts of wind that attacked trees,
telephone poles, and street signs. They kept going, on and on.
Renata thought of the kitchen drawer full of maps that Papoozi
had collected over the years—he who threw everything out and
went nowhere.

&

The room at Albergo Ambrogino was as narrow as a friar's cell, decorated in shades of gray. On the nightstand, a pink plastic rose stood in a glass bowl. "Arte Povera," Papoozi would have snickered. But the room felt bare and lifeless.

Renata imagined the heavy phone on the nightstand ringing with the rough *cra-cra-cra* she'd remembered from Italy. It would be Tito calling, having decided to pick her up and bring her to his house after all. *But of course*, he'd say. A mattress on the floor would be great, she thought. Or anything at all. Panic demanded flexibility.

When Tito did not call, Renata dialed Steve's number. It was just after lunch in America, and he would probably be sitting around in his shirtsleeves looking over rehearsal notes. He always lit up at the director's insights; they were, he said, like snapshots of an object taken from a different angle. When speaking of acting he gave off a boozy euphoria that made her jealous.

Please pick up, she thought. Steve seemed always fully absorbed by work or busy looking for work. Loafing, she'd told him, was considered a source of inspiration in Italy, inferior only to strolling. "What are you trying to say?" Steve had retorted, suspiciously.

Then he picked up but did not speak.

"Steve?" she said.

"Renata, hey. Is that you?"

"You answered the phone."

She heard a rustling in the back mixed with voices, then a layered sound of laughter.

"I'm on a short break," he told her. "I need to be back to rehearsal in five." As usual, he seemed rushed, wired, in between things. From his tone she imagined a smile. She had a crush on that smile." What's going on?" he asked. "Are you at work? Can I call you back?"

"I am in Milan," she said. "I am in a hotel in Milan."

"Speak up," Steve said. "You are in Milan? What happened? Is someone ill?"

"My father is dead."

"Your father. Wait. What?" Steve said.

"He is dead." It sounded like a strangely formal line, she thought, so unlike everything that had taken place in the hospice room.

"Dear God. I don't even know what to say. Tell me everything." Steve's voice cracked with emotion. "Let me hear your voice."

My voice is the last sound my father heard, she thought.

"I don't know what to say." She wished Steve could lean in close, smooth her frown lines with the tips of his fingers, whispering sweet little things in her ear. She tried to tell him what had happened. Papoozi died in one short sentence. She didn't say that he'd looked like a broken puppet or how alone and small he had seemed at the end. The hotel was silent but for her voice.

"Oh, I understand. No, I don't. I can't imagine. I mean—" he said. "I should be there. I want to. Oh God. God. It's not possible. I don't have an understudy."

"What?"

"I'm terribly sorry," he said. *Terribly?* He hated adverbs.

"It's fine," she said. *Izfi-hnn.* "It's all fine." *Izalfinn.* She managed a raspy whisper, her head nodding forward, her eyes drifting closed. Renata was startled by the fragment of a dream—Papoozi, in his good three-piece Ermenegildo Zegna, standing under a shaft of light in the open doorway of Via Saverio, demanding to do his death all over again.

"*Per carita?* What was that?" he inquired gravely of Renata. "A disaster. We can do better than that, yes?"

Renata breathed quietly into the phone, knowing that Steve disliked silence.

"I wish I could be there," he said. His voice seemed guarded, the tone he used with a cop after being caught speeding. "I want to be there with you, but there is so much going on with—"

"What, Steve? What is going on?" she asked.

"Maybe—this is not the best time to talk," he replied.

"Just tell me," Renata pressed.

"My agent has set up meetings," he said, finally. "They are impossible to reschedule. Important meetings—auditions for TV shows."

Renata remembered meeting Steve's agent at a party once— an elegant, forthright woman whose presence had intimidated Renata into gulping down too many martinis.

Steve had more work in LA. Her heart picked up speed. I can manage physical distance, she thought, but even when Steve was in Minneapolis she was home alone most nights. Her solitude in the house so fully absorbed her that she'd begun to sense her very presence fading, like photosensitive paper exposed to light.

"Renata, I'm just letting you know why I'm stuck here. I don't like it either. There's nothing to talk about yet. Zero. Okay? There is no move to California or anything. Don't think about it. Are you thinking about it?"

"No, I'm not," she lied.

"Okay, good. This is not the moment for this kind of conversation. I'm in shock; you are in shock. Everything is a mess." He made it seem as if they were both pressured by unseen forces, while she felt that his situation was pretty clear.

"Yes. Steve. Uh, listen. I might need to stay longer in Milan to take care of things." She realized that she hadn't spoken in English since arriving in Milan; it was exhausting. "My brother needs me here."

She wanted Steve to protest, to be caught off guard by a surge of emotion or a burst of ferocious rage, to say, *Fuck him*, or something equally extreme he'd never forgive himself for.

"Is your brother pushing you to stay?" This was the protective Steve she knew, quick to see domineering traits in others.

"Not at all." Her English felt strange and her accent heavier now that she had returned to Milan. Her words sounded as if they were disintegrating in mid-air. *Nt—aah—aah!—*

The call sagged fast under the weight of all that remained unspoken. There were unknown cities and streets between them, stairways and courtyards, and a vast expanse of water. She heard a door open where Steve was and what sounded like a stage manager call his name in an official tone.

Both agreed they'd talk later. Renata gave him the number of the cell phone that Tito had given her. Then they were silent again, as if peering at each other across a great distance. *Let him go now*, she thought.

"So, I'll call you later. Okay?" he said.

They said careful goodbyes and hung up.

In Milan, when a love ended, every friend came with food or a bottle of wine, and each got a story for a drink or a slice of bread. Toward morning all went home, taking away a bit of the sorrow with them. But nothing had happened tonight. A relationship, Renata thought, should be like a journey in a city where you've never been. The bus driver, just like in Milan, would announce each stop by the name of the street. You would always know exactly where you were and when to get out.

Renata pulled one boot off and threw it against the wall. *Vaffan*, Steve.

"You are pretty," her mother used to say, encouraging Renata to smile for class pictures. "And you would be even more so if you looked at the camera." Renata had refused to do either, as the girl next to her whispered, *"terrona"* under her breath. *"Bastarda,"* Renata had whispered back.

She'd relished the way she'd appeared in the photos—mad as hell.

6

Upon waking, Renata felt cold. She was angry at being broke, angry at being stuck in a cheap hotel with inadequate heating and one thin blanket. Between her crazy sadness and the chill, she had slept only a little. She would not be of much help to herself or to Tito today.

The hum of an airplane, a soft metallic din coming from somewhere far away, filled the room, and Renata felt like the only person left behind in a ghost town. She thought of Papoozi lying alone in this gray light. She grew tired of him being dead.

Peering outside, she took in the monochrome of a winter afternoon in Milan. She opened the window and a rush of chaos and noise met her. It seemed to have been waiting in a suspended state just for her. Trams, kids off from school. Young men and women in leather jackets walked fast, holding small *Esselunga* supermarket bags with last-minute shopping—Palmolive soap, salt, milk? Within the din, she recognized phrases from childhood—*aspettami un momento; ecco l'autobus; no non toccare.* The sounds pulled her in like a tune. *Daa-daa-da-da.* She knew what the passersby were returning to at home and the poems the children had memorized for school. The rhythmic sounds of this familiar life felt intoxicating. If the spirit transformed into a new essence after death, as the Tao suggested, all this would be Papoozi.

An older man poked furtively with his cane at sidewalk litter, disturbing a flock of sparrows. He followed the birds to the next gathering spot and repeated the action with his stick, looking invigorated by his small power of scaring birds.

"I forget *everything*," Papoozi used to say. But he remembered with delight the Neapolitan pet name his mother had given him as a child. *Ucceddruzzo*, little bird.

"*Ucceddruzzo*," Renata repeated aloud, to have little Papoozi there for a moment. Her gaze returned to the old man, now walking away with a smile. Probably he was off to enjoy the classic glass of wine with buddies before dinner. Papoozi had called men of that age and inclination *lycanthropes*, wolves hiding under innocuous clothes. They led quiet lives but hid dark pasts as Fascist Black Shirts, who had locked up Jews, antifascists, and soldiers in cattle cars at Binario 21, train track 21. Those train cars had been hidden below stairs, in the belly of Stazione Centrale, so that the sight of them leaving for concentration camps would not offend the eyes. Transport to concentration camps was a necessity. Why disturb people's conscience? Papoozi and the other prisoners had been led through a side entry on Via Ferrante Aporti, then down to the lower level in the pitch dark.

One Sunday afternoon, when Renata was eight or so, Renata and Tito listened to a scratchy record from Papoozi's collection. Marlene Dietrich sang "Lili Marlene" in German. The children bent their arms like wings and danced in the tiny kitchen.

Vor der Kaserne
Vor dem großen Tor
Stand eine Laterne
Und steht sie noch davor—

"And so what happened to Signor Marini after the war?" they asked Papoozi.

Signor Marini, Papoozi told them, was a big-shot fascist in Milan when Papoozi was carted off to Mauthausen. He shrugged, squinting hard as if something blocked his view, then looked at his children, attentively awaiting an answer, and smiled. All that seemed to matter to him at that moment was the light falling through the window, enveloping the family in a golden shaft like a medieval painting.

"A bear ate him and then died of poison," he responded with a chuckle.

&

"Get in. Be quiet." After a surprise arrest during childhood war games, Renata would push Tito roughly. The rolling pin, made dangerous by attaching sharp Christmas ornaments to it, was her weapon. The cattle wagon was a large wardrobe; in the back there was a terrifying fur stole consisting of two skinny foxes, with eyes bright and jaws clutching each other's tail—an item that had belonged to their mother and had somehow eluded Papoozi's purge. At the door to the wardrobe, Renata collected anything Tito had in his pockets at the moment. "No crying," she warned. "Don't let the bastards have the satisfaction; they'll go after you harder."

Tito came up with the idea of making fake passports for an escape. They had never traveled anywhere that required one, but they saw pictures in a magazine at the dentist's office and labored secretly with glue, paper, and ink. Renata forged the official signatures, her specialty. They made one for Papoozi and Flavia too.

One day a new student named Maria Grazia Marini arrived in Renata's class. The teachers liked her manners, and she was good at composition. She already wore nail polish, and her hair was as straight as blades of grass. She sat giggling with other girls and never spoke to Renata. Renata pretended she was not interested in talking to Maria nor was she impressed with the lacy-collared dresses that others admired. Once, Signor Marini came to collect Maria from school. He was an affable old man and exchanged an amiable smile with the teacher. Renata did not tell Papoozi she had seen him, and how she had blushed at the misery of their worn linoleum kitchen floor, as if Signor Marini somehow knew of it.

"You wear checkered socks? Like a boy?" Maria Grazia Marini asked her once, when they were alone in the school bathroom. "You are a *terrona*?" She seemed intrigued, as if there were something exotic and slutty about both Renata's socks and her having been born in Naples.

Renata stole Maria's new fountain pen, a much-admired Omas, but threw it away as she walked home.

In the hotel Renata took a shower. The blast of water hit hard.

It was too hot, then too cold. We never quit wanting something different till we die, she thought. Everything is almost, but not exactly, right.

Tito had demonstrated a complete lack of curiosity about her life, and even Renata experienced herself at a distance, as if she were still in Minneapolis. This impression gave her the kind of fright she had known after a bad dream as a child. She broke out in a sweat.

Renata picked up the phone as soon as it rang. It was Tito.

"How are you?" he said.

"Very well," she replied with excitement, happy to hear his voice. Given the circumstances, it was, she realized, the wrong thing to say, and the tone inappropriate. "Considering everything," she added, contritely.

"I can pick you up now and you can come to the Pompe Funebri Scotti to choose the casket, but Flavia and I can do this alone."

The word *alone* was stressed deliberately, Renata felt, to discourage her from joining them.

"Right, of course. The casket," she said. She hadn't thought of it and the idea of Papoozi being laid out on a bare table to be measured by strangers evoked an image of medieval brutality that disturbed her.

"They require a casket for cremation?" she asked. "Why? That's silly. I bet the price is exorbitant."

"It's the way it is." *Che Americana,* his tone implied. "It depends on what type of casket you choose. You know you don't have to come. Flavia and I can do it."

Renata experienced a spike of pain mixed with relief. Tito didn't fuss to convince her. She had savored the little drama of it, and all that she wished he might say—*It's just me and you now, Reni. Please. Be ready in ten.*

"You don't mind if I don't come?" she said.

"Not at all. Unless you want to," he said.

Porca miseria, she thought, hurt by her brother's distracted tone, his evident hurry to be off the phone already. She'd fought bullies in the playground for him and she'd given him her last coins to hear "*Sapore di Sale*" play again and again on the jukebox.

"Listen," she said. *Little bastard.* She felt both a sense of dread and excitement at this new Tito.

"Yeah?" he said.

They were expected, at such a time, to act mutually solicitous, she knew. But clearly Tito did not want her at his side.

"Fine with me. Great idea. I can stay here and take a rest while you do what is needed," she said. How about the fact that Papoozi hadn't moved since last night? she thought. How about talking about disturbing things just this one time?

"Sure. It's much easier," Tito said, clearly relieved at her decision. He didn't have to drive to pick her up and deal with *il traffico.* "And you can rest."

"Call me if there is any problem." It seemed an absurd thing to say, but she said it anyway.

"Naturally," said Tito.

Renata knew then that she had said the right thing, in the Italian way. One should offer to help, as a form of courtesy. There was a slight pause. No expectations floated in the silence. Time to end the call, she thought.

"I can't really help," she said. She felt a dark hopelessness mixed with a nip of rage. "There is nothing I can do."

A longer silence followed.

"I know," he said.

❧

It was murderously hot the afternoon Tessa and Renata stopped in at the coffee shop on Hennepin Avenue.

"We'll talk of nothing," Tessa promised. "Stupid news, stupid people, stupid diets. Anything stupid."

They sat by the window and looked at people walking by. Renata could not help thinking of pregnancy, imagining a swelling of the belly of each woman who walked by. Perhaps this woman's or that woman's pregnancy was early still, the baby so small that the protruding belly was not yet visible.

Several teenage girls sat at a nearby table, giggling and shushing one another. They wore large headbands and nail polish in the bright colors of Lucky Charms.

"I am sure it would have been a girl," Renata said.

The day before, she'd dialed Dr. Caro and left a message with the nurse.

"It's nothing, a little spotting," Renata had said, her jaw set against panic. "Just checking." Light bleeding was normal during the first months of pregnancy, after all.

Dr. Caro had returned the call immediately, asking her to come in to the clinic. As Renata listened to his strong, slightly accented voice, distracted by the *tak-tak-tak* of yellowjackets attacking the window, she gazed at the cup on the kitchen counter, the spoon placed neatly beside it. All was in order; there were no accidents, no oversights. Everything would be fine.

"Sorry, but I really don't know that I can come in today, Doctor Caro," she said, primly.

"You need to come in right away," Doctor Caro said.

In the sonogram of Renata's womb, Dr. Caro saw no heartbeat, just a bean-sized mass. There was nothing he could do, he said. Dr. Caro spoke carefully, as if he were trying to memorize something. He explained the necessary procedure and posed questions first in English; then, when she did not respond, he repeated them in Spanish, then in tentative Italian.

Renata did not know what to say. She knew that when she left the room, she would not be pregnant anymore. She would not have her baby. Billions of sperm had raced to that one egg, and one would think that in the chaos none of them would survive. But one did, and that single sperm had come up a winner. But of course, it did not matter. In the big scheme of things, very little ever did.

❧

The next week Tessa kept calling Renata, asking her to come over or to meet at Wellness Within for a quick visit.

"You shouldn't be alone," she said.

When Renata showed up at the clinic, Tessa went to hug her tight.

"Go ahead and pick a treatment bed. It's free of charge for you," Tessa said, with a smile.

"I want to be sick."

"We make people better here," Tessa said.

"Make me better, then," Renata said.

A few days later Renata walked into Steeple People, the thrift store near Wellness Within. She bought a tattered novel in a language she did not know, possibly Czech. Reading it gave her a sense of comfort, for she could not understand much about her own life either. After a while, she noticed a few repeated words, hinting to a pattern that she could almost grasp. She sensed a flutter of meaning, which somehow infused the text with an aura of comfort in the midst of an impossible mess.

She remembered that Dr. Chen had suggested exploring intuition without pushing too hard for knowledge. Do not force an understanding, he'd said. Words appearing again and again in the narrative were like pebbles marking the way in a fairy tale, and on she went line by line.

Eventually, Renata returned to work. She read the possibly Czech novel to Tessa in between patients—*A tak isem ji—rozresal na kusy*—and Tessa listened to it as if it were music. They agreed over a cup of ginger tea that reading this foreign novel was suggestive of the subtle thrill of acupuncture, of something tangible and yet elusive. Renata did not go out much and when she did, she kept close to the walls of buildings. It seemed to her that her sorrow had a smell.

At Wellness Within a thin emotional thread stretched between the patients—the salesman who missed his father, who'd drunk too much but had taught him to swim as a child; the daughter of a pilot killed in Vietnam who had filled her life with a love for books; a pale young woman who suffered from terrible migraines, who wrote down, in thick calligraphy, everything she did each day in the pages of a tiny notebook. Every symptom mattered, and every symptom had meaning. The life force was manifest in everything. She felt that her patients were all thinking, like her: *I will soon leave this behind* and *I will never leave this behind.*

In college, Renata had underlined a passage in her copy of the acupuncture classic *Nei Ching: If man's vitality and energy do not propel his own will, his disease cannot be cured.*

You will make it, Renata told herself fiercely, just as she told each of her patients. *You must want to make it.*

At work, Renata drank herbal concoctions that Tessa prepared to invigorate her *qi.* The tea tasted strong and sweet, infused with tiny herbs that left a musty taste on her tongue; it seemed something a mouse would love.

When Steve returned from Colorado, for a while they did not have a language in common, much less a shared narrative. They kept quiet when together and did not mention what had happened. Renata saw images of the baby everywhere around them. Steve kept disappearing to a friend's house, to a sudden rehearsal, or out on some urgent errand.

His life, it seemed, had picked up speed away from home. He confessed he'd had an affair with a woman fond of horses. He cried; she did not. At night, when she looked out the window, even the shadows of buildings did not seem real, but rather shapes in a postcard, a place she might like to visit one day. Perhaps she and Steve could meet there again for the first time. They'd laugh together and have silly fights, making up easily, as couples do when their relationship is new. There was a sense of ease at asking a stranger, *Why did we speak like that?* and *Why didn't we speak?*

7

In the room of Albergo Ambrogino, Renata looked through a *Gente* magazine she'd found in the lobby. Gossip, British royalty and their pets, and photos of Italian TV stars she didn't recognize. One actress, in a flowered dress, stood with her arms folded behind her head like the wings of a butterfly. She stared upward, her mouth an *O*, just like Renata's mother's when she fed her with a spoon. Too sick to feed herself, and still so beautiful, looking up. *O*.

Renata slapped the magazine shut. Papoozi had claimed that inactivity was the gravest injury to the spirit. He used to take to the streets with a voracious stride, rain or shine, his cane clacking against the pavement or splashing through the puddles.

"*Ecche?* What! Still reading?" He would get impatient with Renata, who had spent many a somnolent afternoon after school reading *fotoromanzi*—soap opera novels in photos—and dreaming of Maurizio Falconeri in *Dramma nella Notte*, telling Renata rather than Luciana Bramante De Florentis, "It's fate."

A pale light came through the hotel curtains. *Go, go.* Renata wore a nice pair of gray pants and a black sweater. Papoozi had always insisted that they dress properly when heading out.

"You look French," Tessa had told her, when she'd worn that outfit to Wellness Within; today, however, Renata felt more Ibsen than Truffaut in her bones.

She hurried out of Albergo Ambrogino, buoyed by the idea of emulating Papoozi's passionate vigor. Since last night a light rain had fallen on and off in spurts, long enough to give the city a disheveled look and the distinctive skunk-like smell Renata remembered fondly from her meanderings as a child, familiar as an imaginary friend.

Milan was plain, mercurial. "An old maid," Papoozi used to snicker affectionately. Rusted tram tracks and old bikes tied to lampposts made the city look working class, but a nonchalance in the ancient buildings left to decay suggested old money that did not have to prove its might with impressive renovations.

Marble plaques, affixed by doorways of old apartments, caught her attention; they honored partisans killed during World War II. The partisan's name, date of birth, and death, and a two-liner was all that could fit. The signs, faded and scarred by weather, seemed almost ancient history, with an abstract quality to the death chiseled in stone. There was no mention, and no room, to say that this one always ran late, that that one had favored bad jokes, strong grappa, or caustic girls. She read the plaques slowly, as if she were taking an eye test. The dead were all terribly young.

"*Non fare il coglione*," she muttered to Vespas zipping close by, stirring up soggy whirlwinds of leaves. A German shepherd relieved itself on the sidewalk in front of her, while its owner was busy peering at magazines featuring scantily clad showgirls at a newspaper kiosk. Girls bumped into Renata and rushed past, without so much as a nod. But it all seemed a game between friends that someone had started, a bit rough but all rather silly. This unfussy anarchy felt like exactly what she needed. The Milan welcoming committee was out in full.

She started to walk briskly, wanting to own the sense of being back. On she went, eager to discover Papoozi's source of energy, but instead she detected something dreary and anonymous in the wet squares crossed by pedestrians with disheveled umbrellas. It felt not like Papoozi's Milan, but simply Milan.

Little squares tucked away at the end of ancient pebbled streets, public fountains in front of ornate gates—everything she saw felt heightened by melancholy. She imagined Papoozi behind her in the tangle of pedestrian traffic, forging ahead, cane in one hand, gray Fedora firmly on his head. *Via via andiamo.* Renata kept going with determination, singing to herself an old Italian song, as she used to do coming home from school.

Ciao, ciao, bambina! Un bacio ancora
e poi per sempre ti perderò—

Then, in her mind, she was home, in the kitchen, watching Flavia stir the *besciamella* for *pasta al forno*. Papoozi had his hat on; he went to the window to check the thermometer before heading out.

And on she went.

Mille violini suonati dal vento—

There was beauty in the store windows filled with boxes of silk ties, kid leather gloves, and silver candlesticks. The city slowly revealed itself to be a source of wonder, the way Papoozi had seen it: white window curtains fluttering in the breeze; pigeons lifting in short flights, as if mysteriously inspired; elegant restaurants where patrons lingered over coffee and waiters strained to sneak a look outside like parrots in their cages; an occasional Alsatian dog with the elegant deportment of a horse.

At last Renata felt a rustling of happy memories while walking past the brightly lit Formaggi Peck in Via Spadari, alive with aging experts of Parmesan. Here, every Friday, Papoozi used to inch through the displays of cheese, stopping to taste the silent offerings of clerks in white, to afterward pronounce, *The Caciotta Romana? Too thick a taste for spring*, or *The Pecorino cacio e pepe tends to gather under the scrape of the knife, too fresh. But I recommend it over the aged one.*

Renata pulled her scarf up to cover her chin against the cold, driven like an old dog following a familiar route. And then she was at Piazza Duomo. She looked up, dazed. The audacity of the tall spires, even the flight of pigeons, seemed orchestrated in a precise choreography to stun the viewer. The years-long cleaning completed at last, the scaffolds had been taken down, and the Duomo's white spirals were pristine against a bruised sky. There was a stern silence to the glory of the marble, which filled her with pleasure touched by melancholy.

❧

The seven-storied La Rinascente department store, adjacent to Piazza Duomo, was composed of large rooms with marble floors, stained-glass windows, and steep escalators. Renata arrived, cash in hand, to honor Papoozi, who'd believed it was imperative that one should count out one's money while paying.

"Thieves, everywhere," he'd mutter, lowering his voice, his eyes alert. "Burglars, spies, fascists—the bastards, like rats, survive everything." He'd refused to frequent La Rinascente. The store's name alone—The Reborn—had a flavor of fascist propaganda, and he was skittish about the high prices.

Occasionally, however, Renata had visited the store at Christmas to browse with her mother, experiencing the marvel other families enjoyed when they strolled through a street fair where colorful balloons swayed in the air and people crowded around braziers of roasting chestnuts.

The aisles of merchandise were luxuriously spaced, so that the people walking between them seemed almost insignificant, their appreciation of the goods less relevant.

Looking at all the things laid out so beautifully, Renata felt that they seemed to belong to a life in some imaginary land yet to be discovered. The colors and textures suggested sensual indulgence. Sweaters and socks appealed to the imagination, while those she already owned had no mystery.

Few customers browsed at that early hour. A nervy young man in an elegant coat looked through a stack of blankets, so much lighter than the thick ones she'd become accustomed to in Minneapolis. Winter in Milan was very different. The famous cold Renata's family had bemoaned seemed, relative to the chill of Minneapolis, a romantic memory heightened in intensity by the passage of time.

A young woman walked fast through the aisles, brisk and confident. They gave each other the quick nod that passengers exchange on a train. Renata admired the women's shirts, then stopped to count her money by a makeup counter covered with sparkling lipsticks lined up like toy soldiers. Turning over the price tag to a blue shirt that caught her eye, she realized it cost far more than she had expected. Would Papoozi appreciate such a reckless gesture in his honor? She'd wear the new shirt for the viewing of his body, after all. Regardless, everybody needs a nice new shirt sometimes, she told herself. It's useful, like a working phone, thick books, and reliable shoes, she argued in her mind against Papoozi's imagined protests.

When she looked up, the young woman she had exchanged glances with earlier stood next to her with a curious expression.

"Renata?" she asked tentatively. Her sweet tone rang a bell.

"Adriana." Renata recalled the two of them walking together, hand in hand, during school outings. They'd always fall behind, their steps reluctant, ignoring the teacher's call.

"Renata, I was thinking of you," Adriana said, and this struck Renata as a trite social lie that irked her. "Oh my God! I have not seen you in so long." Their schoolgirl bond had been cut short when Adriana changed schools, and this encounter felt like unexpectedly bumping into a lover from a passionate one-night stand.

"How are you, Addi?" Renata used the nickname to stop the nonsense. It was Addi she wanted to see, not this woman with glossy dark hair and pink lipstick. Addi, the one who had held her hand at school and taught her the Milanese dialect.

"Oh dear." Adriana laughed. "I'm a disaster! Look at me. I was going to be a teacher."

Adriana was not wearing a coat, Renata realized, because she worked at La Rinascente. Adriana fumbled, putting on her name tag. "But, well, I'm raising a kid alone."

Renata was stunned to find Adriana aged; it was as if she'd expected the little girl she had loved so much to be left behind somewhere, alone and waiting.

"I'm sorry," Renata said, so visibly affected that Adriana touched her wrist.

"Don't be," Adriana said. "It's better this way. And you? Kids?"

"A girl," Renata said. She wanted a trace of the baby lost to her to exist in Milan. In a *National Geographic* magazine, she'd read of the discovery of a 6,000-year-old woman buried in

Denmark. She'd been found hugging her premature newborn, the baby lying atop a swan's wing.

"Married?" Adriana asked.

"I'm married, but—" Renata began, then shrugged. She felt pleased, somehow, to nudge Steve out of her Milanese reality. "And how are things with you? Okay?"

"Reni, I'm not okay, but I'm relieved to be on my own. It wasn't this or that."

"What was it?"

"Who knows. And, look, separating was simple in so many ways. Awful how obvious it felt, once I did it."

"You are still so you, Addi."

"Oh, well. Yeah." She laughed. "And your life?" She glanced around skittishly, perhaps in fear of the attention of a supervisor. "You were going to be—? I don't remember. I just remember wanting to be you."

"Oh no. Me?" Renata said, surprised. For a moment, she wanted an imaginary life to claim.

"Yes, Reni, you. Listen, just do what you need to do with your marriage. I hate to tell you, but I'm glad I got a divorce," Adriana said. "Nobody believes it but it's true. Look, I'm old, and it's a good thing I am. I can't afford to fantasize about hanging in there forever, hoping for things to change."

"You are fantastic," Renata said.

"Age is fantastic, not me. I know I have to go for it, and now."

As children they'd had great patience with each other, with a quiet insistence on their own rules. Both reserved, they knew the social shame of not having a mother, the source of school conventions such as a barrette with a crisp bow attached that all the other girls wore.

An older customer, with a boy tugging at his coat, approached Adriana with a frown. He had a complicated question.

"I'll see you next time you're in Milan, Reni," Adriana said. "We'll go for a drink."

"I moved, Addi. It's difficult, but I'll try."

"Try."

Adriana walked away, taking the customer and the little boy with her. She glanced back for a moment and Renata raised her hand in farewell, then walked to the exit. A new shirt did not seem what she wanted after all.

The young man, now holding two folded blankets, appeared in a large mirror on the wall, growing larger as he headed to the cash register near Renata, seemingly advancing toward her with the warm offering in his arms. *Here, this is what you want: winter in Milan.* Renata felt a rush of desire. Winter in Milan—the strange forms in the fog, the familiar becoming unfamiliar, as it did in fairy tales, and her body comfortable in each space, as if they shared a subconscious life.

Upon reaching the hotel room, Renata was overwhelmed by exhaustion. The room was quiet. It had a chair, a nightstand, a bed. The caricature of a home. *I must move things around,* she thought, as if that would be sufficient to nudge the space toward a place to cherish. It came to her that she regarded her marriage similarly, as a flexible arrangement she could mold to her own desire, if only she would apply herself harder. But it seemed that, fundamentally, Steve was oil paint and she watercolor, and there was no way around that. There was a clarity to this perception, but where it came from she did not know.

The phone rang.

"Pine," Tito announced when she picked up. His tone suggested that pine was the cheapest wood of choice for the casket, and she'd best not object.

"Pine. Great," she agreed. There was a chill in the short pragmatic exchange. *What else was there to say? Oh, come on, Tito,* she thought. *Surely, he didn't think she would object?* Tito asked if she wanted to meet for dinner, but she declined, saying she was too tired. His tone seemed stilted and formal, and she felt frozen at the idea of strained conversation—the fuss about where to eat, what places were cheap enough or close enough. She feared he might insist, but he let it go.

"Tonight I'd like to take a break to try to rest. Jet lag, you know," she said.

"I understand," he said, with the austere tone of a man used to the hardship of long-distance travel. She smiled at that; he never went anywhere. "I'll pick you up tomorrow for the viewing of the body." For a moment the only noise in the hotel room was the muffled rumble of traffic.

"Perfect. Sleep well, Tito."

"Wait. Reni, listen," he said, with sudden intensity. "You remember that day at the beach in Sestri Levante? Papoozi made us so scared. He disappeared for so long, swimming far."

Renata and Tito had splashed in the water, she recalled, poking through crab nests and reefs of algae. Blue-and-white Algida ice cream carts had rolled across the sand, the vendors calling out their wares in sing-song. The midday heat blurred everything, making them look like figures underwater.

Late that afternoon, the waves had gained strength and turned a darker color. Tito and Renata had lost track of Papoozi's head bobbing in the distance. The beach umbrellas had been closed for the day, with the folded chairs clustered around the pole. The ice cream carts were gone.

They'd sat close together on a beach towel, Renata remembered, quietly turning the pages of a worn *Topolino* children's magazine, attentive to Mickey Mouse and Donald Duck's capers as if they were a complicated text eluding their grasp. They'd never voiced their fears.

"Of course I remember," she said. "Why?"

"Were we upset at him?" Tito asked.

"No. We got pissed off at the Germans for making him swim so far and feel so sad and mad. And meanwhile, German tourists were there on vacation, do you remember? They were having fun like nothing had happened, strolling on the beach with their buckets, picking up seashells."

"Wait. Did we get a pen and write the names of concentration camps inside seashells and watch the German tourists pick them up?" he asked.

"Yeah. Dachau and Bergen-Belsen. We decided that Mau-thausen was too long."

"Thank you so much. *Buonanotte*, Reni. I'm so glad you are here."

Renata had no desire to sleep or eat. She wanted to be drinking wine in a noisy bar where voices would drown out her thoughts. She wanted to deface, with mad graffiti, the room that smelled of solitude. She decided to go to an *osteria* in Porta Ticinese, to drink hard and sing an old-time song in front of inebriated strangers who'd cheer and bring her another glass.

When the phone rang, she picked up the receiver fast.

The Italian male voice at the other end sounded vaguely familiar, but she could not place him.

"Do you know who I am?" he said. And then she did. "It's Cosimo. Tito gave me this number."

"Cosimo, yeah," she said. "*Ciao.*" As if his calling her out of the blue was nothing.

Flashes came to her of nights in a crowded kitchen, the aroma of spaghetti *aglio e olio*. She'd wanted him to pin her against the wall and kiss her hard. She'd seen him do this to pale girls who bit his lower lip, then passed their palms over his chest.

"I'd like to see you," he said.

He'd never asked her out. There'd always been someone else, a successive blur of long legs and blond hair.

"Yeah, sure," she said, with studied casualness.

"A drink later?" She heard the *castrato fallito* crack in his voice. He was excited. She'd always been so careful never to say a word about how much she'd wanted him, not even to Tito. "Works for you?"

"Works," she said. Cosimo, she, Tito, and the old group of friends used to meet at Bar Noventa. The place always smelled of mulled wine, cigarettes, and soggy boots. The thrill of memories made her silent.

"Bar Noventa in one hour?" he said. She was eager for him to add something, to give her a hint of what to expect. He did not, but there was a sense of complicity in their short silence.

"In one hour," she said.

The elation of soon meeting Cosimo caused her much turmoil, and she decided it was imperative to check in with Tessa at Wellness Within. Focus on duty and work, she told herself. In truth, she wanted the safety it gave her.

Tessa answered, her voice sleepy. There was an initial clumsiness, then there was the rush of telling everything to each other as usual. There was something unreal in how close Tessa felt.

"Any patients this morning?" Renata asked at last.

"Reynard."

Renata had told Reynard she'd be absent that week.

"*Reynard* was there?"

"He sat on the treatment bed eating pad thai and waiting for his treatment."

"He's not supposed to eat pad thai. He needs to replenish moisture in his meridians. Has he forgotten all my recommendations completely? And did he pay by giving a reading with his Tarot cards?" Tessa had always said that Tarot cards and horoscopes were a way to foster lunacy in the masses.

"Yep, but it was a good reading."

Renata giggled. Suddenly the idea of meeting Cosimo at Bar Noventa seemed an odd and alien reality. Reynard's last Tarot reading now came back to her with disturbing clarity.

"The hanged man," Reynard had said. "This means you will have a big decision to make."

"No. Change it," Renata had insisted, pushing the card aside.

"We can't change the card. It's not possible. Instead, listen carefully to what it says: if you can let go of what you don't need anymore, you'll start a new evolutionary stage." He'd tapped the card with one finger. "It says, let go."

"Yeah, I'll start by letting go of the likes of you, Reynard," she'd said, with a smile. "It's cash next time, remember."

❧

Cosimo had offered to pick her up from her hotel, but Renata protested that she could find Bar Noventa on her own, *naturalmente*. Now she wasn't so sure; she felt disoriented in the grainy light of dusk. A window washer pointed her in the direction of the MM1 subway, but she found herself in Via San Vittore instead, an unadorned stretch of ancient walls that enclosed the prison. *Miseria ladra.* She retraced her steps through rush-hour pedestrians buzzing angrily around bus stops and was confused by sighting a likeness of Papoozi with a tiny dog on a leash disappearing and resurfacing at a distance in the crowd.

Renata stopped at a newspaper kiosk for a moment, once in sight of Bar Noventa. The rusty door was half open, and the menu, written in chalk on a blackboard, hung in the window. There was the same table, painted gray, outside, where she'd smoked her first cigarette, feeling mysterious and somehow French.

Renata walked inside, unhurried in the hopes that a disappointment could be better absorbed in small increments, but everything was the same. The pungent odor of musty wood and grappa, the staccato of arguments about soccer and politics. No sonnets here, no absinthe and unrequited love. Just cheap wine and ugly ducklings. It was a place where a dreary week might be forgiven. Everybody belonged here: middle-aged cynics who secretly wrote poetry, painters in a mood, and amiable bootleggers. A woman peddled roses, calling, "*Rose, rose.*" And there was the table where Tito had told her, "It's no good that you tell me about our mother. I have forgotten her. It's been too long."

In the fairy tales Papoozi had refused to read them, Renata later discovered that the protagonist was always granted three wishes. The third wish was the tricky one, since it turned the first two into something nobody would ever want. It slayed the other two with one stroke.

Her first wish—the one that was always granted—was that Cosimo would want to meet her; the second wish was to find Bar Noventa unchanged; the third she let go before allowing it to take shape.

8

A few customers looked up from the flimsy pink pages of *Gazzettino Dello Sport* when she walked by. Older men, with their hats still on, huddled in a corner over a game of *briscola* or *scopa*, their cards splayed out across the table. The acrid smell of Nazionali cigarettes hung in the air, accompanied by a buzz of raspy male voices. An unsmiling young bartender poured wine into a row of glasses on the counter.

Renata noticed a thin man at a back table with something nervy in his demeanor. It was Cosimo, sitting sideways in his chair, as if he was about to leave. His finely sculpted features resembled those of Giovanni Dalle Bande Nere, mercenary captain, on a medieval medallion.

Seeing her, he leapt to his feet.

Renata met his nervous gaze with pleasure, finding a sense of security in his wordless fumbling.

"Cosimo, *ciao*," she said, pretending an ease she'd never felt with him.

"*Principessa, ciao*," Cosimo said. The nickname had been his way of teasing her for her homemade haircut and her books fixed with duct tape. She remembered instantly his casual aggressiveness, but also her strange pleasure in getting his attention.

"You look the same," he said. His appearance of tousled disorder gave him a Chekhovian allure.

"Oh God, no."

"That's good, I'd say," Cosimo said.

A wave of subtext emanated from him, feeling brutally intimate, just as she'd remembered.

"Oh, thank you."

"You look fantastic," he said.

Renata liked his lack of romance, his hurried directness. He'd never been the flirting type, even when flirting.

"And wow. America," he said, as if she'd won an award. She did not want America to come between them. "Hey, you spoke better English than any of us."

In a small movie theater in Brera the whole group of friends used to watch features in English. *Freaks. The Wizard of Oz.* They'd howled at marching monkeys and put on the headsets for simultaneous translation, making them all look like Princess Leia. Papoozi had paid for her airfare to America. He'd tested her language skills, pacing their small kitchen floor, asking for the English translation of random words. He knew no English.

"America is not what you think," she told Cosimo. She thought of Wellness Within, of the screechy sounds floating from Cholodenko Violin Repair, the crappy door to the clinic, and the wind hammering at the old windows.

"Why? What do I think?" he said.

"I don't know."

He laughed, then looked away, turning serious.

"Sorry about your father," he said. "I just heard."

"Thank you. It's okay. He was very old." It was the expected thing to say, and she received an understanding nod in response. But for her, Papoozi's death had arrived at manic speed, sudden and unexpected like a car crash.

"I'm coming to the funeral," Cosimo said. "Of course."

She shook her head.

"Why not? I knew him," he said.

"There's no funeral. He's going to be cremated."

"Cremated?" Cosimo asked. "Your father, always the original."

"Yup. He wanted to try something new, even when dead," she said.

They shared a tender chuckle.

"Wine?" Cosimo asked. "You still drink red?"

She nodded.

"No whiskey, huh?" His bruised smile made him look vulnerable and dangerous.

"No whiskey." Then she realized she might have given the

wrong answer—perhaps he'd find her more attractive as *una donna americana* who drank whiskey—but he'd already moved toward the bar.

Renata watched Cosimo disappear with a twinge of anxiety, his reedy silhouette bursting with energy, but he was back almost immediately carrying two glasses of wine.

"C'mon, let's sit," he said, like a secret invitation. Her knees buckled, and she sank in the chair opposite him.

"So, Cosimo," she said, breaking the silence. "How is it going?"

Conversation passed in muffled waves all around them, pierced by bird-like whistles from card players admiring a good hand. The bar, the sounds, the smells—they all seemed both real and a memory.

"I'm here," he said, his knuckles tight around his glass. "In Milan." The simple statement evaporated into something sad and prickly. "My job is persuading strangers to buy anything, aside from what they need. The less I care about something, the more passion I find in advertising it. I'm successful at my job. So, I stay. It's Milan for me."

"That's okay, no?" she said.

"O-kay?" Cosimo said, observing her with a smirk. "You are crazy." He seemed to savor every word he uttered.

"Well, I often think of Milan and my life here. Sometimes I want it all back," she said, fumbling for words. "More than you imagine. It's good that you live where you belong."

"I belong here?" he said. "Milan is total crap, and you know it."

"Life is tough everywhere, no?" she said. "The truth is—I might—I don't know. Come back."

"And do what? Oh God." He did not say: *Come back*. He did not say: *When?* "So what do you do? You work? Your brother didn't even know."

"Tito is a jerk. He knows what I do," she said. *Porca miseria*. Tito probably considered the profession of an acupuncturist as akin to that of an escape artist or an astrologer. Worse, imagining it through his eyes, Tessa and Wellness Within now acquired a strange flavor to her too.

"Work! Who cares? You're here, I'm here," Cosimo said.

He raised his glass in a silent toast to that, and she did too.

You are here, I'm here—the magic words. Renata felt light-headed, with a devil-may-care attitude. She was not much of a drinker but drained her glass, head thrown back.

"One more?" she proposed. It somehow seemed hilarious.

"Renata, since when do you drink two glasses in a row?" he asked with a sweet mockery that gave her goosebumps of pleasure. "And what else? A cocktail, maybe? *Principessa*, what have they done to you in America?"

Cosimo's watchful gaze radiated such melancholia that for a moment she felt the possibility of sharing the most unglamorous truths with him. What had they done to her in America? she wondered. She would tell him. Fact is, she had no idea. It seemed to her that it had been Italy that had let her down.

"I don't know," she said, biting her lip, wishing that her last few years in America offered more clarity, as easy to read as a pen flowing across paper, shaping definition and meaning from one letter to the next. She struggled to find words for what she felt.

"I've made you sad," he said. "*Porca miseria.* I didn't mean to. And your father just died. It's perfectly fine to drink more."

"No, it's a good question."

"C'mon, I was kidding," Cosimo said. "Of course I was."

"You were?"

"I know zero about life in America, and I ask you—what?"

She waited, breathing softly. *Ask*, she thought.

Cosimo stared down at the table, as if silence required concentration.

"Only, you know, I hear things about America. Like, Marco was mugged on a trip to New York."

"Marco?" They were done talking about her already, Renata realized with a sinking feeling, and they'd barely even started. It was America, again. "What Marco?"

"Marco, he lived in Piazza Piola," Cosimo said. "His brother owned that corner bookstore, Mercatino dell'Usato. That Marco."

Renata now remembered a pudgy teen, his eyes unfocused behind thick glasses, his mind wandering off mid-sentence; she used to finish Marco's thoughts for him, like an old wife.

"He was mugged the first day on a trip in New York," Cosimo said. "He told me you two were going to start a commune in—where—Sicily?"

"Whatever," she said.

"It was Sicily," Cosimo insisted. "A commune that would host orphans."

The commune had been the topic of one late-night talk, between a *terrona* and a teenager, who slept a lot and spoke in sound bites, both excited at the idea they could offer something to others. She remembered Marco's shitty record player and his immensely fat cat.

"Made me jealous," said Cosimo.

"What?"

"The commune. Don't tell me you didn't know."

She did not.

"He is in India now," Cosimo said. "He started a school for poor kids. I'd like to have the guts to do that."

Renata's American experience now felt slapdash: a failing clinic and a failing marriage. Even Cosimo did not seem to care to hear about her life there.

"Cosimo, are you out of your fucking mind? You can't stand ethnic food and you are horrified of insects. Right?"

"Okay," he said. "But maybe I am a crazy man. I'm not too old to do this kind of thing."

Over the years, Renata had overheard many late-night talks in Bar Noventa about living in India. Safely distant, India cast a light of dreamy possibility over their predictable lives. Weeks might pass without a mention, but then the talk of India would return and bring with it pleasure to the small group, like a lover who gave a night of passion and asked nothing in return. India had been their nest egg for bad days, so they'd kept a cautious watch on it, dipping into it sparingly.

"Of course you can do anything you want," she said, her tone firm. "You are still young. You want it, go for it. Why not?"

"Because," he said, "well, frankly, I don't know what it is I want. I am the kind who just ponders and imagines. I sit here and think this or that. Talk of this or that. Marco is a doer."

"Maybe he sits and thinks, too, eating junk food all day like he used to. Only, he is stuck in India. How can we know?" she asked, fishing for anything to say that seemed safe. "Has he come back?"

"No. Like you," he said. Like someone who'd flicked a bright light on an empty space, Cosimo looked terribly lonely.

"I'm here now," she blurted out.

"Look, so sorry. I need to leave soon," he said. "I have a commitment I could not change."

"Oh, fine," she lied. "Me too."

Renata had told Tito that she needed some rest tonight, and now she found herself thinking about the long hours ahead, alone at Albergo Ambrogino. *Porca miseria ladra.* It was over. She wasn't sure what was over exactly, as nothing at all started.

"So what about another drink sometime soon?" he said.

A couple left the nearby table empty. Renata wanted to be that woman, walking out, leaning against her companion, her gaze distracted by the warmth of his body.

"Or dinner," he proposed when she did not reply. "So we have more time to talk. I am too excited seeing you again. I haven't shut up for a moment—*blah, blah, blah*—and we haven't really talked." His voice was forcefully upbeat. "You live in Minnesota, right?"

"Yes. What do you know about it?"

"*Fargo*," he replied, his eyes glittering with self-mockery. "And it's exceptionally cold. That must change you. It's always the same here. Sometimes I think about the days clicking on and on, like walking on an endless path and it doesn't matter at all who walks on it and who steps aside."

"Oh, Cosimo—" There was a sadness to his eyes, the kind that speaks of years of solitude.

"You still draw? In little spiral notebooks?" he asked. She smiled and nodded. "Cool. I always loved that. Crayons and pencils: a different language at your fingertips and off you go to a private space. Well. You still play chess? It was a miracle to watch you beat everybody. Who do you invoke for chess? Saint who?"

"No saint involved. The teaching of a secular father." She shrugged, looking away, thinking of the saints her mother had prayed to with no discernible results. After her mother's death, Renata had been mad at each one of them—Saint Anthony, Saint Agatha, Saint Theresa.

"No saint. Perfect." Cosimo laughed warmly in response. "C'mon, see? A chat is fun. We have a little time before I take off. Let's talk about, I don't know, things." His voice was full of nervous innuendoes, and she remembered how much she had fantasized about exactly this moment, about finally being alone with him again.

"Like?" she asked.

"Well. Like. I don't know." He leaned in. "Hillary or Obama? Who are you going for?"

She gave him a dry smile. Politics at Bar Noventa: business as usual. An inane fight would ensue if memory served her well.

"It's Obama," he said.

It pissed her off. Because he did not let her talk, and because the man she had pined after for so long acted like a jerk. Even worse, she still found him attractive.

"Of course I choose him. Bingo," she lied.

He grinned.

"Look, *principessa*. He doesn't have a chance to be elected president," he said.

"Really? You know this all the way here at Bar Noventa?" Her tone was so giddy that he looked up. "And I vote for him why, then?"

"Because of your father. Look, he was from the South, no?

The Milanese looked down on him all his life, you feel an affinity with Obama. I get it."

"Wait. It's more important that Obama was the one to vote against the Iraq war, no?" Now they would have a real conversation. "That matters, right?"

"War is not the most important factor," he said.

"It is to me."

"C'mon. Your father fucked you up big time about the war."

"My father did? Not the war?"

"You were always so pissed off like it had happened to you."

"It did happen to me," she said, woozy with adrenaline. "And it pissed me off."

In her last weeks, her mother had shaken Renata and Tito awake in the middle of the night because she was convinced that the SS were going from house to house. She whispered to the children to come fast; they'd hide in a closet or carve a safe crawl space between the walls. For years, Renata woke up in the dark with a strange hope that her mother would again be there, determined to save her.

"I upset you," Cosimo said. "Let's forget about the darn war."

"Sure," she said. "Done."

There was a silence.

"I am an ass," Cosimo said.

"Yeah. You are."

It was a crappy night, in a dark bar full of men with longish hair worn in homage to the youth they'd wasted at the same bar. They expected wishes to materialize like moths in May. A migrant species, dreams would journey to Bar Noventa to find them waiting in their open parkas, with fingertips stained with tobacco.

She stood up.

"I must go," she said.

Cosimo stood up too, a flurry of anxiety crossing his face. A twinge of pleading showed in his eyes, but she leaned over to signal that she was going to impose the indignity of a formal goodbye kiss on both cheeks.

She kissed air twice just as he pulled back, as if slapped. They crossed the line, with kinetic speed, from friendship with subtext to friendship breakup. Before she could turn to go, he pulled her close, kissing her temple. She felt the whisper of his breath in her hair.

"*Ciao, principessa*," he said.

"*Ciao*, Cosimo."

They both knew it was *addio*.

She walked outside, remembering a flicker of the young Cosimo, a rangy kid with a red bandanna dancing alone in an empty room. He'd been exciting and elusive. "An asshole," had been Tito's sharp assessment of him years back. "I'm glad you beat him at chess in front of that jerk of a new girlfriend who thought you were a total loser."

She was elated, remembering that she had.

One evening Papoozi had switched off the radio and stared hard at the fresh bruise on Renata's chin. She was engrossed in her homework, coloring elaborate drawings of saris, saffron, and Hindi gods.

"What's been happening at school?" he asked.

"We're studying about India," she said.

"Who did you have a fight with this time?"

"No fight. It was an accident," she told him. "Girls don't fight."

The boys hadn't wanted to fight a girl, but she'd taunted them from behind her raised fists. She had gained a taste for schoolyard fights as the best release for her anger.

Papoozi stared at her. Her stomach tightened. She went to the bathroom and washed her face. When she returned from the bathroom, Papoozi was waiting in the living room.

"Sit," he said.

He took a chessboard from a shelf and set it on the table between them.

"You can do a lot with this," he said. "It's much more satisfying to fight with your brain rather than your fists." The chess-board looked like a crossword puzzle. She looked at Papoozi, perplexed. He explained the rules.

"Pay attention," he said. "Winning is exclusively determined by how well you understand the opponent's strategy."

He demonstrated moves, swift and precise like a game of war. She watched him with hushed attention, loving the intriguing unfolding of move and countermove, strategy and deception. She reveled in the stories playing out in her head as the pieces moved across the board—the kick of a boot that broke a door open; a queen, abandoned behind a deserted castle; a soldier on the run, with nowhere safe to turn; a horse, trapped and too frightened to move.

Papoozi locked eyes with her.

"Study me. Beat me," he said.

9

S tazione Centrale? This way, yes?" she asked a young woman who had stopped to light a cigarette. The woman just pointed in response.

Renata's old family home was located by Stazione Centrale, but she'd been used to taking a tram there from a different direction. It was windy, and the light from the lampposts brushed the sidewalk. She imagined that the few men and women walking her way were heading to the same destination, evening pilgrims finding their way home.

Renata vaguely recognized a tiny playground carved out of a pedestrian island by the train station—two ancient stone benches, one seesaw, and a swing set. An old woman in slippers fed pigeons from a garbage bag, with a gesture reminiscent of a blessing. The cooing and the beating of wings in unison sounded like laughter.

Disturbed, she wished for Steve. One night, walking in downtown Minneapolis, they'd placed their palms on the window of a coffee shop that had looked abandoned but for a light flickering in the very back. Fingers brushing, they'd whispered of imaginary, marvelous terrors lurking in the back of the shop. There was a tenderness in being caught in a space of fear together.

In a side wall of Stazione Centrale, she found the discreet entrance to Binario 21. She did not want to see it. A little past this was her home—not the place she knew, but something right on the edge of it, now that Papoozi was gone and every room was dark.

Renata wanted the pale light in the kitchen and the chatter of two kids inventing games at night.

"For your birthday, I give you a light bulb always on," Tito had giggled.

"For you, a cat with tiny wings," Renata had replied.

"And for me?" Papoozi had asked, glowing. She realized now that he had fought hard to experience that exact moment, of being silly with his two children. *How wonderful*, she thought now, *that life filled people with desire, that a man wanted children after enduring a brutal war, his body diminished to skin and bones.* This wish had pulled Papoozi along, onward.

"I want a gift too!" Papoozi had said, his laugh so filled with energy and life. Renata recalled the smell of bedtime chamomile, their own giggling, and her father's joy in their innocence.

"A letter never sent!" the young Renata had exclaimed, pretending to hand him one.

"Never written! You must imagine what you wish!"

"Just don't lose it! Ever!" Tito had admonished Papoozi. Papoozi attentively read the imaginary letter, then folded it, and put it away in his pocket.

"What's written in it?" Tito and Renata had demanded. "What? What?"

"It's a secret," he'd told them. There had been a catch in his voice, Renata remembered, a buzz of softness. Papoozi had been moved.

Renata took a tramway to La Scala. From there she could make her way back to the hotel on foot, passing through places she knew. The stores were closed and a few dimmed lights spilled from upper windows.

She was hungry and stopped to buy a Milanese *michetta* sandwich at a corner bar before heading toward the creamy lights of the Galleria. She'd missed the *michetta*—a ball of soft bread inside a crisp crust in the shape of an open flower, filled with thin slices of peppery *salame*. She ate it walking, American style. It was as exquisite as she'd remembered. Under the vaults of the Galleria, she passed by clusters of men, buzzing about politics with a ferocity she remembered from childhood. She stopped, out of habit, at the mosaic of the bull on the Galleria floor. She ground one heel in its balls and took a spin on one leg, for luck. This tradition was well known to the Milanese—an indent in the mosaic suggested as much—but several tourists with cameras stared hard. She exited at the other end of the Galleria. The Duomo again, this time dark, the lights dimmed as if on an empty stage.

She walked by the kiosk selling lottery tickets at the corner of Via Torino, where Papoozi used to buy a ticket every Friday. She gave a slight nod to the old man at the kiosk, before remembering that the lottery always hired a blind man for good luck. "*La Fortuna è cieca*," he called after her in a singsong. Luck is blind. Papoozi never won the lottery, but he took this setback with the fortitude of a man repeatedly denied parole.

In the morning, Tito was late arriving at her hotel. *Il traffico*, he explained.

Renata had paid attention to her appearance. Papoozi, lying in wait, could not see her crisp white shirt with its mother-of-pearl buttons, but she wished he could. Her throat tightened, remembering her emotions in Minneapolis while packing for a possible funeral, given the urgency of Tito's call about her father's critical condition. She'd congratulated herself for selecting such a smart, fashionable shirt, but then felt guilty for packing it.

"Ready to go?" Tito asked.

Renata understood Tito's frown; his rush and hurry was his way to love Papoozi, who had hated to wait.

"Totally," she said.

Tito stopped abruptly at the door to the street. "You look nice," he said. She was happy that he had noticed, but he quickly averted his gaze, as if disturbed by a thought.

Renata wondered if Cosimo had called him with a full report of the previous evening.

They walked to the car under a slight drizzle, just enough rain to create a sense of unhappy expectations for the day ahead. Renata felt at home, recognizing this emotion. It reminded her of living in Milan in winter, and how each day looming ahead had seemed already too long. The light of the overcast morning tainted the streets with a murkiness reminiscent of the scene of a crime, she noticed with a smile.

"You okay?" Tito said. That question used to be the one she always asked him.

"I'm just cold," she said, startled. Cold, hot, hungry—that, too, used to be Tito's response, which Renata could always attend to successfully. The rest, complaints of another kind, were considered irrelevant in their family, as they could not be easily fixed.

"Okay, then. Hurry," said Tito, even though the car was parked nearby, dwarfed by a ripped poster of a Russian circus advertising chained bears and women in glittery costumes.

They rode in silence through a neighborhood Renata did not recognize, a seemingly random conglomeration of old two-story houses sandwiched between towering apartment buildings with tiny balconies, crammed with bikes and plastic toys. Tito was staring ahead, frowning. She realized that it felt natural for them to be silent together, like the very old.

Tito lowered the window at a red light, nodded, and gave money to a skinny man holding a cardboard sign. She could make out the word *refugee* on the sign but nothing of the rest.

"Refugee from where?" she asked.

"Who knows. He is always here, and he changes where he escaped from at every new political turn." They both dissolved into giggles—the man's grit and resilience seemed somehow Papoozian.

In Piazza Piola Tito found parking next to a decaying palace, with an old stone staircase leading up to the front door. A red tricycle lay on its side in the middle of the courtyard.

As they were about to enter the chapel annexed to Ospedale Sant'Erasmo, Tito said, with some apparent effort, "I was thinking about dinner. Tomorrow."

He'd always formed his sentences in a halting way, as if converting his thoughts from some obsolete language into Italian. Today this habit unnerved her.

"Okay," she said. "That's great."

"Is eight too late for you?"

It was, but Renata didn't want to object.

"It's perfect," she said. "And no worries, I eat anything."

Tito took his glasses off, then put them back on. She wondered why the dinner invitation seemed to worry him. He added, cryptically, "We would like to have you over."

Renata didn't know who he meant by *we*. His manner was circumspect, but this wasn't unusual. Even when, as children, they had played at catching invisible angels, he used to pluck his angel gently from the air and, afterward, wipe his hands on his shorts.

"Over—?" she asked, perplexed.

"For dinner," he clarified. "At eight."

The chapel gate loomed over them, with its heavy iron work and the massive medieval latch, designed to protect against the incursions of Huns and Gauls. Papoozi was alone inside. Thinking of him, his delicate hair combed by strangers, Renata felt lightheaded.

"Dinner tomorrow will be great, Tito."

"I will pick you up at seven thirty." He looked relieved. She felt relieved too, as she seemed to be saying the right things.

Tito gave her a pale smile, rubbing his chin with one hand. He wasn't done, she realized.

"Don't bring anything," he said.

She understood from his faint blush that this was a reminder—in Tito's way, in the Italian way—that a bottle of wine was expected. She decided to bring flowers too.

"Oh, I won't," she said, just as expected. She felt a flurry of dread already about this dinner she'd learned of only moments ago. Tito's eyes were vivid, searching. There was more.

For a moment Renata thought that he might ask her about Minneapolis and Steve, but he did not. Maybe he felt that she, too, was simply floating in a suspended state, only occasionally catching the momentum that allowed her to land again in his life.

"Hey," she said, with a laugh. "Thank you. So, dinner at your place? Tomorrow?"

That was obvious, but there was something else that Tito was working toward. She wanted to help him get there, a line at a time, the way she used to make a recalcitrant Tito memorize poetry for school. *D'in su la vetta—della torre—della torre—antica*—Now, Tito seemed to become smaller and smaller, until he was in front of her, a sad little boy—*Passero solitario*—

"I would like you to meet, okay, my girlfriend."

"Your girlfriend?"

"My girlfriend," he repeated. "Loredana."

"You have a girlfriend? Oh. Really? No, I mean, you did not tell me."

"I just did."

Loredana. The name contained no Neapolitan flavor.

"She can't wait to meet you." He seemed distracted, as if his voice came from someone else filling in for Tito at the moment.

"Is there a problem?" she asked.

"Yeah, I guess. No big deal." He cracked his knuckles—*tak-tak-tak.* "Okay. Remember I told you I could not host you?"

"The apartment is too small?"

"We live with her parents." The street was deserted, but for a rail-thin homeless man with a broken Prada bag, intent on rummaging through garbage bins outside the closed doors of the Supermercato Alimetari Bindi.

Renata glanced at Tito, but he was looking over her head as if at something ominous in the distance.

"That's fine, that's fine," she said.

"Well, okay, then." He kicked away an empty can of aranciata that had rolled against the iron gate and was rattling back and forth in a sudden icy breeze.

"No problem, parents are fine," Renata said.

Oddly, her reassuring words seemed to make Tito attack a loose button on his coat with ferocious intent.

"They don't like me," he said at last.

Freaks, total freaks. Renata imagined a creepy woman who collected porcelain figurines and a husband in his pajamas all day, chain smoking.

"They don't like you? What? Why not?" she asked. "When they get to know you better, they'll come around."

He pulled the heavy gate open and let her in.

"No, they won't. They're the kind of Milanese that have been set in their ways for generations. Pure *Meneghini*. I'm a *terrone*."

"Oh God. Come on. I was told things had changed. I've heard things were moving in a different direction now. Very old fashioned, these jerks." But *bastardi di merda* came to her mind. Papoozi had fought a war for these pretentious Milanese too. It pissed her off.

"Oh yeah," Tito said. "Very much so."

"Okay, don't worry, I—" She was rambling. "Everybody can change." But then she remembered how, years ago, she'd refused to even consider switching to a different brand of cigarettes.

"You can't tell people how to feel," Tito said.

Renata couldn't care less about Loredana's family. It was Tito she worried about, the younger brother who counted on her and believed she could fix anything.

"*Ciuccia nebbia*! Fog suckers!" Renata grinned, using the familiar slur against Milanese. But *ciuccia nebbia* was a friendly insider joke; it didn't taste bitter like *terrone*. "Watch me work the room at dinner tomorrow; it will go fine," she said, dulled by the sudden certainty that the evening would be anything but fine. "You'll see, I'll make them rethink it." It was an idiotic thing to say, but Tito nodded in response. It was a way, she thought, he could love her back.

They walked up the uneven steps to the chapel, once a pale yellow, now chipped and slippery in the sprinkle of morning rain. Vines hugged the thick walls.

"Flavia?" Renata suddenly remembered.

"Here already."

"I mean, is she coming too?" Renata asked. "For dinner tomorrow?"

Tito gave her a puzzled look. "No."

She expected him to say something more. He didn't.

"Okay," she said, feeling somehow reprimanded.

To her surprise, Tito leaned in and whispered in her hair, "Don't mention it."

There was a slight pause.

"She is not family."

He now pushed open the door to the chapel, the silence between them like a blast of cold air.

10

Papoozi had chosen a closed casket viewing when their mother had died, in the center of the mortuary at Ospedale Fatebenefratelli. The room had appeared enormous for its emptiness and was damp like a dungeon. There had been nothing at all to remind Tito and Renata of the woman who had hummed tunes while ironing, with a liquid voice that made their scalps tingle.

Tito pushed open the door to the chapel. It was dark and quiet. Through a door on the side they entered a long, whitewashed hallway. Tito entered a side room that looked like a hospital chapel from a period movie, but for the absence of religious symbols. Two tiny windows let in dull streams of light. Gray foldable chairs sat around the open casket in the middle of the room.

Flavia, a delicate figure, was peering inside the open casket. Renata could not imagine what comfort Flavia obtained from this slightly bloated Papoozi, in a brown jacket and silk tie, resting in this oversized crib.

The pine casket was richly adorned in a way that seemed grotesque, even mortifying. *Che pagliacciata!* Buffoonery! Renata expected Papoozi to sit up straight, mad as hell, throw out the white lace pillow—clearly too stiff for comfort—and demand that the tacky satin cover be removed from his chest. *Imme-dia-tamente!*

That he lay quietly, withstanding the affront, made her understand that Papoozi was truly dead.

"'*A livella*,'" Tito announced beside her, taking a piece of paper from his coat pocket. Every time Tito had had to speak in public, he'd always appeared to be in an acute state of physical distress.

"*A livella*" had been Papoozi's favorite poem, written in Neapolitan dialect by the comic actor Totò. Papoozi had known its verses by heart, a mix of wit and philosophical musings about how all, count or beggar, are equal in the face of death.

Tito cleared his throat, glanced at Papoozi with a slight nod, then started reciting.

"*Ogn'anno, il due novembre—c'è l'usanza—*"

Renata noticed that the chaplain had slipped in, and after a quick greeting to Flavia he was now standing in the back, listening with respectful attention, hands clasped in front of him, as if "A Livella" were a prayer in Latin. It might as well have been, given that the chaplain likely spoke not a word of Neapolitan. Neither, Renata knew, did Tito or Flavia. Only she could understand Tito's words.

An aching tenderness gripped Renata as she observed Tito's flushed cheeks and his determination to recite the entire poem, despite his halting awkwardness.

Renata fixed her eyes on the Papoozi that was so clearly not Papoozi. He was done now, done with worrying about money, food, disputes about tramway seats, and the vexations with his doctor.

Traditional Chinese medicine believed the soul to be present in the bloodstream, so perhaps some vital energy of Papoozi remained there; perhaps that part of him had heard the poem.

Having finally finished the poem, Tito leaned toward her. "It's the closing of the casket," he whispered. She nodded, confused. "I don't think Flavia can take it," he added. "She might need to sit outside."

Renata sensed that Tito was attempting to guide her, aware of her ignorance of what was supposed to happen. He probably found her nods irritating, she thought, when it was clear she understood nothing.

"She can sit outside. We can both sit with Flavia," Renata said.

Tito now stared at her.

"No, we cannot," he said. "A witness is needed at the closing. It's the law."

"I'll stay," she said. "Of course I will. Flavia needs you."

She wanted to say: *Don't worry, this is not Papoozi. This is merely an abstract sketch of him, like a pencil drawing on paper.*

"Are you sure?"

"I'm sure," she said. And she was.

In truth, Renata was relieved. The thought of sitting alone with Flavia on the marble bench outside left her with a knot of apprehension. She felt only a tenuous bond with the Papoozi lying inert before her, his face devoid of all mystery. The closing of the casket would be bearable.

Renata watched Tito take Flavia's arm and walk out with tiny steps to match hers. They seemed to soften, leaning against each other. She followed their movement until they stepped outside, when a shaft of light swept across the floor of the chapel, exposing cracked tiles and ancient stains. Papoozi would have leapt up this very instant to follow them if there were any shred of life in him, she thought.

With everybody gone, Renata breathed carefully. She felt the moist silence, thick with candle smoke, push softly against her chest. She could not resist staring at the still face of Papoozi, his lower lip curled as if he had detected some foul odor.

The door behind her opened to admit three men with large bags. They looked like plumbers, and their synchronized actions were silently efficient. They stopped upon seeing her. The taller one moved toward her, exuding the doleful air of an exhausted butler.

"Signora, may we begin?" he asked, with a slight bow of respect, his eyes liquid with what seemed to be a genuine sadness.

"Please, go right ahead," she said.

The men took big drills out of their bags. The domesticity of the sight would have heartened Papoozi. The tall man kept gazing at her, seemingly trying to pinpoint something that deeply disturbed him.

"The noise is difficult to hear," he said at last, in a low voice.

"Thank you, it will be fine," Renata whispered back

Renata couldn't care less about the noise. Papoozi lay in his casket, covered in miserable lace and crappy satin, as if this indignity was but an ordinary occurrence in his hard working-man's life. The incongruity of this sight had severed any link to the person her father had been. Papoozi—a *terrone* who'd never received a promotion—was now subjected to one final affront, and Renata could only watch in strange fascination.

"Please, go right ahead," she repeated.

The men went to work, making slight adjustments to align the top and bottom casket lids perfectly. Renata observed every detail with a cool detachment, in order to describe it later, at home, to the live Papoozi, the way she had always done when witnessing a curious event. Papoozi, like the Papoozi of old, would listen, rapt.

"Precise? How precise were they, Reni?" he would ask.

"Very."

"It would have been good if I had been there, to make sure."

"You were there."

When Papoozi had been a young man, he thought he could fix anything with a hammer, a saw, and a nail. With good tools at hand, he used to say, you can make everything right again. "*Ecco fatto!*"

Renata closed her eyes. When she opened them again, the men were drilling the screws to seal the casket. Tito stood beside her, squinting painfully as if peering into the sun. The men at work shot him a piercing look of reproach, and the tall man sighed with relief. So this was what they'd expected, she realized—the man of the house. After their task was completed, the men shook hands with Tito. Renata wondered if Tito had slipped them a discreet tip.

As they left the chapel, Tito proposed breakfast at a local cafe. "Yes," Renata agreed. "I think we should."

She enjoyed yielding to his plans and asked, casually, "How's Flavia doing?" She felt both happy and guilty that he had chosen to leave Flavia alone to spend time with his sister, just like old times.

"Oh, you know," Tito said.

Renata didn't, but for once she was relieved by his silence. She brought a hand to her cheek where she felt a muscle twitching.

"Do you want pills?" Tito asked.

"What?" she replied, surprised.

"I've got Valium," he said. "I went to an open pharmacy last night." He took a small bottle of pills out of his pocket.

"No, thank you," she said.

On the marble bench Flavia was hunched over, as if she were attempting to light a cigarette against the wind. She looked up and shook her head, disconsolate. Renata elbowed Tito lightly.

"The pills?" she said.

But he shook his head, agitated. Flavia's mute pain wafted to Renata like a sound she could not bear to hear. *No pills for this* was Tito's sharp diagnosis.

"We should have coffee together," he offered. Flavia nodded.

Renata hoped that once they had a moment together, Flavia would put aside her restraint and ask Renata the many questions one might pose to a long-lost acquaintance. At the same time, she wanted to be invisible; unseen, so that she ran no risk of saying things that could disappoint.

"Where would you like to go?" asked Tito.

"Oh, it does not matter," Flavia demurred. She turned to Renata. "You?"

"Any bar is fine," Renata said, hoping to go somewhere pretty, somewhere she could remember later that would make the sharpness of the morning recede a little.

"I was thinking of the cafe at the corner," Tito proposed. "It serves fresh pastry."

"Perfect," Flavia said.

"It's just two steps away." Tito reassured her, taking her arm.

"I like any place," Renata said, with an inadvertent nod to the invisible script. "I'm not hungry." Flavia and Tito exchanged a glance: *Who could ever be hungry at this moment?* Nonetheless, they turned warmly to her, with a tender concern for her lack of appetite. The focus of their attention felt good. For once, she loved the Italian preoccupation with food.

The cafe was a tiny space, cluttered with tables, carved out of a hole in the corner by an entrepreneurial mind. It smelled of grappa and ham sandwiches. No fresh pastry was in sight. Renata imagined this was the designated coffee shop for Sant'Erasmo, and she pictured the chaplain sitting at a table, whispering comfort to distressed families just like them. There was, she thought, a peculiar solitude to sorrow.

There was a tiny cafe by Wellness Within she used to go to after a difficult day. Sitting by the window, she would watch the wind sweep leaves down the street and people waiting at the bus stop. She could overhear snippets of conversation among the customers—*Do you think he is her boyfriend? Want my advice? I cannot try again.* She found comfort in the way lives blurred into one another.

"Do you wear a stethoscope around your neck?" Papoozi had once asked her on the phone.

"No, I don't."

"What do you use?"

"The tip of my fingers over the wrists."

"Show me one day."

Renata had never had the opportunity. The mystery of illness, explored while sitting in the kitchen in Via Saverio, eating walnuts, would have been cozy. She had loved to fall into the late-afternoon rhythm of shelling and eating while chatting about this and that and the other.

In the bar near Sant'Erasmo, Renata, Tito, and Flavia sat at a small table by the window, awkward with one another, as if they had never spoken before. They seemed acutely aware that each one experienced Papoozi's death in a very different manner, so they chose silence. They ordered coffee. They waited for the tiny cups to come, looking around skittishly and avoiding one another's eyes.

"I think," Tito said, when the coffee finally arrived, "we should go to check out the house."

"Ah, yes." Flavia sighed. "Naturally."

"When we are done, no rush," Tito said. "Reni, you'd like to see the house, right?"

"Of course." She looked away. This time, Papoozi would not explain his absence with a frantic call from a phone booth battered by rain, saying that he was caught in a winter storm, with no tram in sight. And then he would appear at the door, one hand up to signal, *Here I am, all is well,* rivulets of water trickling to the floor.

"Has the house changed much?" Renata asked.

"Not at all," Flavia said.

Yes, it had. Papoozi would not be waiting inside, pacing in his slippers, impatient for them to come home.

The coffee turned out to be an exceedingly bitter percolation, startling Renata with its aggressiveness. Tito squinted at his cup, looking mortified at his selection of this cafe. Renata tried to hide her discomfort as they all concentrated on drinking their coffee. Flavia peered into her cup with sorrowful determination, taking small sips. After a moment she turned to observe a little boy having a tantrum right outside the window of the cafe, his mother partially hidden by the sign painted on glass. The boy seemed possessed by a furious despair he would not let go of and it was marvelous. Their composure was an artifice, and it offered not a shred of relief. They all stared, transfixed, at the little boy arching his back and jerking about like a hooked fish.

11

W e are starting all over in a new apartment!" Papoozi had declared after their mother's death, clapping his hands. "All new! The tables, the beds, the lamps!" His sudden extravagance confirmed the children's fear that nothing would remain the same after their mother's death, not even Papoozi.

The new furniture arrived within a few days, all flimsy pale wood. These polished pieces, untouched by anyone, looked wrong, not real furniture but something approximating it, like the alphabet small children scribble when they first learn to write. In the new space, meant to erase her presence, Renata imagined her mother everywhere as a comfort.

The building looked just as she remembered it: the iron fence still needed paint; the narrow gate leading to the paved yard was left ajar. She marveled at the sameness but wasn't sure that she liked it; her absence and return seemed equally insignificant to Via Saverio 7.

Steve had suggested using their scarce savings for a trip to Italy to meet the sensual and witty Italians who hung out in cafes, but she knew they would visit only with Tito and Papoozi, who would insist upon being constant company. Steve would grow testy sitting at a rickety table laden with leftovers that should not go to waste. Trains would blast past, drowning out conversation, and the heat would be torrid, locked in the dense cement sprawl of a city that frowned upon foliage and air-conditioning.

The glass doors leading to the modest apartments were adorned with the dark blue curtains of mourning, and the notice of Papoozi's death was affixed under a large ribbon in a matching color—all of it looking ordinary in an upsetting way. Renata thought of Papoozi going through each day of his life while the curtains waited for him, folded on a shelf at the Pompe Funebri Scotti.

A small ledger had been set up by the door of the *portinaia*, the concierge, with an open book for Papoozi's friends to sign. There were no signatures.

An aging *portinaia* Renata did not recognize came to greet them in house slippers, feet and ankles so swollen as to seem almost deformed. She wore a nice black dress and a thin gold chain and eyed Tito and Flavia with sullen eyes, as if expecting obscure accusations of negligence.

"*Buongiorno*," she said.

"*Buongiorno*, Signora Ines," they responded in unison, as if in prayer.

Signora Ines offered an indiscernible murmur of condolences to Tito, the new man of the house, and a small bundle of mail for Papoozi, bills and flyers held together by a rubber band.

"The casket will be brought home for the last time tomorrow morning, Signora Ines," said Tito. "We will be here by nine tomorrow. The casket will arrive by nine-thirty."

Renata was aghast. "Here? Wait! The funeral is here?" Papoozi couldn't have a decent ritual in this entryway.

"There is no—uh—funeral." Tito hurried to explain. "This is ritual in Italy and, of course, here in Milan. You wouldn't know this, no worry." Flavia and Signora Ines were staring at Renata in such hypnotic wonder that Tito became confused and stammered. "The—casket is—brought home for the last visit—before being taken to—"

"The crematorium," Renata interrupted. "I know that."

There was a little silence.

"Ah, the daughter from America?" Signora Ines said.

"She just came," Tito said, with a meek smile.

"*Grazie* for taking care of everything," said Flavia. "Always so attentive, Signora Ines." She attempted an apology for the disruption the funeral would bring to her work. Signora Ines, Flavia shared later, was well-known in the building for her moods. Signora Ines sighed, with a half-hearted never-mind gesture. Tito sighed also, possibly at the thought of the considerable Christmas tip her extra effort would require.

The tiny elevator was a creaking, tight space with wrought-iron doors that needed to be manually closed. Renata chose, by habit, to operate the doors. Little Tito had often left one of the doors slightly ajar when getting out, inadvertently deactivating the elevator and causing an uproar among the residents of the building.

"I have the keys," Flavia said, brushing the hair off Tito's eyes, a casual gesture that made Renata stiffen with her own desire for such maternal intimacy.

"I have the keys too," said Tito, giving Flavia a timid smile. It was clear to Renata how close they were, each stretching out moments with useless exchanges, for no reason but the pleasure of sharing the emotion a little more, the way a parent and a child do. She remembered her mother and herself reminding each other about keys, umbrellas, and whatnot, to savor the sound of their voices responding, like a bird call.

The familiarity of the apartment gave Flavia the confidence that Renata remembered more clearly than the tenuous public figure she'd exhibited so far.

"Here we are," Flavia said in a singsong voice, leading the way with an energized gait. As if on cue, the screeching sound of a *Treno Diretto* entering the train station ripped through the house.

Everything, Renata saw, was absolutely the same, yet not. The furniture seemed oddly put together, even if there had been no change—a chair set against a wall now looked derelict, the tiny bookcase prim. The furniture gave the impression that the inhabitants had gone, leaving behind what they didn't care to take.

Papoozi's armchair retained the indent his shoulders had left on the pillows. The newspaper, on the table beside the chair, had last been folded by his fingers.

Her years in America seemed to have worked like a mind-altering drug. Papoozi—whose city walks appeared to have the quality of an aphrodisiac, who read encyclopedia entries as if he were sipping anisette—seemed to her now to have been unable to experience pleasure. He was not the tough, attractive man, full of vigor, that he had been in their eyes, but a shunned outsider. In fact, he'd never asked company over, as if that were a sign of good manners. At a rare dinner out, they'd lingered so long that Tito fell asleep with his head in her lap while Papoozi was fussed over by a waitress. Excited by the attention, he'd told her about gathering sea urchins at Posillipo and the beautiful sea off the Amalfi coast.

"Do you believe in God?" Papoozi had asked Renata once with piercing intensity.

"Sometimes I pray in Latin," she'd said.

"And what happens?"

"I am not sure." *You can't always know the result of prayer*, her mother used to tell her.

"Why do it then?" he'd asked.

"It feels good," she'd replied. In the Latin words, she found a sense of mystery and comfort in her mother's remembered hope.

The sweet and musty smell of rooms that had remained closed for a few days gave her pause. Papoozi had breathed this very air, she thought. Through the crack of a door left open, she saw the *salottino*, the tiny receiving room with a small couch, an armchair, and a coffee table—all covered with white sheets to keep them pristine for visits. The room had been used only once that Renata could recall, when two Mormons in white shirts and ties had come to the door. They'd looked terribly young and hopeful, and Papoozi had let them in so Renata could practice her English.

"I need to freshen up," she said. In the small bathroom with pale green tiles, she studied Papoozi's toothbrush and his Pasta del Capitano toothpaste in its plastic cup ready for his evening ritual. The delicate smell of his aftershave lingered in the air, and a trace of gray fuzz clogged the corner of his razor blade. She stayed in the bathroom a bit longer, relishing the suggestion that Papoozi might show up.

While she was in the bathroom Flavia and Tito busied themselves cleaning, the tiny garbage pail under the sink already full. Renata wished to experience everything the way Papoozi had left it a bit longer—the severe curtains left open, the *fette biscottate* and walnuts in a bowl on the table, the folded newspaper awaiting his attention. He could walk in any minute then, back from one of his strolls.

She opened the freezer door and dipped her face in the cool mist from the ice cube tray, just as she used to do in the hot summers of her youth. She had forgotten how small everything seemed in Italy, like in the fairy tale of the three bears. In the refrigerator she touched a few things. The yogurt, *Yomo naturale alla Fragola,* was the size of a jar of baby food.

"You can have it," said Tito. "It's fresh. I checked."

"I was just looking."

Flavia had washed a plate, a fork, and a drinking glass, all of which now dripped in the drainer which hung above the sink Italian style. She thought of Papoozi eating from that plate, using those utensils, that last evening, unhurried, with the radio on as usual, not knowing it would be the last time.

"Sit down, go ahead." Flavia was primping a pillow on an armchair Renata did not recognize. "You rest a bit now. All the way from America—"

Renata chose a chair at the dining table instead. She used to study in that spot and had always enjoyed the rush of noise from the massive *Stazione Centrale*. It was in the midst of turbulence that she found a perfect calm.

"Here's the 16.35 *Diretto* from Bologna, what a brontosaurus," Papoozi used to say from behind his newspaper. "I don't know how you can do any work here." But she did.

Studying acupuncture in America, she'd loved the mess and chaos there too—intrigued as she was by the different habits, the mix of cultures, and the variety of food. She'd applied herself to learn a language that seemed a mimicry of birdcalls in an aviary and had found a centered space in the midst of everything so new and surprising. Indolent in Milan, Renata had studied exceedingly hard in Minneapolis. A baker gave her bagels when she treated him for free, which started the barter system at the clinic. This exchange of goods brought unexpected wonders to her life.

Renata felt tempted to go to her old room but was afraid to. It had been a lonely room in the winter nights.

"Going to your lair?" Papoozi used to ask her.

With a gesture that seemed automatic, Flavia went to the small TV.

"You two watch a bit of TV?" she asked firmly. "Relax, there is nothing for you to do here."

Both Tito and Renata said they would be fine without the noise. The TV set had been new when Papoozi bought it with his first *tredicesima*—the extra paycheck given to employees in Italy to cover Christmas expenses—but was now obsolete, with its thick frame and tiny screen. A doily drooped down each side, resembling a prayer veil.

She could envision Papoozi enjoying the noise from the TV, hands crossed in his lap. He'd never seemed to choose a program, but simply liked the babble of voices, the way a canary in a cage is appeased by the company of a tiny mirror or a bone.

Flavia was at work in the kitchen, suggesting that nothing out of the ordinary was going on.

"Will Flavia be fine with her pension?" Renata asked.

"Of course," Tito said.

She felt a little ashamed that America didn't provide pension plans, but she loved her patients very much, whether they paid a regular fee or not. She loved Tessa declaiming, "This clinic is madness!" and she loved the red flowers that looked like feathers, so unusual to her, that grew on the trees outside her window. These things of her American life all shared something in common, even if she did not quite know what that was. Her life seemed a collage, where the individual pieces created meaning in their asymmetric, disconnected placement.

"Sometime we'll get a pension plan in America too," she said. "Soon, I think." She'd seen Obama raise his fist high at a rally. *Change.*

She caught a glimpse of herself reflected in the window, a blur against the railway tracks. In the last years she had been only a voice on the phone to Papoozi, their last conversation a few months earlier.

"Do you have peach trees there? Or sycamores?" Papoozi had asked. *Do you have things there that remind you of us?* he was asking.

"Yes," she'd lied. One night, while she waited for Steve to come home, her window framed a scene of snow falling among the maple trees. She had, at that moment, wanted fog and the familiar rumble of a *Direttissimo* train. Her home in Milan. "Sycamore trees and peach trees, all here," she'd told him.

Flavia, meanwhile, dusted and swept, showing respect to Papoozi the only way she knew how.

"Reni," Tito said quietly, with an odd intensity to his voice. "I need you to sign something."

Sign? He wanted the apartment, she thought. She lived in America now, as he often reminded her during their occasional phone calls. America, the mystery land of prepared dinners, tall men, and stiff cocktails. Tito had made it clear she did not belong in Milan anymore. She knew he was thinking that she didn't even speak Italian in her daily life and could not possibly return. He had not asked if she wished to.

"Now?" she said. "C'mon."

"It's important."

"Later." She did not intend to sign anything.

"Reni, *porca miseria.* Listen!" Glancing over, she saw Tito becoming increasingly irate—a grown man who didn't like to ask for anything.

"I'm going to see my old room," she said, jumping up. She was a mess of torpor and melancholy, but Tito could not make her do anything at that moment. He was a bastard for trying, and she was not giving up the house.

"Yeah, well. I think it's a bit dusty," he said, with a forced smile.

"Always was."

Her room was as she'd left it—a faded coziness in the tiny desk and flimsy curtains. Bella, her porcelain doll, perched still above the wardrobe, ashy with dust. A sepia photo of little Renata hung on the wall, reminiscent of a long-departed ancestor's portrait. It all made her feel as if she had been alive a long time and possibly outlived herself.

She closed the door, sat on the bed, then fell backward with her arms open wide, floating over the sound of trains, the voices coming from the street, and a sharp metallic noise from the courtyard that she could not identify yet felt familiar. It was a perfect moment of peaceful abandon.

I'm staying here for a while to sort things out, she imagined telling Tessa. *I need it.* Tessa would understand. Renata pictured herself reading in Papoozi's living room in the soft light of a late afternoon; it had the allure of things lost.

"Reni?" Tito pushed the door open and sat on the end of her bed.

"How do I look back in here?" she asked. Alarm at his unexpected arrival in the room had given her a shot of energy.

"Very nice."

"You know—I might stay. Don't I fit right in?"

"Yeah, good," he said. "And Steve?"

"Oh, Steve. You know."

"No, I don't know," he said, pulling a folded piece of paper from his pocket. "You and Cosimo are totally ridiculous. Are you still crazy for the jerk?"

"I never—"

"Ah, right," he said. "He never did either." He scanned the paper in his hand.

"Why? Did he talk about me?" Renata asked, with studied casualness.

"Oh God, this is total nonsense," Tito said. "We need to take care of urgent business."

"Go for it. I'm used to pressure, you know. I'm a doctor." She sat up. "You should say that to people when they ask what I do."

"We need to talk," Tito insisted. "I have to ask you something. We have very little time. Papoozi wanted his ashes to be dispersed in the sea in Naples, but the Italian government does not allow it. The *Pompe Funebri Scotti*, the funeral home, was helping get a passport for Papoozi, so that his ashes could be taken, say, to Switzerland, where casting the ashes into a lake is legal. The permit must be signed by Papoozi to prove that he agreed. Do you understand what I'm saying?"

Renata was still thinking about what Tito had just said about Cosimo.

"Yeah, I do."

Renata imagined Papoozi escaping to, of all places, Switzerland, and could not think of anything more incongruous. But she liked that the Italian government was determined to check on his whereabouts after death. He would have been amused at that, after a lifetime of neglect.

Tito showed her the official-looking piece of paper he held. "You used to be able to fake any signature. Can you fake Papoozi's?"

"Yeah, of course," she said, with a grin. "I just need an original to copy from."

They were a team, and she was solving a problem, just like she used to. She saw them again as two *terroni* kids, alone in the playground at school.

"I have it," Tito said.

Renata sat at her old desk, pulled up her sleeves, and copied Papoozi's signature, following the labyrinth of curves and lines, careful not to smear or stray. She bit her lip, concentrating on the solo of the capital *C* soaring impossibly high, then followed the swing of vowels with her eyes half closed. At the end, she leaned against the back of the chair to examine her work critically. The *S* of Cesare was a bit too sharp, but she felt otherwise satisfied. It cheered her that she had truly done something for Papoozi. Her mother had taught her how to write the alphabet by copying words, and Renata had found her old concentration returning, so that when she glanced up, her task completed, she was surprised to find Tito standing there instead of her mother.

"Don't tell Flavia, it would make her too sad," Tito said, pocketing the signed paper.

Renata nodded. "Yeah. She would be sad, wouldn't she?" She had done something for Flavia also.

"You are kick-ass good, Reni. Good thing you are back."

"Oh, sure," she said. "Thanks." She crossed her eyes in self-mockery but felt a surge of happiness at his words. In a recurring dream, she lived again in Milan. She worked at a job where she washed the hair of the dead. Silence, a gray mist, warm water. In the dream, she made her mother beautiful again.

"Switzerland!" She laughed. "That's where everyone pretends the ashes of their dead go?"

"Can you believe it?" Tito shook his head.

Renata imagined a train of the dead wending its way through the Swiss hills. Papoozi, even if reduced to ashes in an urn, would demand the best window seat.

Switzerland, of all places. That land of banks and mountain peaks. And that vigorous choral Swiss song that was so popular but that Papoozi had found so irritating. Men singing in unison had the sting of war.

"God, he was such a pain in the ass," she said.

"Nobody could live with him," Tito acknowledged with a chuckle. "Not even himself. He never stood still."

They both laughed. They tried to stop but couldn't.

☙

Tito proposed a simple dinner at Strippoli, but Flavia preferred to be taken home. Renata remembered Strippoli as a small *tavola calda*, buffet-style restaurant, serving typical dishes from Puglia, much spicier than Milanese fare. There would be no pressure at Strippoli to order antipasto with a meal or follow precisely the sequence of dishes that only tourists skipped, to the distress of waiters. The restaurant—squeezed into a dark square between two churches and the buildings of Università Statale—was a student hangout, dark and moist, with a pungent smell of *peperoncino* and spices one would take home, nested in one's clothes. Renata remembered a few lonely glasses of sour-tasting wine and an occasional pensive grappa there as she watched the flow of pedestrians outside.

"Sure, I remember Strippoli," she said, to Tito's palpable relief. She recalled leaning in at a table, and the soft and ticklish sensation of a man's beard brushing against her cheek. "I like Strippoli."

The restaurant seemed smaller and more crudely lit than she'd remembered, with just a few mature customers sitting alone. They turned their heads with a frown, as if brusquely interrupted.

"I'm having problems with Steve," she confessed to Tito over a beer. She wanted this conversation to be different from their usual cautious talks, but she was not sure exactly how to proceed. He rubbed his eyes, as if she had used a dirty word.

"You want to talk?" he said, after a moment, sitting up with a strange stillness.

Renata grasped for something to say, already regretting what now felt like a forced intimacy. The buzzing of overhead fluorescent lights amplified the silence.

"Nah. I'm too upset," she said.

"Are you too upset to make it to the dinner tomorrow?" he asked. His breathing was suddenly short and rapid—a staccato of panic.

"Of course I can. I would never let you down, Tito."

When their food arrived they both stared at their plates—

orecchiette pasta with broccoli rabe for her and roasted peppers with garlic for him. Old-time favorites.

"Did we ever eat this at home?" she asked, in an attempt to lighten the mood.

"I don't think so," he said. "But it would be nice to be able to place a call to the dead, don't you think? One innocent call, every now and then, and have the opportunity to ask something stupid like, did we ever eat broccoli rabe? No big stuff. One wonders about the little things."

Renata wished they had chosen an *osteria* that smelled of Nazionali cigarettes and old wood, where people were loud and silly.

"Okay. Something was wrong with our mother's liver. Did she drink, smoke?" Tito asked. "I don't remember."

"No, no. The doctor caught her cancer too late. By the end it had spread. Bones, liver. Who knows where it had come from. Papoozi said that bombs were not made of rose blossoms, they affected civilians too. Smoking and drinking would have been fine. They would have offered some shred of pleasure to her days. Like, I don't know, a cigarette after dinner."

"Don't be silly. A cigarette? C'mon, what joy is there in that?" he asked, raising his eyebrows.

The first time Steve and Renata had met for a date, at a bar in Dinkytown, he leaned in to light a cigarette for her with the bemused smile of a nonsmoker in love. They'd maintained eye contact in elated silence, as if they were about to make love.

"Smoking is a real pleasure," she said. "I miss it. But this is true for so many things that, at this point, I don't know which ones matter." She looked down at her hands folded tightly in her lap. Maybe it was herself who she wanted to be missed.

"Hey, Reni. Look. We don't have to talk about your life," Tito said, pushing his empty plate to the side. "I just wanted to know if you were still up for the dinner. That's all."

"It's okay to talk about my life," she said. "It's totally fine."

"Things with Steve are your private business," he said.

They finished their beer quietly. He drove her back to the

hotel with the radio on. He stopped in front of Albergo Ambrogino and they sat, saying nothing.

"I'm sorry about Steve," he said, after a time.

"Thank you," she replied. "But no worries. I'll do great at the dinner. You know that."

"Tomorrow you want the day to yourself?"

Feeling a surge of gratitude for the offer, she agreed that a little time to herself would be great.

"I'll come to get you tomorrow evening then?" Tito asked.

"Yes," she said.

He waited a moment more. The silence between them grew in intensity.

"Are you sure?" In his frown, she saw now that he feared her presence at the dinner. He did not trust her.

"I'll do great," she bristled. *Nice shirt, hair brushed, and a fabulous bottle of wine.*

She forced herself to visualize an animated dinner. No awkward conversation or blunders.

Her desire to do everything right made her aware of her inexperience. Her mother had taught her things of little use, such as cooking in anger spoiled the food. Papoozi had taught her that Eskimos used one hundred different words for snow, and that the Chinese language had no word for goodbye. She'd learned nothing from them about the right clothes to wear, about men, wine, or life.

They like you, she imagined Tito saying after the dinner was over.

They like you, Tito, she would reply.

12

As Renata entered La Rinascente, a melody fluttered mid-crescendo, accompanying her up the escalator to the floor where Addi worked. A naked mannequin—without hair, its eyes glassy—reclined on the second floor. "Everybody looks strange when naked," Steve used to say.

Renata noticed Addi by two mannequins in designer coats, pulling leather gloves over their hands, her movements following the rhythm of the song. The sight made her smile. The unperturbed immobility of stylish mannequins had always appealed to her. At parties, as a young woman, she'd tried to imitate their distant, sexy attitude.

"Addi," Renata called out. "Oh, it feels so good to see you!"

Addi turned.

"Hey, you came back—" she said.

"Yeah, here I am! Already!" *Too loud*, she told herself. "Well. Okay. See, I thought we might do a stupid errand together that's killing me. We could make it fun, like old times." *Too much too soon?* "It's so silly. I'm all hot and bothered about having to choose a bottle of wine for a big dinner, and it's ruining my day."

"Oh no! Today I have a lunch date. Want to join us? It's fine. This boyfriend is just like a temp job. A little boost while I figure things out. Come."

"Maybe some other time," Renata said. *Goddamn.* She had run out of the hotel, not thinking. She started to go.

"Wait!" Addi called. "We can grab a quick bite. You pick where."

"No, it's okay. You guys go ahead," Renata said, with her head down and shoulders up, like a boxer.

"What is this all about?" Addi asked.

Lunch with Addi and her boyfriend meant listening with a

frozen smile while they went through anecdotes about their
lives and pet peeves. Renata had told Addi nothing real about
her life in America. *Every interaction is theater*, Steve had said. Is it
really? she wondered, her eyes fixed to the floor.

Addi reached out to lift Renata's chin with the tips of her
fingers, her face soft with tenderness. *Addi and Reni.* Renata
felt tears fill her eyes. Then she told Addi everything—that she
could not come back another day. She lived in America and
had been in Minneapolis for seven years. Sometimes she cried
at the thought of forgetting her voice in Italian, the way the
tongue softened, holding vowels. She sang childhood songs to
herself. She had no child. Her husband was not in love with
her. She had started to agree with him and liked herself less and
less. A patient of hers, a palm reader, had told her she'd lived
many lives, one after another, but Renata felt that she slipped
in and out of different lives all the time—the happy wife, the
American woman, the expat. Her father had just died, and her
brother talked to her as if they were polite strangers. He had
invited her to an important dinner that night with his future
in-laws, Milanese elite who disliked him. She wanted to fight
for him. She wanted to bring the best bottle of wine on earth
and impress. She wanted to be the older sister he remembered,
the one he'd thought impossibly brave. Instead, she was in a
deep panic.

Addi dialed a number on her phone and talked fast.

"I canceled the date," she told Renata. "We'll grab French
toast at the bar downstairs and do something just the two of us.
Then we buy the damned wine."

Addi's boyfriend had reserved two tickets to go see Leon-
ardo da Vinci's painting *The Last Supper* at the church of Santa
Maria Delle Grazie, and Renata and Addi agreed it might be
fun to have a new experience together. On the way, they talked—first, tentatively, of winters, summers, and nights in Milan
and Minneapolis spent with open windows, warm air, and men;
then, of listening, as kids, to the mysterious rustling of sick
parents. Addi remembered Papoozi indistinctly, the blur of a

man vigorously pacing outside school one day. Addi's mother had opened the door to Renata once, in an old nightgown, her feathery hair held by clips. Addi's mother had told her daughter about how they had made clothes out of old bedsheets and coffee out of chicory during the war; they'd read books with pages thin as rice paper. Making do, she'd felt, was a point of honor, and she'd looked upon desires with disdain. *There was nothing to them*, she used to say, *and they made you feel awful.* This had scared Addi into keeping secrets.

The solid grace of the church of Santa Maria Delle Grazie was a welcoming sight. A few tourists paced in the waiting room, talking in French, German, or English with a terse urgency, consulting their maps to their next destination. "There are secrets in the painting," an old Italian woman murmured to a shy little girl. "Look closely. The spilled salt, the food on the plates, they are all clues." Renata smiled, intrigued.

Renata and Addi sat close on the bench, fingers entwined.

"You picked up and moved to America," Addi said. "Radical. It's exactly something I imagined you would do."

"Moving, not moving, and where. It makes little difference," Renata said. "If that's all it would take, I would live attached to a suitcase."

"C'mon. You are supposed to tell me it makes a big difference."

They chuckled, shushing each other.

A young lady in a blue outfit signaled that it was time, and they followed the small group of visitors along a tight hallway.

The chapel was bigger than Renata had expected. She remembered Papoozi telling her that Napoleon's soldiers had created a makeshift stable in the chapel, and that Jesus's feet, on the mural, had been cut to make a door tall enough to accommodate soldiers on horseback. Renata liked to think that the painting's faded hue was caused by the gaze of thousands of visitors who had been transfixed by its beauty.

"The disciples all look like squirming butterflies pinned to a board," Addi whispered.

"I think that, in that instant, they see the future, crystal clear. There is nothing to say or do. They were having dinner, and then suddenly, their lives have changed and there is no fixing it," Renata said. "They know that. Look at them. They know. This is the moment." There was some satisfaction, she felt, in witnessing grown men's despair—men of faith, to boot.

The old lady pointed at the painting and spoke quietly to the little girl about various details she believed were important. Renata, however, was captivated by the Apostles, each swept up in the emotion of inevitable sorrow and loss. Da Vinci's painting didn't seem merely old or encompassing artistic bravado, but, instead, a tragedy caught in mid-act. Gazing at it, Renata felt moved.

Addi must have thought the same, and they exchanged a glance like secret spies.

"You know," Addi said. "I woke up in the same bed, in the same house, but after my mother's death everything changed. I suddenly felt as if I lived in a different country, say Greece or Norway, and had to adapt to different rules of behavior. I couldn't go back. In this new country, I tried to imitate the cool girls. But it wasn't what they did that made them cool, it was a thrill they had in their blood."

"One day, I heard my mother drop a glass," Renata said. "I ran to the kitchen, and she was standing there, staring down at the pieces. I swept them up fast. I thought that if I threw them out, hidden in a plastic bag, she would not be dying anymore. I tried to act normal at school. I got good grades. I tried so hard to do everything that I thought would give me a pass to go back to my old life."

"You know, there are billions of black holes in the universe," Addi said. "It's scary. We could fall in one any time, they say. We could disappear somewhere with no air, no light. What could we do about it? Nothing. It's not like when we were girls and first learning to kiss; we can't try it out and figure our way.

There are infinite things we can't control. Let's go do something we can. Not that I know a thing about wine," she said, with a smile, slipping her hand through Renata's elbow as they left the chapel.

&

The Supermercato Conselve was open, the lights dim, like a regret.

"*Porca miseria ladra assassina*," Renata blurted out while they hurried across the street, enveloped in a blast of cold wind. Cars, swerving around them, honked hard.

Renata was heartened by the warmth inside Supermercato Conselve, buzzing with young people in thin puffy jackets, rushing through the produce aisles before closing time. She saw that aisle six was still reserved for wine, just the way she'd remembered. I know this city inside out, she thought with satisfaction.

"I don't think my father ever had to buy wine for a special occasion," Renata said. "To be honest, I don't even know what his days were like. Now I wonder, what did he do all the time? Walk, and then what?"

"The mail," said Addi. "My father got bills and catalogues only, but he used to sit at the table every evening and go through them, disparaging products advertised by idiots and morons while the TV played in the other room. He'd smoke a cigarette and sip a glass of cheap wine, the kind with a twist-off top that finds its way into every apartment where crusty widowers stay up too late."

"Oh God," Renata said. "When I stay up alone at home and start complaining about everything, I get afraid I'm turning into exactly that—a lonely crank."

"Same," said Addi, "but I also like it. There is some appeal in making do, don't you think? Nothing is desired but what you already have. My mother thought it the ultimate satisfaction."

They strolled up and down the aisle, the rows of gleaming bottles intimidating in number and variety.

"Jesus," said Renata. "It's just a bottle of wine." But it was more than that, she knew. It was her first step toward being a warrior again for her brother.

Pausing between Sicilian and Valtellina reds, Addi lifted one bottle, as if close scrutiny might bring clarity.

"Why not that one? I think I have heard of the label before," Renata said.

"This wine is a good one," a young man pointed out helpfully, his tone one of casual expertise.

"This one?" Addi said, picking it up. "A long name. It's a good sign, no?"

"Yes. It's a great wine." A slight yet elusive accent drifted through the young man's words, as if a familiar tune shifted from adagio to fortissimo. I sound like this in English, Renata thought. Empathy softened his gaze—foreigners could easily detect others feeling stranded. "Off to a date?" he asked. "The wine is key."

"Obligation," Renata said.

"Ah, much worse," he said.

"Oh yeah," Addi said. "Serious business."

"You want to impress?" he asked. He appeared scruffy in his leather jacket, with his somnolent smile—not exactly what Renata imagined a wine connoisseur might look like.

"Perhaps I don't want to impress," she said, with a shrug, opting for a gutsy, jaded *Vaffan—fuck them all.*

"Yes, you clearly do want to impress." He handed her a bottle. "This is excellent. Hearty, with a suggestion of berries and figs. I am a bartender at La Traviata, and this is a favorite."

"Oh wow. La Traviata?" Addi lit up.

"Yeah," he said. "Come and eat there sometime. Ask for Marius, I'll give you a free glass."

"Your name is Marius? Nice," Addi said. "Why a Latin name?"

"Latin? Oh no." He laughed. "I'm Bulgarian, rather a beast to some Italians. The usual idiots, who exist in every country, right? They think that outsiders come to murder, steal—that kind of thing. Without imagination, they presume the same of

everyone else. If lucky, we are sexy beasts to them." He pressed
a bottle to Renata. "This wine is special." He winked, casually,
as a friendly nudge to lighten the conversation. "You know, this
is all foolishness anyway. I'm sure the lady of the house couldn't
care less."

"He's right, Reni," Addi said. "What matters is the gesture.
The lady of the house wants to brag with her girlfriends the
next day, say how hard you tried to impress her."

"Is the lady of the house all that important after all?" Renata
asked airily, trying to sound casual.

"To you," the young man said.

Renata hated how easily others could read her. She felt
particularly apprehensive about engaging in conversation with
mature women of Loredana's mother's age. They were poised
and confident, everything that Renata feared she was not. After her mother died, Renata used to ask women for directions,
when she knew the way perfectly well; she'd told them she was
lost so they would be concerned about her. She'd dropped her
backpack to get help putting it back on; she'd said odd things
in order to be remembered. Later, she would imagine conversations they might have about her with their family at the dinner
table.

"Well, how badly can this dinner go? Right? Good wine or
not." Renata put the bottle under her arm. The dinner might
seem to last forever, but it would end. Standing in a little group
under the sharp fluorescent light, talking freely, her apprehension felt silly.

"How bad is it if you don't go?" Marius asked. He possessed
a kind of raw energy, like a musician. She wanted to talk like
he talked, move as he moved, and everything would acquire a
sense of lightness and ease. "How bad?"

"Very bad," she said, with a laugh. "For one thing, my brother would kill me, perhaps many times over." But her chat with
a stranger, for whom she felt an affinity, had reduced the wine
to an errand, no mystery to it, and the dinner was just a dinner,
after all. How dangerous could a meal possibly be?

"Ah. Let's be brave then, shall we?" he said, picking up a bottle of the same wine he had recommended to them.

"Come on, go get them," he said.

They all exchanged a goodbye wave that he turned into a playful victory sign. Renata studied his slender back as he walked away, his elbow cradling the special bottle of wine. *Go get them.*

"You got this," Addi said. Renata, through Addi's eyes, pictured the dinner in a jauntier mood. They hugged goodbye like warriors, without tears.

13

Tito arrived to pick her up at seven-thirty on the dot. When Renata spotted him in the glaring light of the hotel lobby, he looked much younger in his careful attire—a little boy in a stiff suit and tie, dropped off at the wrong place. She rushed to him and squeezed his fingers, feeling his bones, sharp and delicate like a bird's. He glanced nervously at the bottle of wine she was holding, and she showed him the label for approval.

"You shouldn't have," he said, with a look of such astonishment that she knew a bottle of aged Brunello Di Montalcino, with its *suggestion of berries and figs*, was not only the perfect thing to bring, but an impressive choice.

"It's nothing," she demurred, "really." But she felt uncomfortable about something she could not pinpoint; she understood only when a man crossed the reception area, holding a bunch of red roses.

"The flowers," she breathed. She'd forgotten to buy them and now all the shops were closed. Only pharmacies alternated night shifts, that much she remembered. She experienced a rush of hatred toward the efficiency of Italian unions that made her blush.

"I got them," Tito said. "I thought you would be too busy." He looked down, contrite. "I also got wine, but not as good as yours. You don't mind?"

"No, sure. It's fine." She felt a strong swell of tenderness pass between them and for a moment thought they might break the family tradition and hug.

☙

During the car ride, Tito became expansive, describing Loredana's parents as *gente perbene*, people with solid principles and a good reputation—the Milanese password for families of respectable wealth or a white-knuckled aspiration to it.

"Ah," Renata said, alarmed. "Are they quiet or chatty?"

"Quiet," Tito answered, confirming her fears.

When the car stopped, Renata was surprised by the neatly manicured look of the neighborhood. She did not recognize it, yet it seemed familiar. These were suburban small villas, the *villetta* status symbol of well-to-do Italians after they'd retired. There were manicured lawns and sleek cars parked at the curb.

"Here we are." Tito sounded more resigned than happy.

"Where?"

"The Lorenteggio."

The Lorenteggio. Papoozi had forbidden them from venturing into the Lorenteggio neighborhood, even during the day. Once Tito and Renata had accidentally found themselves there after catching the wrong bus in Piazza Castello. Fascinated by forbidden territory, they'd explored a little, finding abandoned syringes among the white pebbles of a playground and under the bushes.

"This is the Lorenteggio?" she exclaimed in disbelief. "But it is all so fancy now!"

"It changed. Everything does."

Only seven years had passed, and this radical transformation felt truly unsettling in a personal way. It gave Renata a glimpse of experiencing her own death while still alive. She remembered how her patients in Minneapolis seemed upset at any change in the clinic, as if it were a sign of their irrelevance. They wanted the reassurance of continuity—the same carpet, lights, and chairs. They overreacted to even minor changes at the clinic. Now she had an intuition of the fear that triggered that response.

"Well, of course, I'm surprised," she said. "Nobody likes change, even good ones. My patients—"

"Listen," Tito said quickly, retrieving the flowers from the back seat of his car, "do you mind saying you are a nurse?"

"I'm sorry?" she said.

"You know, it's nothing. Who cares?"

"Maybe I care," she said.

"You told me and Papoozi it was quite the same."

"That was in a phone conversation. It was a way to make my job sound familiar."

"You can push it a little and say you work in a clinic. Why do you always have to tell everything?"

"What do you mean?"

"Like, you know, that Steve is a pig. Why tell Papoozi? What did Papoozi need the truth for, at his age? Why didn't you let him dream a little longer and brag in every store about a daughter in America, married to a successful actor who adores her? I saw him tear up after you told him. Papoozi, who never cried." Tito's voice was pitched with emotion. Renata was glad she'd never told them of her miscarriage. "Keep some things to yourself. What's the harm?"

"Fine. You want me to say I'm a nurse?"

"Only if it comes up," Tito said, after a short silence. "It's easier."

"Don't bring it up, then," she said. "Why would they ask? Loredana isn't working."

"She is younger."

Renata felt as if he'd slapped her. Tito started to walk ahead of her.

"Where do I work, a clinic?" Renata asked, through clenched teeth, attempting a conciliatory tone. Tito, from behind, looked terribly lonely, his steps staggering in distress.

"I don't care what you say," he said over his shoulder.

"Tell them I am a nurse," she said. "Whatever." They were both pathetic, she thought, hurrying to catch up with him.

Tito, however, had stopped dead in his tracks before a young man parking his Vespa.

"Gianni," he said, with a dread that seemed at odds with the gentle figure in jeans and a peacoat, walking toward them with one hand in his pocket, his collar turned up against the wind. "Loredana's cousin."

Gianni waved, a lit cigarette between his fingers. The tip twirled in the dark like a sparkler.

"Tito!" he called cheerfully.

"He will talk the whole time," Tito said.

"Yeah, well, good, let him do the talking."

"He speaks terrible English and is dying to practice." Tito shot her a sharp good-luck-to-you glance before greeting Gianni with a quick hug.

"Gianni! Good to see you." Tito laughed too hard.

"Surprise!" Gianni opened his arms wide. "Zia Marta invited me."

Gianni glanced at Renata, who now regretted her decision to wear the prim shirt and skirt she had been so proud of.

"Who's this?" Gianni asked Tito, a flash of bemused interest in his smile.

"My sister, of course. Renata."

"The one you didn't host?"

"The only sister I have."

Tito's dry tone suggested he was stung by the observation that he had not hosted her. Gianni dropped his cigarette on the sidewalk and ground it under his heel.

"Next time, I host her," Gianni said casually, nodding a *ciao* in Renata's direction.

"So, how are you?" Tito said.

"Uh, okay." Gianni shrugged, a light of defiant optimism in his eyes. Hands in his pockets, he sauntered ahead of them to the entrance to the apartment building and quickly pushed the buzzer several times.

"Zia Marta!" Gianni said into the intercom, with a warm cheeriness that made Renata look forward to the dinner, the evening, and even Zia Marta, whom she had feared just a moment before. She looked away when she caught Tito looking at her darkly. He'd nailed Cosimo's character, she recalled, but this time she wanted him to be dead wrong about Gianni, which would mean an uncomplicated evening ahead, with a relaxing dinner and casual chatter. Normality.

"They have a dog," said Tito, when an excited barking sound obscured the voice of a woman responding in the intercom.

The door opened with a metallic snap and Gianni raced inside, then, promptly catching himself, stopped to hold the door open for Tito and Renata.

"After you!" he said, with a flourish. Walking past him, Renata caught the scent of wind and aftershave.

The door of a ground-floor apartment was pushed half open, and a black dog was seized and hauled back on the verge of escaping. He looked like a pet pig.

"Emanuele!" a woman called to someone behind her, her tone resigned, as if she already knew Emanuele would not do a thing, "Emanueleee, get Oscar!"

Gianni leaped forward, picked up the squirming Oscar, and plunged his lips in his fur. "I love your stupid, stupid face, Oscar!"

&

The woman greeted Tito and Renata with a nervous smile, peeking from around Gianni. She was small and slender, with high cheekbones and a delicate mouth. Her enormous eyes were a striking pale green and it was clear how beautiful she must have been in her youth. In a dove-gray skirt and pale lilac top, she had a casual elegance.

"Gianni!" she sighed. "Take Oscar inside, he is impossible today." Her tone suggested that Oscar was impossible every day, and much loved.

"This is Renata, my sister," said Tito.

The flowers and wine were quickly admired and handed to Gianni.

"What a pleasure," Zia Marta said, offering her cheeks for a double kiss which revealed she favored an expensive perfume. "I have heard so much about you."

All of it false, Renata thought with a broad smile.

Inside, a small dining room, decorated in excellent taste, was adorned with antique prints of the Navigli Canals. The table was set in crisp white linen and gilded porcelain plates. Renata thought with tenderness about Papoozi's Capodimonte good dinner set that resembled, by comparison, excavated relics from Pompeii. A shimmering glow enveloped the space, a softness of shapes and colors that melted into each other. A subtle smell was coming from the kitchen, fragrant with cloves and meat.

An old man with a soft protruding belly, a trim mustache, and gold-rimmed glasses hurried in to greet her. He wore the stiff smile of someone who would rather not entertain altogether. It was matched by his firm let's-get-it-over-with handshake.

"Marta, Gianni is exciting the dog," he said to his wife, who left to attend to the yelping and laughter from another room.

Everybody seemed relieved when Loredana made her entrance. She was skittish, with the intensity of a dancer, and lithe with long dark hair and large brown eyes. She wore a cinnamon-colored top and matching sweater. Gianni was on her heels, without the dog. Zia Marta followed.

"We locked him in your room," Gianni said to Tito, as if it was the best of news.

"Oscar?" Tito was not pleased. Renata tried to meet his eyes, perplexed. He slept in a separate room from Loredana then?

"Gianni, I hear you graduated," Zio Emanuele said, in what sounded like an accusation. "The Bocconi that liked you so much has let you go at last?"

Gianni smiled, looking somewhere above everybody's head. He didn't strike her as the type to attend the elite Bocconi University.

"Dad," Loredana said.

"Dinner is ready," Zia Marta announced, with cheery elegance. She shot a glance of reproach at her husband, who shrugged, unrepentant.

"Renata, sit by me," said Zia Marta. "I can't wait to speak to you. Tito, you should go stay at the hotel and have your sister sleep here. Where are your manners?" Her playful tone was threaded with steel. "Gianni, be our sommelier and pour the drinks, will you?"

"Sommelier would be nice." Zio Emanuele frowned into his empty glass. "Some are held in high regard and make an excellent living." Gianni blushed.

"A toast to the guest!" Gianni said, hastening to pour Campari in everyone's glass. Bright red and cheery, Campari looked like a fake drink in a child's game.

"*Cin-cin!*" everyone cheered.

The drink was stronger than Renata had remembered; it rushed to her head.

"Do you miss Campari?" Gianni asked. There was an effervescence to his manner, the grace and daring of youth that Renata recognized and wanted back for herself. She remembered how that brash confidence let one slide anywhere with ease, fleeting and intense at the same time. She sighed at the longing for a life still unformed, like his.

"I miss it very much," she said. She had not, but at that moment she wanted all the Camparis she had never been offered, and dinners with a nice man who spoke her language and gave her his full attention. No absorbing schedule calling him away to a rehearsal room with creaky chairs, where a director and actors were waiting.

Loredana and Tito took turns going to the kitchen, bringing back dishes of velvety risotto with mushrooms. Renata, not allowed to help, could see them whispering in quick, urgent bursts, their heads close together. Their behavior suggested a hint of secret trouble brewing between them. Suddenly she didn't feel hungry anymore. A serving of fish, one of veal and a dish of baked eggplant and grilled radicchio smoldered on the kitchen counter. A tower of different kinds of bread was heaped on a tray. Gianni, who had sneaked in for *grissini*, was chased out of the kitchen by Loredana with a few friendly dish-rag slaps. He raced to sit in the empty chair beside Renata.

"Save me." His enormous eyes sparkled in delight.

"You save me first," Renata said with a chuckle. The mix of excitement and Campari seemed to combine to wonderful effect.

"*Buon appetito!*" said Zio Emanuele, clearly impatient to begin. As a good Milanese, he knew the warm risotto would easily get mushy and lose definition.

"*Buon appetito!*" all echoed.

"You like risotto?" Gianni whispered to Renata in English, leaning so close she flinched. The use of a foreign language and whispering in one's ear was considered rude, and he got a quick glare of reproach from Zia Marta. He pulled back with a vulnerable smile, glancing up from under a shock of black curls.

"I like it very much," Renata whispered back in English, under the cover of a sip of wine.

Compliments to the risotto were murmured and all eyes remained fixed on their plates between forkfuls—each savoring every bite with a frown of pleasure.

Only Tito seemed not to share everybody's ease, shooting glances around the table, his eyes narrow and agitated. With the exquisite risotto and its perfect blend of tastes, Renata found her appetite again, together with a confused sense that everything was and would be fine. Whatever was worrying her brother, that could be discussed later.

There was now the distraction of the conversation while each diner selected their preferred second course. Small waves of laughter accompanied the repeated changes of mind. Gianni demanded to open the Brunello di Montalcino, even if he ate fish for his second course. It was a clear compliment to Renata that Zia Marta deflected, saying it was best to wait, with no reason given.

Papoozi would have demanded an explanation instantly. He, Renata remembered, had defined the Milanese as irrational, and, collectively, pains in the asses.

14

As the second course was passed around by Tito and Loredana—and welcomed by all with whispers of ecstatic wonder and compliments to the cook—wind whipped at the windows, making them rattle as if someone were attempting to get in. This ghostly disturbance brought an uneasy silence to the table. The diners kept their eyes fixed on the windowpanes, as if something portentous was about to manifest. Renata imagined Papoozi trying to join the feast. He'd loved eggplant and radicchio.

Oscar made himself heard in the other room, and Gianni left to attend to him.

"Emanuele," said Zia Marta. "The window."

But it was Loredana who went to check the locks on the windows, heels clicking against the marble floor. Fortunately, Renata thought with relief, talk of death or condolences would have been inappropriate before coffee was served.

"There is no need to pay attention to the wind right now. Put some music on, Tito," Zia Marta said in a firm tone. "Chopin."

"Chopin would be great," said Zio Emanuele, his voice distracted, as if he were lost in thought. Renata wondered if he was thinking of Cesare's death or the inevitability of his own.

"Chopin is old," said Loredana, shaking her head. Her hair gave out a smell of freshly cut grass that Renata liked.

"I am old, too," said Zio Emanuele, taking off his glasses and rubbing his eyes.

"We know." Loredana laughed.

"Loredana," said Zia Marta.

Renata smiled at Loredana, and their eyes met for a moment, a flicker of shared amusement passing between them, then Loredana looked down at her plate with a slight frown. Gianni returned from the other room.

"You mentioned Chopin was your father's favorite," said Zio Emanuele to Tito.

"Thank you for remembering," Tito said, his gaze meeting Renata's, then flicking away. Papoozi had not known a thing about Chopin. As far as classical music went, Papoozi had been fiercely jealous of Caruso, suspecting the singer to be his wife's true love.

"Would any piece be fine?" Tito asked.

Zio Emanuele waved his arm in an expansive gesture, as if to force Tito to cheer up.

"Naturally," he said.

Tito walked glumly to the CD player, and it upset Renata. *Mezze seghe bastardi. You get up and get your Chopin. My brother is not your butler.*

"Ah! Wonderful," said Zia Marta, when the music wafted across the room.

The thundering chords sounded to Renata not just unfamiliar but morose.

"You are doing great," Tito whispered as he passed her chair. His eyes spooked her a little.

"Your sister is lovely," said Zio Emanuele.

"She is fantastic," Gianni said. "*Simpatica da morire.*"

"Absolutely," said Zia Marta, her firm tone signaling that quite enough had been said on the subject.

The veal piccata was tender, and the lemony aftertaste was perfection, but Renata liked it less than she wanted to. She met Zia Marta's eyes—clearly, she was expected to pay a compliment.

"A marvelous recipe," she obliged.

"The Brunello now, please," said Zio Emanuele. "A toast to the second course!"

"It deserves it," Renata said.

"I'm glad you like my piccata. It's been a family recipe for generations," Zia Marta said.

"Her family goes far back," Zio Emanuele said. "Garibaldi probably ate from this same recipe."

"I don't think so. My family would have gladly poisoned

Garibaldi with it, dear. He and his entire razzmatazz army of revolutionary *camicie rosse*."

An uneasy chuckle floated around the table, with the exclusion of Renata, who did not laugh. Papoozi had held the Red Shirts of Garibaldi in high regard.

"It's such a pity you are going back so soon," said Zia Marta, locking eyes with her. "Now you live in America. In Minneapolis, yes? You like it?"

Renata shot a quick glance at Tito, hoping that he would not bring up her commitments to her American husband, her nonexistent nursing profession, or both as a reason for the shortness of her visit.

Looking around the table, she felt a ripple of emotion for their lives in Milan. She experienced a sudden desire to be there, not as a strange presence, but as one, just like them, who lived there.

"Milan is still my home," she said, surprising herself, the wine slowing her words. "I am used to Milan," she added, a curious thought that gave her pause. Everybody sat in silence, staring at her. "It's my true home," she concluded firmly and a bit defensively. Minneapolis, at that moment, seemed a sequence of strange cafes, rooms, and streets that others owned and had graciously lent to her for a bit. *I like being in Milan*, Renata imagined saying to Steve. *The danger of truth*, he used to say, *was the thrill of theater*. Take this, Steve, she thought.

Zia Marta gave her grave approval. "*Milan xe un gran Milan.*" *Milan is great indeed*, an overused Milanese saying that was already considered a geriatric chestnut when Renata was in school.

The bottle of Brunello di Montalcino was passed around, receiving nods of pleasure to a final toast. All raised their glasses and drank.

"Fantastic wine," said Gianni. "Light, with a hint of tobacco."

"Absolutely. A delight, smooth and layered." For once, Zio Emanuele agreed with him.

"You don't drink your wine, Lori?" asked Zia Marta. Loredana's expression tightened, and she fixed her gaze on her plate.

"Renata brought it," Zia Marta said to the whole table, "and it is a very good wine. I say, very good." She turned to Renata and said warmly, "America hasn't ruined your taste one bit."

"Truly." Zio Emanuele took another sip with joyful surprise. Renata detected in Zia Marta's features the faded but still visible arrogance of a wildly popular high school girl.

"Excuse me," Renata said in a crisp tone. *What crap*. She bristled at the implied disdain for American wine, food, and life habits. In short, for herself. "We do have excellent wines."

"Yes. They have great wines in America," Gianni interjected, receiving polite nods in response.

"How do you know, Gianni?" Tito said. "Have you been there?"

"Not yet. But I want to."

"Loredana doesn't care about this, nor does she care for the wine," Zia Marta said, in a voice that brought everybody to silence.

"What do you mean, Zia?" asked Gianni.

"She's barely touched the wine."

"Thank you, thank you, Marta, we don't need a remark on everything." Zio Emanuele came to his daughter's aid. "She took a sip for the toast, it's fine."

"Pour," Loredana ordered Gianni.

The conversation limped listlessly around nothing in particular, and Renata noticed with dread Tito's intense expression while he took small sips of the marvelous wine. Something was very wrong.

"I've been thinking," Renata said, compelled to say something by a feeling of impending doom, "that you have been very kind to invite me and I want you to know how much—" Tito's gaze fixed on her and she stalled. "—I truly appreciate it."

"To Renata!" Everybody raised their glass.

"To America!" Gianni's cheer floated alone.

"How long have you been in America?" asked Zia Marta.

"Seven years."

"You don't have any accent," Gianni pondered, his eyes gazing upward, as if to better concentrate on the issue. "Can you believe it?"

"Very odd," Zia Marta remarked as if detecting deceit.

"America—" Zio Emanuele said in a pensive tone. All attention immediately transferred to him. He gazed at Renata with a flicker of awe but didn't complete his sentence. "You know," he said finally, "I have thought of visiting America many times."

"Did you ever go?" asked Renata, feeling that giving some kind of a response was polite, even though she knew full well the answer.

"Never did," said Zio Emanuele, seemingly touched by his own act of renunciation. Having just spent a prickly evening of imaginary regrets with Cosimo at Bar Noventa, Renata looked down at her lap so nobody could read the flash of amusement in her eyes.

"Never did?" said Tito respectfully, keeping company with the old man amid the apparent lack of interest.

"Never." Zio Emanuele said, his voice choked by yearnings, which his loving gaze suggested he had forsaken for his family's sake. He looked as if he might say something more, but then he simply shook his head.

"You still can travel, Emanuele. Why not?" Zia Marta patted her husband's hand. Her expression suggested this was a lament she had heard many times before.

"We will both go to America," said Gianni, with great resolve, turning to Renata. "We'll all come and visit! This summer!"

"You'll come too?" Renata asked Loredana.

"I'd love to," Loredana said. "But. You know. We'll see." She smiled, then went back to studying her plate. Renata glanced inquiringly at Tito. Clearly there was an issue at play that she could not understand. She felt tense and uneasy, and the wine wasn't helping any.

The room appeared bleached under the chandelier, and everything took on a quality of liquid agitation. In this light, everything and everyone seemed to her like something else entirely, as if she were trapped in the scary part of a dream. Renata reached for her wine, then stopped. *This is the last thing I need.* Then she gulped it down.

Looking up, she saw everyone's eyes on her, watching her in a curious, expectant way. It seemed that she was supposed to say or do something. Oscar began to bark again, then stopped.

"Tell us an American joke," she heard Gianni ask. He leaned forward, as if repeating a request she had not responded to. His words, she saw, were received with a buzz of consent and smiles around the table that seemed to confirm this impression.

"American joke," Gianni repeated in English, his cheek resting on his palm, a twinkle in his eyes.

"I don't know any jokes," Renata said which, for some reason, made everybody laugh.

"I have a joke," Gianni said, jumping in, his cheeks flushed, the wine and excitement rendering him seductive in a disheveled way. The evening was coming to an end—it had been a good one, after all, and Renata could not remember why Tito had made such a big fuss about it.

"Tell the joke," Renata said with a smile.

"Okay," Gianni replied, his chin resting on one hand. Renata noticed his long fingers, the polished ovals of his nails, and the watch band around his wrist. She imagined him putting it on in the morning.

"A man walks into a bar—" he started.

"Oh no! No!" Loredana and Zio Emanuele shrieked. "Not that joke again!"

"It's a good joke," Gianni protested.

Renata leaned over and whispered in English, "You are also fun without the joke." Gianni leaned back in his chair, with his hands behind his head, and took a deep breath. She felt a vague discomfort at her older age, at the excitement of his flirting. She floated, an inch further away from everything happening around her, but Gianni's attention made her feel fully present again.

"Are we having dessert now? Coffee?" Zio Emanuele asked, clearly restless to end the evening.

"I'll get the dessert," Gianni said.

"I'll make the coffee," said Loredana.

"Let me do it." Renata got up. "I'd love to help."

Renata owned the same Italian Bialetti machine in Minneapolis; she enjoyed the coziness of her tradition, adding a soupçon of salt to make the coffee taste creamier. But then, standing, her knees buckled, and she leaned against the table. She chuckled to suggest her stumble had been intentional. Then her knees buckled again. All eyes were transfixed on her, as if on a piece of paper on fire.

"What is it?" asked Tito in a thin voice, coming to her side.

She didn't know. "I'm just cold," she said, grasping for something to say.

Zia Marta stood by her now, a glint of steel in her eyes. She seemed to hesitate, then took Renata by her arm. "Why don't you sit?" she said.

"I am just a bit tired," Renata said, shaking herself free.

"Naturally," Zio Emanuele said. "Don't crowd her."

The room was still, waiting for something to happen.

"A glass of water?" Zia Marta asked, with quiet formality. A decision had been made—water.

Gianni rose and quickly filled a glass with water, then touched her shoulder with a moth-like delicacy as he offered her the drink. There being nothing else she could do, she dutifully drank the water while everybody watched.

"She should lie down," Zia Marta said.

"I don't need to lie down," Renata said.

"Listen to Zia Marta." Tito moved closer, his tone avuncular.

"Lie down just for a moment," Loredana said, blushing, her voice low and urgent.

"I am fine," Renata whispered to Tito.

"Come and lie down in my room," he insisted.

"Great idea," said Zio Emanuele.

"What's going on?" Tito hissed in her ear.

Renata pushed him away and walked off alone, unsteady, toward the room where she heard Oscar barking.

"It's the emotion," Zia Marta diagnosed, following her with

a second glass of water—given that the first seemed to have been a success. "Her dear father. What a terrible loss."

A sudden melancholy wafted down the hallway. They all looked at her, shaken by her terrible loss but still holding up bravely, swaying before the door to Tito's room.

"Don't crowd her," said Zia Marta. "I'll stay with her."

The others headed back to the dining room, exchanging whispers.

Oscar bounded out immediately when the door was opened, and Renata found herself in a hybrid space that operated as a storage closet and as a makeshift bedroom. A cot, covered with an old afghan, fit snugly against the corner, a scratched metal closet in another. Crates filled with odds and ends, skis and rolled-up posters added to the clutter. A pair of Tito's shoes lined up neatly beneath the small bed, shined to perfection. She felt the urge to pick them up and cradle them on her lap to give them comfort. Instead, she sat on the bed.

"Thank you for the water." She took the glass from Zia Marta, tipped her head back, and drained the water in one long gulp. Then she slammed the glass on the rickety table she assumed was Tito's nightstand. Tito spent every night here.

"Better?" asked Zia Marta.

"Yes, it was nothing."

Zia Marta glanced over her shoulder, then took a deep breath. Her tightly coiffed hair resembled a helmet under the light.

"Renata," she said. "What do you think of Tito and Loredana together? I hear you are very close to your brother. You know him well."

A gentle knock at the door startled them both.

"We are fine. Just give us a moment," Zia Marta called, nervously clasping her hands together. "He is a nice young man."

Renata said nothing. She wanted the talk over with.

"We are just wondering if he is right for Loredana."

Renata could tell from Zia Marta's tight expression that her mind was already set. "And what do you think?" she asked. "I think Loredana needs a man who is more driven," she added.

There was a silence. Zia Marta seemed disappointed by Renata's lack of response.

"I see you understand what I'm saying?" Zia Marta said.

"Yes," Renata said. She did. She felt the rush of an old fight after school; she missed the naked simplicity of facing her opponent behind raised fists.

"Loredana is graduating from Bocconi with top grades," Zia Marta said with pride. "It's hard. Tito's such a nice man in many ways."

Renata kept silent, but the look in her eyes made Zia Marta stutter. "I just thought you might—be able to help him understand how we feel."

Renata thought of Tito, sitting in the living room in the bright light, in that peculiar way he had of seeming always alone. "I suppose I could," she said.

"That's what I thought." Zia Marta nodded. "Would you like me to leave you alone for a bit?"

Renata didn't want to lie on that bed, with her head on that pillow, in that room. "I am fine," Renata said, standing up. "Shall we go?"

"You must forgive a mother looking after her daughter."

Renata just wanted her to stop talking. "It's fine. We should join the others."

She thought of Papoozi's fury at the narrow-minded Milanese. She recalled how much even the cryptic Milanese dialect had flustered him, causing one of his tirades.

"What kind of language is this?" he used to rage, with a liturgical crescendo. "Did you hear what the cashier said? *Xzink tzent? Cinque-cento lire* becomes *xzink tzent.* The bastards come up with all sorts of things so outsiders can't understand."

"There is no rush," Zia Marta said. "You can take your time."

Even the sound of Zia Marta's breathing was misery to Renata. She went to open the door.

"Everybody is waiting," Renata said.

They were welcomed in the dining room by a warm buzz. The men were drinking coffee and talking politics. Loredana was sitting in the chair by the window, Oscar at her feet.

15

In the car Tito was quiet. If only she could do the dinner over again. Renata would not drink; she would become friends with Zia Marta; she would make magic. They would swap recipes, write them down on napkins, rushed and giddy. *Thank you*, Tito's eyes would say at the end of the fabulous dinner. *No problem*, she would smile back and happily fall asleep on the ride back to the hotel.

"They were nice," she said, trying not to slur her words.

"Naturally. They always are."

She shut her eyes at his tone. At school, she'd held kids' heads under the water fountain when they threatened little Tito. She'd punched like a man on his behalf. Her lip was split open many times. She'd been called Rocky Marciano, and in the end, the *coglioni razzisti* stayed away from her little brother. His eyes said, then, *I owe you*. Now he kept them locked on the empty road. Milan looked raw, uncivilized, a failure of a city. Cars were scrambled in makeshift parking at the curb, street signs resembled weathered crosses. It all seemed shabbier than she'd remembered.

Perhaps it was agitation, rather than the wine, that had made her act out at dinner, after all. The silence continued. She and Tito were two tiny boats, paddling off quietly to opposite sides of a lake.

"Did you know that Eva Peron had been buried for years in the Cimitero Monumentale in Milan?" Renata said at last.

Tito would be interested in this. Papoozi had read to them about Peron, and little Tito had giggled at the name, making up a little singsong and dance in the kitchen.

"No, I did not know," he said.

"Under an assumed name, of course. Maria Eva Duarte, her maiden name."

A car tore past them, music blaring. They passed Bar Noventa, where someone was talking in animated gestures about
soccer or politics or exotic travel destinations. Perhaps Cosimo
had returned and was now drinking wine at the table in the back.

"Only the Pope and the Junta knew," Renata said brightly.
"We could have walked right by her grave without knowing it."

The Junta, the Pope, a secret burial—and the two of them,
innocent bystanders. Now he would surely say something. They
would discuss destiny. She hoped this could lead, somehow, to
the subject of Zia Marta.

"Oh God," he said. "When did we ever go to the forsaken
Cimitero Monumentale? It's where rich people are buried under
marble angels pointing to Heaven."

He drove, in deep concentration. He seemed to have shrunk
a little behind the wheel. Renata wanted to tell him what Zia
Marta had said to her in his makeshift bedroom and get it over
with. Would it have made a difference if she'd drunk less at dinner? No. The cards were already stacked against Tito. Renata's
being tipsy had just rendered hearing Zia Marta's verdict easier;
she should have drunk more. Zia Marta had asked Renata to
speak to Tito, and she would. Now. It seemed the mature thing
to do. "You know what?" she said.

"What, Reni?"

The affection in his voice changed her mind.

"Our problem in Italy is that we never went to the moon,"
she said instead, fishing for something. Anything. "We never
even dreamt of doing it. Our expectations are too pedestrian."
Tito was silent. "Actually, we have none."

"The possibility of a woman president is going to your
head," Tito said.

"Come on, Tito. We have no expectations," she insisted.

"What are you saying? We have too many expectations in
Italy. We are paralyzed by them." Renata did not wish to engage
in a row over some vaguely political topic—an Italian pastime
she now feared.

Closed bookstores, cafes, offices—Milan was silently racing

by. Papoozi was gone. Renata disliked the definition of death as
a state of uninterrupted sleep. When asleep, even dogs tossed
and twitched at the sound of wind and rain at night. Street
lamps flickered and swayed.

"I like Milan like this," Tito said.

Their sudden closeness felt sweet and a bit painful. They
remained silent, watching the city go by.

"Make me cry," she said.

"Oh, please." Tito shook his head.

They'd invented a game, after their mother had died, to
toughen them up. One sibling tried to make the other cry; the
winner was the one who held out the longest. Renata had always won.

"Mom loved me more," he'd insisted once. She'd almost lost
it and cried that time—it was absolutely true.

"Psycho," Tito had raged, when she kept winning.

The idea of the game had come to him when he read about
kamikazes. "A kamikaze," he glowed, "is trained to face anything, even his own death, without batting an eyelash." They
were not sure the Make Me Cry game was the kamikaze way,
but they'd agreed it would serve the purpose.

Renata dropped the subject. Maybe a chat about the Mino-
taur would stir things up? The myth had made an impression on
them both. Or an innocuous talk about flowers, whose delicate
petals yielded no practical use? Referencing what Zia Marta had
said could easily tiptoe into these musings of fear and pointless-
ness. No—she discarded both.

"Do you know I learned to drive in Minnesota?" she said.
The topic was lame, but it was one that could edge toward a
necessary conversation. Inadequacy, a quirky choice—either
one might open the door to more weighty subjects.

"Nuts," Tito replied, glancing her way. "At a driving school?"

"Steve taught me."

"Cool."

Renata had always appreciated Tito's diffidence toward
words; in fact, she, too, felt words were often clumsy and wrong.

The only thing she wanted to say about Steve was that he unbuttoned his shirt slowly, slept uncovered, and spoke gibberish
in his sleep. The rest was *stupidaggini*—idiocies.

"What did Zia Marta talk to you about?" Tito asked, his gaze
fixed on the road. Renata did not have to look into his eyes. She
wanted nothing more than to climb out of the car, crawl to her
hotel room, and lock herself in until all was resolved.

"Oh, she mentioned that Loredana studies at Bocconi," she
said casually. "Impressive."

"Yes," Tito said. "And Gianni never graduated."

"Really? But he said—"

"He said it so they would get off his back. Zia Marta even
gave him a present. She adores him."

"Well." Renata liked Gianni even more at that moment,
feeling that he was fighting tooth and nail to escape the cage of
shoulds. Once she'd told a friend in Milan that she was engaged,
just to shut her up about dating advice, but later she'd been
forced to invent obstacles to the nuptials, cribbed from *fotoromanzi* magazines. "Tito. He'll tell them, eventually."

"No, he won't."

"Why not?" she said.

"It's a huge lie. They'll never accept it."

"Oh, come on," she said.

"In Italy, it is." His tone was terse.

She looked down at the nice outfit she'd worn to impress
his future in-laws. "Who cares," she said, not wanting Tito to
know that she was stirred by Gianni, with or without a college
degree. "Tito? Really. Who cares!" She wanted all her true and
imaginary weaknesses indulged along with Gianni's.

"Everybody does," Tito said, under his breath. "Everybody
cares."

She felt his frosty wave of disapproval brush over her, too,
and she wanted to tell Tito that Zia Marta found something
reprehensible about him too.

"That's why in Italy everybody is such a pain in the ass," she
said instead.

"You don't say."

"Yes, well, Gianni can do something different, no? Is it college or death? It's always this one path or nothing at all in Italy." She could not stop talking—wine, sadness. She also wasn't sure that any of what she was saying was true. "Think out of the box. *Si puo' fare*, one can. We are such monotheists; we worship this one designer and chef and the rest are trash. And why? No reason. Maybe. I don't know. Gianni could go to America and find something exciting and fulfilling there." Tito kept silent. "Or somewhere else," she finished, sensing that her life in Minneapolis was not a good example to give him. She fished for something that might appear impressive in Tito's eyes but found nothing.

"Why are we still talking about Gianni?" he said.

There was the hush of a fight in the car, and they were almost at the hotel when he spoke again.

"Do you want to trade places?" he asked, morosely. "I sleep at the hotel?"

"No, no. Tito, Zia Marta didn't really mean to invite me." She shrugged. "She couldn't care less about having me over." She wanted to add: *Or you.*

Tito was waiting. It was clearly time for her to say something positive about Loredana. It used to be that they would go somewhere to talk quietly about an important evening over a glass of wine. But she knew they wouldn't—she was too drunk.

"They are good people," she said finally as they were in sight of her hotel.

Tito pounced on this minuscule encouragement.

"They are," he said. "You should meet them again, I am telling you. We could take them out for dinner somewhere nice." *Somewhere nice.* There was apprehension in his tone. *Somewhere nice* meant expensive.

Tito parked by the hotel, and it was only when she got out of the car that he said, "Reni!"

She stopped. He got out too and closed his door.

"If they had asked," he said. "I would not have told them that you are a nurse."

Renata was both irked and moved by his solemn tone.

"I'm in Minneapolis; it doesn't matter what I do," she said. *Vaffan*, she thought. *Don't be nice to me, I won't like Loredana anyway.*

"And I would never talk about your marriage." He was doggedly determined to right a possible wrong between them, his eyes moist. We should have learned to take our gloves off, Renata thought, wishing they had inherited some of Papoozi's fierce rage. Life would feel less like a stacked deck. Emotional memories rose to choke her. "You know I wouldn't, Reni," he said.

"It's really okay to say I'm a nurse." After all, Papoozi had loved nurses—they gave you water, told you stories, listened when you spoke. "It's just normal to mention Steve, or not. We don't need to be lunatics about this. We can talk about anything. And never mind those damn bores and their risotto. They pissed me off big time." What she felt most keenly, however, was a deep disappointment with herself for putting up with them, and the misery of their victory. "That old bastard probably made his money by being a *pescecane*, a shark during the war, a frigging bootlegger, while Papoozi was eating dirty snow in Mauthausen. Chopin!"

She turned to go.

"Wait!" Tito called. "What do you think of Loredana?"

Renata gave him a smile that held no hint of joy.

"Oh God, Tito," she said. "I just met her. We said nothing to each other. And it was at the end of a tough day."

"What don't you like?"

"I like her. I like her."

But Tito was determined, grabbed her arm.

"It's just—" She panicked. "You are not right for each other."

"Okay. Why?"

"Her parents don't like you," she said.

"I know that."

"She has ambitions," Renata said. "You work in a furniture

store, for fuck's sake, and she is going to graduate from Bocconi."

Her voice was Zia Marta's. He heard that. His eyes were electrified; his silence, scary.

"Say something. Why are you just staring at me?" she asked, her hand at her throat.

"You look like shit," he said.

"Yeah, I spent a whole evening with jerks."

"You act insane," Tito whispered, his breath hot on her face. "You flirt like a slut. Look at your goddamn sorry clothes. And you still can't even brush your hair. You look, frankly, very single."

"Well, I am going to be. It's not that bad a thing, you know. Not as bad as saying I sleep in a family's broom closet, dating someone who might perhaps want me. She doesn't say a word, so you'd never know."

"We are getting married," he said.

"Oh, really? Bullshit. Have you told the family?"

"Not yet."

"Speak to them now." She felt as if she'd smoked a full pack of cigarettes on an empty stomach.

"They don't matter; we are getting married," Tito said. "Loredana is pregnant."

"Tito!" she cried. "What are you going to do? You can't live in that closet! You have no money."

"I am going to get married. I'll solve it. I don't need any help." The *from you* he omitted hurt.

"Okay," she said.

"Okay."

"Just—" she began. *Just what?* Nothing came. Car horns blared in the distance, skimming the night like birds of prey.

"Okay, then." Tito nodded. "I just wanted you to know. I will pick you up, say, at eight tomorrow?"

"That works." The fight was now settling under her skin, stinging hard. "Tito. Let's not worry about Zia Marta."

"I'm not."

"Me neither," she said, with tipsy hopefulness.

"Excellent," Tito said. "See you tomorrow morning at eight, Reni."

Tito got back in his car and took off, without waiting to watch her walk safely into the hotel.

Renata's thoughts turned to Loredana, at her refusal to drink wine at dinner, at her withdrawn demeanor. She imagined Loredana looking outside in silence, thinking of the baby, haunted by Zia Marta's prattle.

She remembered how, when she'd been pregnant, she used to pace back and forth, back and forth in her tiny apartment, describing Italian landscapes to the baby, and pointing at her few framed photos from Milan—the Navigli Canals, La Scala, Via Manzoni.

Renata adjusted the buttons of her coat, trying to steady her breathing. The news of Loredana's pregnancy had at first felt like a punch to the stomach, but now her heart slowly opened to a luminous tenderness. Renata could see Tito in a world filled with the domestic pleasures that made life seem less haphazard and hostile—Tito would be safe.

The street of the hotel was quiet now, and standing still, she could almost detect the feral vapor of her altercation with Tito in the air. In front of the old Hotel Ambrogino, a most venerable Milanese institution, in the virulent exchange with Tito, she'd experienced a Papoozi tough, no-nonsense moment. He was in their DNA, after all.

16

In the deep of the night, wrapped in a dark robe from the hotel, Renata went downstairs and wrote Steve an email on the hotel computer. Firm and suffused with nocturnal restlessness, she suggested they not phone each other for a few days, because of the time change and some nonsense about both being busy. She liked the efficiency of the typed letters marching across the screen, estranged from her emotion. She pressed her finger on the Italian command for send: *invia*. Off it went. *Via*.

When she arrived at the reception desk the following morning at eight, Tito was not yet there. A garrulous clerk with a large tie told her she had no messages. He showed her where a note would be and insisted she look and agree it wasn't there. On he went, excited about rules that made hotel life seem as unyielding as a crossword puzzle. Her life, too, felt fettered, yet didn't seem enlightened by a plan, she thought. She recalled a school trip to the Acquario Civico di Milano, where a large fish had kept coming to the glass. Their eyes met briefly before it floated sluggishly away. The fish left her with the impression that it was alive to be watched, rather than to live.

She walked to the door, alarmed that Tito might refuse to meet her again, but equally relieved, because seeing him would remind her that she couldn't do a thing for him. The sister from America was a dud.

Tito ran in, flushed, smelling of coffee.

"Parking," he said, "—a nightmare."

They avoided eye contact. His agitation was spilling out. His hair uncombed, no gloves.

Their father used to chastise efforts to rehash arguments as "salvaging pieces from the wreckage," but Renata felt an equally Papoozian determination to rummage through last night's disaster, which could, in the light of day, be a sign of hopefulness.

"How are you?" she asked, carefully. "How are you feeling today?"

"Rushed," he said.

"I could have taken a taxi." She meant it innocently, but his startled look reminded her that taking a taxi was considered an extravagance, and a deadly insult to a relative. Traffic and inclement weather were equally dismissed before the obligation of family bonds.

"I'm glad to give you a ride," he said, attempting solicitousness. "Okay—uh—"

"Well, what?"

"Loredana insisted on joining us. She is waiting in the car." He selected the words carefully, giving them mysterious innuendoes.

"That's nice," she said. Now they wouldn't be able to talk at all. Would it kill Loredana to rest at home for the baby's sake? But Tito's searching eyes and the creases of sleep on his cheek made her say again, this time kindly, "Really, it's nice."

"Yes, considering that mornings have been difficult for her—you know—"

Tito's words took her breath away. She did remember that.

"Yes, I understand," she said. "Mornings."

"*Sbrigati*, hurry up!" His sudden anxiety flew in her face with birdlike fury. "Loredana and Flavia are sitting in the car in a no-parking zone."

Following Tito, she avoided looking at him, with his irritating gait and sulky eyes. She stared straight ahead, as if the words she wanted to say were written across the morning sky.

"Tito. I'm truly glad you are getting married." She felt impossibly clumsy, her voice stilted. But on she went. "I love that you are having a baby. I think it's wonderful. I do wish I could help." There—she'd said it, even if it seemed threadbare.

"Thank you." His voice was soft with gratitude, or simply relief, that she was now walking faster to keep up with him. "And I hope it works out with Steve." The moment felt beautiful and strange—they were talking.

"It won't. I miss him, but I'm sick of him," she said, feeling brave. Renata thought of their bicycles in Minneapolis, hanging on the wall side by side, like large melancholy animals. She counted memories like loose change.

Her shadow on the sidewalk was a fleeting smudge, quivering after his, swirling over rivulets of water and cracks.

"You are going to be fine," he said, the words somber, as if there was something noble in being stuck and suffering.

"Don't say this bullshit," she said. *I don't want to be fine*, she thought.

A kid struggled to keep his hat on against the wind; a woman in a flapping coat was pushing a stroller, head down; an anguished schoolgirl with glasses ran past, breathlessly repeating a rhyme. Everybody was caught in the rush toward the next step. The girl might not memorize the poem in time. The little boy might lose his hat. She might not tell Tito what she most wanted to say.

"If we talk of something important, we should stop and do it," she said, walking rapidly, wanting to be able to look him in the eye. "Why not? What's the problem?"

"We must go to the house. Papoozi—" he said.

"It's a dead body." She was shocked at herself. "Me and you are here. Papoozi is gone." She was dreading the upcoming ritual. Papoozi had held a profound distaste for funerals. Whenever they'd encountered one on the street, Papoozi used to instinctively fold his middle and ring finger under his thumb—*scaramanzia*, the Neapolitan gesture to ward off bad luck.

Tito stopped, threw his scarf over one shoulder, and waited impatiently for her to catch up.

"What would you do if you needed to make a decision, but fear held you back?" Renata asked.

"Fear always does," Tito said. "No?"

Renata thought about Gianni's eyes when he'd said *save me*, and she'd replied, *Save me first*.

"Yeah."

"Look, Reni. Do something so it's impossible to take back your decision. Okay. Here it is. A mess is fine, that's what I mean," Tito said, his eyes shining. "I'm glad of what happened in my life. Of course, now I worry. But so what. I always do." He laughed. "I'm grateful it made the decision for me, no?"

"What did?"

He looked confused, then irritated.

"Loredana being pregnant," he said. "The mess did it, and now I know."

"Oh, and I—what?"

"Make a mess too. Let something happen that you truly want, Reni. No thinking. No decision. Do something you cannot take back. You can do messy. You can do crazy. You took off for America to study *acupuncture*," he said. "You can do anything. You always did, Rocky Marciano."

He gave her a timid smile. She remembered tossing handfuls of dried leaves into the air, to fall like rain over their heads and shoulders—an excitement they'd shared after she'd scared a tough bully.

They hurried to the car.

"Did Papoozi know about you having a baby?" she asked.

"No. I was going to tell him."

She thought of Papoozi's copy of the *Enciclopedia Dei Ragaz-zi* and the jar of dry figs he'd kept beside it. He used to read them entries after dinner when they were little. Afterward, he would show them how to spread sugar on the halved figs, then place an almond exactly in the middle. "In the middle!" he'd exclaim, with a gentle smile. Perhaps he'd kept these items for his grandchildren, Renata mused.

Loredana was sitting in the car, behind Flavia, who occupied the passenger's seat. Her gaze turned to Renata, wide and uneasy. Renata gave her a *don't worry* nod and a smile, as she would do with her patients. She recognized in Loredana's eyes the fright of the body taking over.

Renata remembered her mother, pregnant with Tito, guiding her hand over her belly. Under her palm, the baby was a tiger wrestling in a tight cage. That unborn Tito felt inexplicably different from the baby born later, who slept soundly and barely squirmed.

"*Buongiorno.*" They all nodded to one another.

"Renata," said Flavia, shaking her head. "We never let you catch any sleep, do we?"

"I don't sleep much anyway," she demurred, as if insomnia were a mature choice. Her nights had been plagued by agitated dreams from one to the next, leaving her ravenous for a night of deep, dreamless rest.

On the drive Flavia, Tito, and Loredana chatted quietly about some politician she knew nothing about. The three of them shared an intimacy in their whispered tones and half-finished sentences—political agreement, she knew, forged a strong emotional connection. She stared out the window.

At Via Saverio, Tito found parking near the gate, sandwiched between the ancient van of a Stimata Vetreria Filimberti and a pale-blue Fiat Cinquecento. They sat in the car for a moment, frozen like people who hear a strange noise in the night.

Signora Ines dragged herself out of her apartment to greet them with a solemn nod. Renata marched straight to the ledger. The condolences book now had a few signatures—*Mario e tutti alla Salumeria Ghidetti, Andrea e tutti alla Pasticceria Fazio.* Mario and everybody at the Ghidetti grocer, Andrea and everybody at Fazio Pastries. The butcher and the pastry chef were Papoozi's special friends. Papoozi loved to eat, and the only concentration camp story he'd ever shared with them was about bread and the power of solidarity.

Once, when Tito and Renata had engaged in a murderous fight over a Toblerone bar, he'd told them that the Nazis wanted the prisoners in the barracks to be mad at each other, they wanted them fighting over a sip of water or a sliver of stale bread.

"They wanted us to die faster. They wanted us beating each other up over garbage, like dogs," Papoozi had said. "At Mauthausen," he told them, "we were given only one piece of bread per barrack, and we decided to split it into tiny pieces. One prisoner held a tiny piece of bread in each hand behind his back and we took turns choosing which hand, so we would not fight about who got the biggest piece. We were dying, we were starving. They wanted us to become animals, but we did not. We fought to remain human beings. We did it. We beat the bastards."

The storekeepers all left notes of condolence in elaborate, old-fashioned penmanship. Kids in America, Renata thought with amusement, were trained to write in block letters, rather than cursive, as if practicing to pen anonymous notes for blackmail.

Glancing down the page, she noticed: *Addio Cesare!* It was signed *Davide*. This particular entry stirred her.

"The funeral van will be here soon," Tito said.

"Who is Davide?" she asked.

"Davide? Davide who?" Tito signaled with his palms for her to lower her voice.

"Just Davide," she said in his ear.

"I don't know who he is. Perhaps Flavia does. What does it matter now?"

A light-gray funeral van slowly entered through the large gate that Signora Ines had opened, and several men in dark suits jumped out. Silently, they brought out what looked like an iron bed, then unfolded the metal legs.

They disappeared into the van and reappeared, carrying the casket, now covered in a wreath of red roses, balancing it carefully on the iron stretcher. A delicate scent wafted from the wreath, and there was now a sense of anticipation—but there was just the four of them, standing awkwardly in a terse silence. Tito glanced around, looking disheveled in his open coat and loose scarf, his eyes those of a man on the run. Nobody else was present; there was nobody they could walk up to and say, "Thank you for coming to give your respects to my father." They all stared at the casket, transfixed; their collective breathing was the only sound to break the immaculate silence.

A young couple with a poodle walked toward the elevator, then stopped, confused as to what they should do. Going around the casket seemed indelicate. They looked at each other, lost, then crossed themselves, heads down. A delivery man also stopped in his tracks to show respect, his eyes frightened by the casket. His package must have contained meat, because the poodle growled, pulling wildly at the leash.

The situation reminded Renata of a crappy movie—an indie cobbled together by scrimping on sets and actors. Steve had been cast in one a few months before, as the victim of a violent crime dispatched within the first three minutes. Renata had showed him how to smoke, as his part required it. Steve didn't even like to hold a cigarette. "Touch is everything," Papoozi used to say. Now he was nailed in a box.

"Are we done?" Renata whispered to Tito.

"In a minute."

And in a minute the room bustled with activity as the men reappeared to take the casket back to the van.

The four of them returned to Tito's car to follow the van to the crematorium. Most families, Tito said, chose not to accompany the body to the crematorium, suggesting this decision was a special way of honoring Papoozi.

We should have poured wine on the ground instead, Renata thought, as the ancient Romans did. We should have found Papoozi's old Beretta and shot up at the sky; we should have made chaos. Papoozi had told them that the declaration of the armistice had ignited such uncontrolled excitement in Naples that all the men flocked into the streets, shooting any weapon they could grab.

"Emotions, you know," he'd explained, with an indulgent smile.

The funeral van was swallowed up by the traffic ahead of them. When they passed the Cimiano subway, Renata remembered that the tracks rose to street level. From the car she glimpsed movie posters covered with graffiti, and beneath them, a bench. A lanky teenager in combat boots sat at one end of the bench, and a tiny nun clasping a black briefcase sat at the other. Language courses to study French, German, and English were advertised alongside, each equally defined as the language of the future.

One night, as they'd been sitting at the table after dinner with a language dictionary at hand, Papoozi decided to teach them English by touching different objects: a glass, a fork, a chair. Tito squinted at the sound of each word. "These words are wild animals," he said. *Napkin, spoon.* Renata liked the fact that in English her voice didn't sound like her own. Perhaps the new language did other wonders too?

"Am I tall in English?" she asked, to a cascade of giggles.

"Am I fat in English?" Tito asked, grinning.

After a moment, Papoozi chimed in, "Am I young in English?"

In middle school, Tito had picked German as his language of choice. Usually timid, he took the bus alone after school and went to Piazza Duomo and Il Castello Sforzesco, where he proceeded to chat up the German tourists. He'd planned to protect the family, and Flavia, in the next war by persuading the German soldiers not to take them prisoners.

"Partisan, *ich*? Me? No way," Tito used to repeat over and over in German. "*Ich suke pilz*. I am here looking for mushrooms for my poor family. *Die kraken*? The gun? A protection against the partisans, *naturlich*, of course."

He'd been determined to keep them all safe, and he practiced until he was fluent. "I sound as if I'm from Salzburg," he said proudly, reiterating praise he had heard from his teacher. At snack time, Flavia gave him an extra smear of Nutella as encouragement.

"Signora Ines has been at the crematorium many times," Flavia said carefully, as if Signora Ines should rise in their esteem for having a membership card to the crematorium.

"Really?" Renata pretended to be impressed, for Flavia's sake.

17

At the crematorium, the funeral van shot ahead and out of sight while they found parking. A few old Fiats were parked side by side against a brick wall, and Tito pulled in beside them. They walked through an imposing iron gate wet with dew. The crematorium was located in an unadorned, sullen building at the end of a patchy lawn. A heap of discarded wreaths wilted next to a swampy gravel path. Renata wanted to sink to her knees and refuse any comfort.

"Let's go," Tito called out.

"Let's go," she echoed reluctantly, feeling as if they were all sleepwalking. *Let's not go in, Tito. Let's not have to remember this. Let's get out of here. We are done. Tito, it's over.*

A thick oak door was opened by an old man. He motioned behind him, toward an unfurnished space with large glass windows covered by cafe-style louvered blinds. Papoozi's casket had been placed at an equal distance from other identical caskets. No special place for him.

Their anxious steps sounded too lively in the silence, and the little group seemed to find an unexpected alchemy in feeling similarly inadequate. The place was so stark as to suggest irreverence toward the dead. Visitors did not seem to be expected and there was no seating space. They stopped, staring at Papoozi's casket, bathed in a cloud of dust visible in the muted sunlight. Like wolves around a fire, they kept their distance.

Renata noticed with a painful jolt that one of the caskets was small.

"You were so sick once as a baby I almost picked out a casket for you," Papoozi had told her. She remembered the smell of wilted flowers, a bowl of steaming medicine by her bed, and a tall doctor saying quietly, "We're doing all that we can," followed by her mother's high-pitched cry.

She'd dreamt, she remembered, of wind and rain, and of seeing the roots of trees. She'd goofed around, buffeted by the wind. There were no words to describe it—no verbs, adverbs, or even the subject: I.

Her mother had placed a holy image by Renata's bed. But the Christ on the cross had looked too exhausted to do much of anything.

"It's okay if I die," she'd told Papoozi.

"It's not okay," he'd said. "Pay attention. I'm giving you something very special, this one time only. It's magic."

He'd forced her fingers open and closed them around a small metal object—a war medal he'd received for bravery, actions he later scoffed at as "youthful folly."

"Hold tight! Don't let go of it, and you'll be fine. I promise."

Renata held the medal tight. In the morning, when the doctor had declared her out of danger, Papoozi took back the medal. She'd never seen it again. When she'd asked about it, Papoozi had told her, "It's just a war medal. You did everything yourself."

Renata felt overcome by tenderness for Papoozi, who had fought to save her life against all odds. She wanted to go back to the old house and find his medal.

"We need to go now," she said to Tito.

They all nodded in assent, looking relieved to be able to leave. Emotion, Renata thought, felt slightly inappropriate to the space. She didn't want to stand there, waiting for Papoozi to be burnt down to ashes.

"Why did Papoozi wish to be cremated?" she asked Tito.

"*Che ne so?* How do I know?" He shrugged, perplexed. "I don't really know. Once, he said that a funeral was a fuss and a waste of money. But then he got emotional and said it was the best choice, so at least his ashes could go back to the sea he loved."

That sounds like something your father might want," said Loredana gently, a thoughtful intervention for which Renata was grateful. She exchanged a timid, warm glance with her future sister-in-law.

"Yes, he did want to go back to the sea in Naples," Flavia said, her tone a little heated. "That's the reason. He wanted his ashes to be scattered in the sea of Naples, where he swam as a young man. He wanted to return there. That's why."

"He chose cremation because he wanted to go back to Naples? It was not just a manner of speaking?" Tito asked.

"No. He insisted. After death, he wanted to be forever in the sea he loved," Flavia replied. "That's why he chose cremation. It was the only way to go back and be there forever."

"Sure. I'll take care of it. Do not worry." Tito patted her hand gently. "As soon as I can, I will go to Margellina and scatter his ashes. I was just wondering."

"There is nothing to wonder," said Flavia. "It is all clear."

Outside, they were met by sunshine. Renata took a deep breath, enjoying again the brilliance of days in Milan when the air smelled of unripe citrus.

The little family of Tito, Flavia, and Loredana walked together, unsteady on the uneven path, making soft murmuring sounds like the cooing of doves. Renata thought of Wellness Within and the deceptive simplicity of the rooms, like a Morandi painting. She thought of Tessa making tea, of new patients. There was a suspended moment in time before new patients spoke, shy, as if their illness was a secret. *Do you like birds? Do you like plants?* they'd sometimes ask her, wanting her to have pets, to care for small things. She'd feel their pulses under her fingertips, pressing and letting go, pressing and letting go. She'd find in the Meridians signs of things they had not revealed in the intake. The body talks, talks.

"Coming?" Tito turned back toward her for a moment, pausing by the crematorium gates.

Renata realized how terribly lonely the closeness of Tito, Flavia, and Loredana made her feel. She was overcome by a yearning to hear Tessa's voice. Digging her cell phone out of her bag, she dialed Tessa's number. After what seemed like an endless time, Tessa picked up the phone, her dog Bugsy barking in the background.

Renata held up one finger to Tito, indicating a quick, important call.

"Squirrels, he hates them," Tessa sighed, half asleep. It was dawn in Minneapolis, Renata realized, with a pang of guilt. In that moment, Renata suddenly loved Bugsy too, a mutt whose snout she found repellent. "What's going on?" Tessa asked.

"I'm leaving Steve," Renata said. It seemed, suddenly, as if this course of action had been agreed upon a long time ago.

"Uh? I can't hear you." Tessa sounded barely there, half asleep, and trying to rouse herself. "Are you okay?"

"Yes, I am fine."

Renata heard her own frightened little girl's voice and hated it savagely.

"I wish I were a man," she said, biting the soft part of her thumb to hold back tears. "If I were, it would feel manly."

"Wait—?"

"I'm leaving Steve," she repeated, loudly enough that Flavia turned, aghast. *Fuck crematorium etiquette.* "I am leaving Steve!"

"Why?"

"I'm alone and I'm afraid of being alone," Renata said, feeling her sadness fill the air.

"Without him?" Tessa asked.

"With."

There was a silence.

"I don't know what to say," Tessa whispered, as if Steve could somehow overhear her. Her voice sounded like a swarm of bees, then trailed off, her breathing deeper.

"That's okay. That's good. Don't hang up." Renata felt the space between them grow wider. She closed her eyes, seeing the maple trees in Minneapolis, with squirrels scrambling across the branches in a soundless wind. "At least in Italy, they don't put makeup on the dead," she said, irrationally. "Just don't hang up." The silence started to calm her, as if it were a space she was allowed to fill, her words floating in air and darkness. "I hate myself with him. I become whiny and needy. I used to be a vodka-and-martini type." This wasn't quite true, but Renata wanted it to be so. She imagined Tessa blinking, panicking with her, but then she realized Tessa was breathing deeply because she had fallen back to sleep. Renata smiled. That was so like Tessa and it felt good.

જ

In the car Renata rummaged in her bag. Gianni had slipped her a piece of paper with his phone number. *Find it, miseria ladra,* she thought, energized by the resolve to see him again.

"Reni! Flavia!" Tito called out. "I need to get back to work. Where shall I drop you? Reni, you want to walk around and go somewhere special?"

"You can drop me off in Via Saverio again," said Flavia, her cheeks flushed, her tone one of uncharacteristic determination. "I have to take care of a few things." She turned her gaze toward the window, avoiding eye contact as she fingered her hair.

"Great. I'll join you," Renata blurted out.

Flavia, looking studiously out the window, did not respond.

"So?" Tito asked, impatient. "Via Saverio for both or where?"

Flavia turned to Renata, gazing at her for a moment, as if scrutinizing every nuance of her expression. "Via Saverio for both," she said finally. Renata smiled, determined to discover the whereabouts of Papoozi's war medal.

Loredana placed a delicate hand on Flavia's shoulder.

"Signora Flavia, we would like to have dinner together tomorrow evening. And you too, Renata, of course. Somewhere simple."

Renata felt a knot of sorrow. The visit to the crematorium made the word *simple* sound heartbreaking. At that moment, the phone in her pocket buzzed like a small trapped animal. Tessa? Or Steve? She shut it off.

"Dinner tomorrow works for everybody?" Tito's voice pleaded.

"Sure," she answered cheerfully. *Let's get it over with.* She rummaged through the contents of her bag as if the piece of paper might float up, in a flutter of Gianni's effervescent energy.

Renata sighed, certain this would be another awkward dinner with meandering, self-conscious conversation and forced banter until the wine kicked in.

"Men like to watch TV together in an *osteria*," Flavia whispered with trepidation. "If there is a soccer game, it'll be crowded."

"No, no, not an *osteria*. We are going to a real restaurant," Tito hastened to say. "Reni? No TV is on in a nice restaurant, right?" Renata, distracted, looked up from her handbag. "Reni!"

"No TV in a good restaurant. It's an excellent choice," she said.

She stopped rummaging furiously in her bag, feeling this would somehow frighten the piece of paper to go deeper into hiding.

"Great!" Tito said cheerfully. Renata sensed he was cajoling her into joining some secret plan. "Any kind of food is fine?" he asked.

"I don't know," Flavia whispered, fatigued. "Yes."

"I'll think of somewhere to go," said Tito quickly. "I'll ask at work." His voice sounded tense and Renata feared the evening would be a fiasco.

"We can move the dinner to another evening, so you have time to figure it out," she offered, breezily. Tito glared at her, his eyes intent.

"Tomorrow night is perfect," he said.

Tito parked in front of Via Saverio and Flavia hurried out on wobbly legs, as if escaping a sudden downpour. Renata jumped out after her with a quick "*Ci vediamo*" to Tito and Loredana. Her previous visit to the apartment had left her with a kind of hallucinatory nostalgia. The rooms were saturated with Papoozi, and she felt both apprehensive and excited—not unlike the experience of seeing him in person.

Signora Ines had removed the mourning adornments, and the doors to Via Saverio were back to their usual appearance. Renata felt a pang of quiet animosity thinking of Via Saverio

waiting for the next tenant to move into Papoozi's apartment—
and life would simply go on as usual there. The thought struck
her that Papoozi and Dr. Chen would have approved of this
swift change with equal enthusiasm. Onward. *Xiang qian*. Renata smothered a chuckle with her hands. Flavia nodded, with a
sigh, at the sound, presuming, clearly, that it was a choked cry
of pain.

Signora Ines slouched in a chair, just inside her door, much
like a passenger stranded overnight at the airport. Hearing their
steps, she strained to rouse, but Flavia motioned for her not
to bother and proceeded to the elevator without looking back.

18

When Flavia opened the door of the apartment, they both stood for a moment. The silence seemed thicker than it had been during her last visit, and no surge of impressions rushed forth. It was as if Papoozi's spirit had been hauled away somewhere along with the funeral ornaments.

"My own four bricks," he'd used to say, looking out the kitchen window at the clouds, as if he owned them too.

I'll never have the chance to be in the apartment alone, Renata thought.

She walked into the kitchen, wanting to empty her bag in private and find the paper with Gianni's number.

"Hungry?" Flavia asked, standing just outside the door.

"Not yet," she said. It seemed too early for lunch, but she remembered that in Italy meals were timed with military precision and Flavia looked expectant. "But you bet I will be."

Renata dumped the contents of her bag on the small counter. The tiny piece of paper appeared among a jumble of subway tickets, a pencil stub, crumpled tissues, and assorted candy she did not remember buying—*caramella Rossana, liquirizia Tabu, pastiglia Leone.*

Imagining the sequence of events her phone call to Gianni would initiate, she hesitated, immobile, as if eavesdropping on her own thoughts.

"Need anything?" Flavia asked.

The question startled her. Flavia's insistent attention always made her miss her mother.

"I'm fine, thanks," she replied absently, examining the piece of paper with narrowed eyes. The phone number was smudged, unreadable. Excellent. Now she would not be tempted to do something she could not take back.

From the kitchen window Renata could see a worker in a blue uniform walking along the railway tracks, tapping the metal rhythmically with a long stick.

"I can make something later," Flavia said. She was standing in the kitchen door, and, for a moment, it seemed as if they were appraising each other. We're not that comfortable together, after so many years apart, Renata thought. It had been a long time since, as a little girl, she'd found reassurance in Flavia's energetic cleaning. Flavia's ritual suggested that each day would start anew in a similar fashion, and that there was no finality to anything, even dust.

Now Renata just wanted Flavia to get busy so she could spend time in Papoozi's room, imagining, discovering. It was the little things that she found most revealing—a button, a note, and, first and foremost, the medal.

"No worries about lunch. I will pick up a *trancio* of pizza later," she offered. "Or sandwiches."

Rather than reassuring Flavia as she'd intended, Flavia appeared alarmed. "Pizza! Sandwiches! I will make pasta," she announced.

"That's great," Renata said. "Of course. No problem."

The shrill ring of the doorbell startled them both, the intercom crackling with a voice.

"Who is it?" Flavia asked, her eyes fixed on the intercom, where the *portinaia* mumbled something incomprehensible. Renata went to open the door, relieved by the presence of another. Alone in the apartment with Flavia, she felt like a guest who had overstayed at the end of a party.

She opened the door to a frail man in an old parka, standing stiffly as if posing for a portrait. Cold air and solitude wafted from him. He held a cellophane-wrapped flower arrangement.

"Signora Flavia?" he asked, in a thick accent. "Delivery. Fiorista Cortellazzo."

"For me? How come?" Flavia asked. Through the thickly decorated cellophane, they could see a cheerful, brightly colored arrangement. Renata was surprised not to see white chrysanthemums, the traditional Italian flowers of mourning.

"It's for Signora Flavia," the man confirmed with wooden determination. He gestured toward a small note tied beneath the golden string. "Signor Cesare was supposed to pick them up, but we haven't seen him for days. We left messages on the machine."

"My God. Give them here." Flavia's words slurred.

She brought the arrangement to the table, holding it with the delicate reverence of a holy reliquary. Renata gave the man a tip—too small, she gathered, when he took off without a *buongiorno*.

Flavia sat at the table and looked at the arrangement, fretful and unhurried at the same time.

"The note?" suggested Renata. The word *Flavia* was visible on the paper beneath the string. She recognized Papoozi's angular handwriting, sizzling with life, but Flavia kept looking over the flowers, squinting in concentration and emitting the soft humming sound one uses to soothe a fussy infant.

She looked up at last, her eyes jumpy. "We had a spat," she said. "Right at the end."

Renata hoped that Flavia would not say more. "Don't think about it," she said.

"No, this was important. He wanted us to get married."

"Oh God," Renata said. "At his age? Flavia!"

"Yes, I thought it was nonsense too. And I said as much. That's how the fight started. I am a big mouth." The idea of Flavia being a big mouth seemed even more absurd than Papoozi proposing. "He proposed right here and I said no."

Renata could see him pace, could imagine the heightened tone he used in solemn moments. *Flavia, for God's sake, marry him*, she found herself thinking. *Say yes. Yes.* Her father's reckless wish, at his age, sounded exhilarating.

"Why get married and change our lives?" Flavia said, wringing her hands. "Why?"

"You know him," Renata said, "always different." She remembered his glorious madness, years back, when he'd dared to buy a home for their new life, trembling and uncertain, yet determined to start over again.

She sat by Flavia, but no words would come.

"The TV is on all day," Flavia burst out. "America. And your father catches the word *change*. We change, at our age? Your father would never even switch his brand of soap. It's Palmolive, Palmolive!"

Renata gazed at the object of Papoozi's love—she looked small and frightened. Renata delicately caressed Flavia's hand, the way she had been yearning to do since she arrived.

"It just means he loved you. Enjoy that. Don't ruin it." She racked her brain for more platitudes, thrilled that Flavia hadn't pulled her hand away.

Moving onward had been a vital necessity to Papoozi. She'd remembered he'd gotten rid of everything at her mother's death. Then he'd sat in the dark, his hands on his knees, as if listening to the sound of his own sorrow. He took his temperature every few hours, refusing to eat. Tito and Renata had hidden in their mother's wardrobe, certain that Papoozi, too, was going to die. Then he'd pulled himself from his stupor and bought an apartment; energized, he'd made them a family again, binding them all together with the smell of fresh paint and rooms to fill anew. He'd left crumbs on the new kitchen window, Renata remembered, so sparrows would come to greet the children after school.

"I'll never forgive myself," Flavia said.

"You must," Renata said.

"It was a small thing he asked," Flavia said. "He was such an intelligent man. Much smarter than I am."

"Oh, you are smart. You told him no." She could not imagine the blind force of romance in this room, with its ancient TV and threadbare curtains. Yet she loved it.

"Don't tell anybody about the marriage proposal and the fight," Flavia said. "I don't know why we are going out to dinner tomorrow night. Call and say I'm sick."

Renata remembered Tito's anxiety about their evening plan and felt frantic to fix this for him. "We're going! It's just a dinner," she said.

"I'm sick, I cannot go," said Flavia. "Call Tito."

"I will. Just give me a moment," Renata said, stalling to think of something that might change Flavia's mind.

But it was Tito who called her on the cell phone a moment later.

"It's me, Tito," he said. "Two girlfriends are joining us tomorrow night, and Loredana just let Gianni know we are having dinner, so he is coming too." In the pause that followed, Renata felt a raw exhilaration. "We are going to hear some music," Tito said, his voice shaky. "Dinner at Il Tarocco." Il Tarocco was expensive—Tito was splurging.

"Flavia is not well," Renata told him. "She is not coming." A vision of wine glasses, crumpled napkins, and lit candles in tiny glasses flitted through her mind. And jazz.

"I am not well," Flavia confirmed.

"Get her on the phone," said Tito.

Their conversation seemed interminable. Flavia nodded intermittently, but said nothing, then returned the phone to Renata.

"We are all going to dinner," Flavia said, with great poise. "It's Loredana's birthday." She seemed to savor saying Loredana's name—a new sign of intimacy. "Tito said not to, but we should get her a little something."

"Well, of course we should," Renata said, happy at the prospect of a birthday celebration. Onward.

Flavia removed the cellophane enveloping Papoozi's flowers and filled a vase with water.

"He was so old, so sick. I thought marriage was a crazy idea," Flavia said.

A memory of Papoozi in his camel-hair robe flashed through Renata's mind. Even so old, he'd believed in new beginnings.

"I liked my life the way it was," Flavia said. "I have a home all to myself, and nobody tells me what to do."

"You know what you want," Renata said. "It's good."

"A marriage would have added absolutely nothing," Flavia said. "But it's sad to think that I said no."

"You might not have gotten along and that would have been a disaster." Looking in Flavia's grateful eyes, Renata smiled reassuringly. "I am married, and I know there are always problems in a marriage."

"Yes, I know you are married," said Flavia, becoming attentive. They'd never talked about anything personal, and Flavia spoke as if grappling with a foreign language. "A man named?"

"Steve." Renata felt a rush of desire to be madly loved by him, right at that instant.

She visualized Steve in a cafe in Los Angeles, with the washed-out palette of sleek, modern furniture. He sat at a table talking to his agent. His hand rose to gesture over his head—it seemed he was waving goodbye to her.

"Your father said Steve was not the right man for you." Flavia pronounced it *Stay-vv* which seemed to render him an innocuous abstraction, someone Renata didn't know.

"Why?"

"Your voice when you talked about him."

And what else did my father say? Renata couldn't bring herself to ask the question. Flavia gazed at her, a flutter of feminine expectation in her eyes. Renata's shoulders went soft with desire at the idea of Flavia's tender embrace—if only she could let herself cry. She saw again the younger version of herself struggling at this same table to memorize Cicero's *Catilinaria*. *Quo usque tandem abutere, Catilina, patientia nostra?* Back then, her tears had found a warm understanding in Flavia's arms.

"I guess sometimes things don't go as expected," said Flavia at last.

"They rarely do."

Their eyes met briefly, and Flavia must have seen her distress, for she spoke kindly. "You look tired. I must do an errand for your father, but you can go to the hotel and rest," she said.

"What is the errand?"

"He kept a medal from the war and asked me to throw it in the Navigli canals after his death."

"You're kidding me."

"No. I must find it and throw it in the canal. He asked many times, and I promised," Flavia said.

"Give it to me," Renata said. He is my father; it is my medal, she thought. She had clutched it while ill.

"He made me promise that I would," Flavia objected.

They stared at each other. Renata was touched by the strength in Flavia's rheumy eyes, the fingers searching for comfort in her scarf. Papoozi's last soldier.

"Then you should," Renata said. She felt the urgency to hurry with the disposal of the medal and be done with it. She'd go to the Navigli with Flavia.

"Yes." Flavia nodded.

"Tell me. What did he say about me?" Renata asked. Flavia gave a thoughtful sigh and Renata thought she might actually get an answer.

"He was very worried," Flavia said. "He hoped you would come back."

"And do what?" She waited.

"Come home, that's all. I never had children myself but I think that's how a parent feels," Flavia murmured, looking at her with tender eyes. "'Perhaps Titina comes home,' he kept saying. He wanted to see you again, to spend time together."

Titina, her Neapolitan nickname she had forgotten.

"But how is America?" Flavia asked, with forced brightness.

"Oh, you know, different." Renata gave her a timid smile.

"Different. Oh, sure." Flavia rose and came to caress Renata's arm. Then she moved away and Renata missed her.

"You know, your father said that the best thing about death is that you don't take your memories with you."

No memories of me? Renata thought. He didn't want to take memories of me? When I lost my shoe on the merry-go-round and he found it? Not even memories of his wife? Renata remembered her mother's melancholy gaze, which bloomed with light when she read to the children. She would want to remember this, even after she died herself. It was his memories of war he wanted to forget, she realized then. Sometimes he'd start telling them a story, then stop, refusing to go on. This had frightened the kids more than anything they'd read or heard.

Flavia sighed, then headed to Papoozi's room. "I'd better get the medal now, there is so much to do before the birthday dinner tomorrow." Then she hesitated and said, "Your father always repeated to me, 'Remember, throw it.' He was right, wasn't he? What's to keep, after all? To cry, that's all. A war medal. Your father liked the idea of America having a president who voted against the war. After he watched the news, he said it was good that you lived there."

But Renata still wanted to keep the medal.

"I'm sorry for Signor Davide," Flavia whispered. "Poor man, there is no way to comfort him now."

"Signor Davide?" Renata asked.

"Can you believe it?" Flavia said. "He made it all the way downstairs to the ground floor to sign the condolence book. He is an invalid."

"He was a good friend of my father?"

"Oh yes. They met because of a mistake with the mail, a letter to concentration camp survivors, and after that, they played chess together every Saturday evening. Some people in the war lost their faith, like your father, but Signor Davide didn't. He lost his entire family and his speech, but not his faith."

Flavia paused, and Renata thought how terribly old and frail she seemed, as if bruised by the intimacy of revelations.

"Did you ever go back home?" Renata asked.

"Oh no." Flavia shook her head. "I never went anywhere."

"Not even for a pilgrimage to Rome?"

"No." Renata liked Flavia's timid courage, a schoolgirl standing up straight, knowing she was giving the wrong answer. "There was a pilgrimage to Assisi organized by my church, but your father was sick and I said no." Her voice took on a musical timbre, suggestive of a story repeated many times.

"I have an idea." She wanted Flavia to do something she'd never done before. "There are a few *osterias* along the Navigli that open at noon. I'll take you out for lunch."

Flavia shook her head, an indulgent smile crossing her lips at the extravagance of the suggestion. She fingered her pale-blue scarf. Papoozi had probably given it to her for Christmas. "Me, eating out for lunch? No," Flavia said. "It's not for me, but thank you."

"Okay." Renata felt a pang of guilt for making Flavia uncomfortable. "We don't have to. Let's go to the Navigli together to get a gift for Loredana." She needed to get out of the apartment. The guilt for not returning home earlier, combined with Flavia's innocence of the world, made her ashamed of her life. "First we throw the medal."

Renata proposed to share a drink, as a goodbye toast to the medal. Flavia agreed—a thoughtful gesture, despite her protest that she rarely drank and never on an empty stomach.

Renata found a small bottle of Prosecco and poured two glasses. They raised them in a toast to Papoozi.

"Drink it all, out of respect," Renata said, the beginnings of a plan forming in her mind.

They drained their glasses, maintaining eye contact.

19

They took the tramway to the Navigli stop, where everything was as she'd remembered it—tiny stores selling antiques and vintage clothes, windows of old houses closed against the mist, walls with graffiti. Kids kicked a soccer ball back and forth; old women walked home, carrying grocery bags.

They walked by a small *osteria* already open for lunch in Ripa di Porta Ticinese, a dark place with wooden benches, fragrant with freshly made coffee. Renata had been there a few times when she'd lived in Milan. The radio was on, and Renata recognized the voice of a favorite, Lucio Battisti, one of the first singers to let her know how vulnerable men could feel.

"This is very nice," Flavia said. "Everything, and you here."

They walked around, trying to choose the right place to toss the medal in the Navigli. Flavia seemed wobbly after the wine, and Renata offered her arm, Papoozi's special medal held tightly in her other hand. Flavia had asked Renata to throw it for her, because she did not feel well.

"What do you think? Here?" Flavia asked at last, as they approached the Ginocchio della Lavandaia—the Washerwoman's Knee, a dilapidated historic site Papoozi had liked. It made him think of girls washing clothes, he'd told her once, of their laughter and teasing he'd remembered from his boyhood in Naples.

"Yes, here," Renata agreed.

"Close your eyes," Renata said. Flavia did. She only opened them again at the light plop of the metal hitting water.

"We did it." Flavia looked overwhelmed.

"We did it," Renata said.

Renata lowered her eyes, feeling a slight heat in her cheeks. Deep in her pocket, she clutched Papoozi's war medal. When

the moment had come to throw it in the Navigli, Flavia had
closed her eyes as instructed, overcome by emotion heightened
by the Prosecco, as Renata had hoped; Renata then threw an
American quarter into the canal. *This is my memory. I decide when.*
Papoozi hadn't specified when the medal should be thrown into
the canal, she reasoned. Could Papoozi mark time in eternal
rest? Stung by the thought of him reproaching her, she turned
sharply to Flavia. You are the one who is certain that he is bask-
ing in the light of the Lord, she thought. Why would he quibble
over an old medal?

Afterward, they browsed the tiny stores crowding the Navigli,
looking for an appropriate gift for Loredano. Flavia chose, at
last, the boutique Maglieria di Lusso. A tiny bell tinkled as they
entered. The shop smelled of cedar. An attractive saleswoman
looked up at them suspiciously over her glasses when they entered, as if she could read their modest home in their features.

Renata started toward the shelf of cashmere sweaters.

"There is no Entrata Libera sign in the window," Flavia
whispered. "Which means no browsing allowed." Renata hesitated, eager to be agreeable.

"We are looking for a gift for a young woman's birthday,"
Flavia told the saleslady, who leaned forward attentively. The
woman proceeded to drop scarves and gloves of delicate beauty on the wood counter, one after another, in a steady, hypnotic
sequence. She wore a thick layer of makeup, which suggested a
fear of looking her age.

I'm getting old too, Renata thought; perhaps this was not the
time to be thinking of making changes with Steve or anything
at all. But then she thought of Papoozi and his marriage proposal—making a radical change had not frightened him. She
clutched the medal in her pocket.

"What about these?" asked Flavia at last, selecting an exceedingly expensive scarf and matching gloves. Renata noticed
the mauve threads of the yarn, the knots of gray, the tufts of
mohair.

"They are perfect," she said, touched by Flavia's recklessness.

A look of shared intent passed between Renata and the saleslady, both equally eager to conclude the sale. Renata wanted to be done and have a moment to admire the medal hidden in her pocket.

Flavia glanced at her, as if she could detect the deception, then went back to inspect the acquisitions up close, with the diffidence Renata remembered while buying fish.

The wind outside was so strong that walking felt like wading through freezing water. It reminded Renata of the icy winds of Minneapolis. She had only two days left in Milan.

"Will you take the bus back home to Via Saverio for a quiet time at home?" Flavia shouted, struggling to be heard against the wind. *Home*. A tram was visible in the distance, windows flashing in the sunlight that streamed through the clouds. "Here comes my tram home." She handed Renata the gift package for Loredana and the keys to Via Saverio. "Give the gift to Loredana. I am old; she will understand. I need a quiet day for myself, resting. Il Tarocco and young people are not for me. You must be tired too. Go to the apartment to enjoy a little time to yourself. Home is better than a hotel room." Renata would be alone in the apartment after all.

The tram slowed in front of them with a prolonged screech. Renata studied Flavia, wanting to commit her features to memory. Flavia turned before boarding the tram, as if offering herself to be remembered like this—timid smile, hands holding white hair, thin as smoke, off her face, her eyes tearing from the cold.

After Flavia departed, Renata walked along the canals. She had only a vague memory of their home before Via Saverio, but it was around here somewhere. She stopped at a small bar, thinking she'd been here with Papoozi. She recognized a pastry, shaped like a swan and filled with cream, which she'd been fond of as a child, and she remembered a cordial exchange Papoozi had had with the bartender, an old man with a mane of gray hair and wire-rimmed glasses. The bartender, he'd told her later, was a former partisan who had been unable to find work after the war. For a while, using his wartime knowledge of the mountains, he carried contraband cigarettes from Switzerland to Italy and sold them on the black market.

Renata recalled walking by the coffee shop. In her high school years it had been crowded with punks in towering mohawks who smoked Nirdosh, thin aromatic cigarettes from India, and dogs excited at the noise of the pinball machine. The coffee shop was empty now, but for an old man who sat with a cane between his knees, staring outside.

Renata exchanged nods with pensioners walking small dogs. She sat on the steps of a narrow wooden bridge and watched a kid fly a kite that looked like a bomber. This was home too. She sat on the steps of a small chapel that looked like a toy house for the Madonna and Child. People pushed small flowers through the iron grate. She walked to an open field where kids played soccer, screaming like swallows. She could live like this, she thought. She wanted to bum a cigarette from a young man, but he walked off before she could ask him, taking the sharp aroma of Marlboros with him. She passed old apartment buildings, their railings running the length of each floor, that looked familiar.

Renata was determined to find the old building where they'd lived before their mother died. Her search felt like following instructions smudged on a blackboard, but at last she discovered it. The old house was just as she'd remembered it—the barren courtyard with a small statue of the Virgin Mary rising like the lone survivor of a bombing. The corner window of the fourth floor, her parents' old bedroom, was open, a white lace curtain fluttering in the wind.

Papoozi, who did not believe in an afterlife, once examined with the children the reproductions of the paintings of Giotto in the *Enciclopedia dei Ragazzi Mondadori*. "They express the life of the spirit through perfect geometric shapes," he'd told them. Afterward, Renata had drawn their house with a circle outside—which she'd imagined as her mother, resting right above the perfect square of the room where her children slept, watching over them.

✿

In a small square off the Navigli, almost lost in the midst of cheap housing., Renata looked for a cab. A lonesome cab driver in a cream raincoat waved his hand at her. Going home had lost its sense of urgency, but his gesture sealed the deal. During the ride she noticed that his eyes kept glancing her way in the rearview mirror. "Men find a sad woman exciting," Papoozi had told her once.

Renata envisioned standing alone in the doorway of the apartment in Via Saverio.

I can't do it, she thought. She told the cab driver to stop in Piazza Piola. She wanted a moment to think about what to do. The driver did as asked and turned to look at her. They stopped right in front of a florist.

"Here?" the driver asked. He seemed confused.

An idea had come to her.

"Just for a moment, I'm getting flowers," she said.

His eyes seemed to light up with a suspicion that she would bolt without paying. Flowers, she thought, were the perfect way to say goodbye to the house in Via Saverio.

"You can see me go in," she reassured him briskly, stepping out. "I'll be right back."

The tiny store smelled of exotic flowers like the women in the foyer at La Scala. A girl with the coolness of porcelain sat on a tall chair, black fingernails tapping her chin. She had so many piercings that Renata felt indiscreet just looking at her directly.

"I'm paying a visit to an old lady," Renata said. She had spoken in jest, but now she thought of the cracks and water stains on the walls of an apartment that had grown old along with Papoozi.

✿

Renata didn't turn to look up at Via Saverio until the cab had driven off. She listened to the crunchy sound her steps made on the gravel. She breathed in the scent of winter in the air. She crossed paths with hurried women. Stray cats dipped in and out of their way. There was something charming about both.

Inside, a stocky man with gray hair in a buzz cut walked toward her in the hallway, hand outstretched. "You are the American daughter of Cesare?" he asked.

"I live there." She shook his hand. "In Minneapolis." Standing again in Papoozi's apartment building, her life in America seemed a stretch of time she might have skipped altogether without detectable consequences.

"My condolences. My father Davide misses him so."

"Ah, Davide. Yes, of course. I saw his signature in the condolences book. He is your father?"

"He took me in when I was this little." The gesture of his large hand, hovering parallel to the ground, was tender. "I thought you could be Cesare's daughter! I wanted to say something to you."

"Thank you. I hear Davide was a good friend." Renata imagined the chessboard resting on a counter, waiting for Davide and Papoozi to continue their game.

"My poor father is heartbroken about losing Signor Cesare. He remembers every chess game. I watch him move his fingers over the pieces sometimes all by himself." He showed the gestures. Renata could see precisely the invisible game. "Perhaps you might come by later? It would mean so much to him."

"Perhaps," she responded weakly. This man's innocent faith that she could do something for his grieving father made her quite aware that she could do nothing at all.

"2B," the man offered. "For coffee? Later? Or tomorrow?" he suggested, an urgent plea in his eyes.

"If I can," Renata whispered. It was the Italian *no* and they both knew it. "I have to take care of things upstairs. It's my last day and all that. You know how it is." She could not bear the thought of seeing someone who missed Papoozi as much as she did.

"Sure, sure, but come if you can! 2B." He forced a cheerful smile, then turned away with a little wave goodbye.

Renata rode the elevator with a child in short braids and an old woman who didn't say a word. The little girl stared at the flowers, then, her chin to her chest, lifted her beaded purse above her head and held it in front of Renata, as if she were a vision in a dream.

When the elevator reached her floor, each gesture felt familiar to Renata, from the way she closed the small doors of the elevator behind her, to the moment she took to observe the keys before opening the door. She had somehow imagined entering the apartment as a new person. But it was the same old Renata who walked in and dropped her bag, flowers, and Loredana's gift on the nearest chair.

The bouquet of flowers, she realized, was why the little girl in the elevator had shown Renata her own beautiful purse as a sort of exchange. "I would be a terrible mother," she said with a smile.

She peeked into every room. They were chilly and immaculate, the beds tidy, the chairs lined up straight. The apartment now reminded her of a used-furniture store. Even Papoozi's fountain pen had been placed square, next to his notebook on his desk, the life gone from it. Everything had been sanitized by Flavia.

Renata stood at the kitchen window, looking out at the trains. A red neon sign blinked in the distance, advertising Brillo, the scouring pad trusted by housewives for thirty years. A local train went by, wobbly like an old dog.

"Sitting here like a rabbit in her cage all day?" Papoozi's sharp voice sounded in her head.

She felt the vibrations of a *Direttissimo* train under her feet and stared out at the view of the city, the shapes softening with the change of light.

"Yeah," she answered Papoozi, with a grin. "I'm doing exactly that. What else did you think I would ever do?" She pressed her palm to the glass of the window, catching and letting go of distant lights as she used to do as a child. Her hand moved in a circle, as if washing the surface with a sponge soaked in soap and water. Old games, old silliness. For a moment, the past felt real.

Renata turned on the TV, the screen cloudy and flickering. She tested the armchair, which felt scratchy.

She grew restless at the idea of the upcoming dinner. Performance anxiety, Steve called it. Renata imagined Gianni's eyes on her and felt an anticipatory thrill. His energy entered her bones for a brief moment, but then she felt the weight of the day. Loredana's friends would be curious about Tito's American sister, and she found the attention of strangers exhausting. The forced exchanges felt like a presidential debate, with predictable questions and answers and a palpable sense of relief when it was all over.

Renata wished for the intimacy of Italian girlfriends, like the ones who sat close together in coffee shops and walked in chatty groups, high heels clicking on the pavement. Together they would chuckle at her apprehensions, teach her how to apply makeup, instruct her on what to say to attractive men. They would giggle, then get intense, as she'd seen them do in cafes. She'd watched them stir their coffees, adjust their necklaces, and say something like "And that was nothing—" or "I couldn't live with that anymore." She would tell them all the things that went through her head. She'd tell them about Steve being gone all the time and about eating alone at night, peas pushed to the side of her plate.

20

Renata thought about apartment 2B.

Perhaps you can come later? the man with the buzz cut had said. *Perhaps tomorrow?*

Dusk crept into the room. She looked at her watch. It was time to go. There was nothing urgent to accomplish in this house. She'd visited each room and ran up and down the short hallway to render the visit a bit adventurous, but the house had stopped giving her something in return for her attention.

Her phone rang with a number she didn't recognize. She picked it up, eager to talk. A wrong number was fine—she'd be indulgent and chatty. Even a telemarketer would do. Sure, sure, I understand how helpful your product is, she would agree.

"*Principessa?* You don't say goodbye before leaving?" Cosimo asked. "Not even a call?"

"You were a jerk the other night," she said.

"Still am. Don't you want to have a drink before you leave?" he asked with forced cheer.

"I am too tired to do anything tonight," she replied, pleased to be able to say no to him. "Tomorrow is also impossible." Then she drifted into an awkward set of fake excuses, not wanting to mention the dinner Tito planned that Cosimo had not been invited to.

"I know about the birthday celebration," he said, with a chuckle. "Me and your brother talk, don't you know? I'm busy tomorrow too."

He had a date that night, of course.

"I am going back to the hotel to catch some sleep," she said. This is how it ends, she thought.

"Where are you staying?" he asked, in a tone so tender it was as if he were passing his finger gently over her cheek, the way one does to a tired child.

"Albergo Ambrogino," she said.

"That claptrap? Who are you, Sid Vicious?"

"Nancy Spungen. I'm in Via Saverio now," she said, as if it were the Taj Mahal, then realized that Cosimo knew her house well. His parents lived only a few blocks away.

"Dear God, get out of there. Your father didn't want to live in that chicken coop anymore."

"Of course he did," Renata snapped, getting angry at Cosimo's nonsense.

"Nah. Why would he? I bumped into him at the Supermercato Loreto all the time, and he told me he was going to give the apartment to Tito and Loredana when they got married."

"Really? What else did he tell you?"

"That's all. He mentioned going to see America and the Mississippi River, and of coming to see you. He was excited that you lived in a different country. His daughter was *sangue del mio sangue*, blood of my blood, as he put it. An immigrant like him." He paused. "Hello? You still there?"

"Yes." She could always count on Papoozi surprising her, even in death it seemed.

"So, is it beautiful?" Cosimo asked. "The Mississippi River? Your father knew everything about it from his reading. We are all settling for less as we get older, me included, but your father never did."

"Yes, the Mississippi is beautiful." Renata imagined Papoozi, his glasses pushed high on his forehead, studying maps.

"Your father, what a character," Cosimo said. "You mind that I told you about the apartment? I hear you object to your brother mating for life with that drip, Loredana."

"She is not a drip," she protested.

"I hear you have the hots for her cousin," Cosimo said. Through the phone she heard the double click of a lighter as he lit a cigarette. "You inbred." The conversation felt warm and uncomplicated, as if they'd already spent an uninterrupted lifetime together. In the past, she remembered, they used to sit close and speak very little. "Hot date for you tomorrow night," he said as he took a puff of his cigarette. "Wearing a skirt like a girl? Lipstick? Or your bad-boy stuff, as usual?"

"*Vaffan*," she whispered.

"You are still one crude little boy," he said. "Your parents should do something about it, Rocky Marciano."

"I don't have any parents," she said, casually, but her fingers were tight and bloodless clutching the phone.

The view from the window dimmed with the evening light. The railway station, the skyscrapers, the treetops faded into a smudge.

"I'm sorry. When I talk to you, I'm like a cat, all skittish and overexcited at every thread you throw my way. So, can I see you the day after tomorrow? For coffee, maybe? Before you go." Cosimo sounded tentative, demure. She rather liked that he was such a jerk, like a kid.

"Yes, you can," she said, bemused. He knew, after her intense scrutiny at Bar Noventa, that she liked him, Renata thought. She sensed in him something new; he was self-conscious about being seen by her. She seemed to know him better than he thought, and that made him nervous. Her power amused her. "The day after tomorrow is fine. A quick coffee in the morning before I leave."

"Brush your hair for me," he said, cheerfully, then added, "Just kidding."

"I always brush my hair."

"Nah, don't bother," he said, his tone light. "It's not a date, right? But really, it does not matter what your hair looks like. I like imperfect things more and more, especially in myself. I mean, as far as I'm concerned, I'm willing to settle for less. It must be an age thing."

He said a soft goodbye and hung up. After a moment of listening to the dial tone, Renata hung up too. She exhaled as if she'd held her breath the entire call.

"Your father is raising you like a raccoon," Cosimo used to tease her when she'd show up to a gathering. "Good thing you are sexy. Is that a hairstyle? What are you wearing? Your father does not know yet that you are not a boy? You all go shopping together or something?" It sounded like a dumb joke at her expense, but Papoozi, Tito, and Renata would do exactly that.

"Sweatshirts are sweatshirts," Papoozi used to pronounce. "Boots are boots."

"New clothes should be bought with caution," Papoozi warned them, "as they can attract the wrong kind of attention. You do not want to look wealthy or you could end up being kidnapped and held for ransom, hidden in the mountains of Sardinia like Paul Getty, Jr. You could end up having one ear cut off and sent to me in the mail." Kidnappings were all over the news, that much was true, but somehow other parents seemed oblivious to the danger, judging from what their kids were allowed to wear, carelessly and with gusto.

Renata slid out the door and into the elevator, pushing the button for the ground floor. She thought she might stop somewhere on her way back to the hotel so she could buy a good hairbrush. The Upim department store was nearby. She thought about buying a dress but decided it was too tricky finding the right fit. Should I wear something more tailored? she wondered. Less colorful? The negotiations between her desires and how the dress looked on her always upset her.

When the elevator stopped on the ground floor and the light switched off, Renata remained inside, wanting to stay in the dark comfort of a neutral space. She thought of apartment 2B.

"What a waste being alive if you don't go for things that have a little risk," Papoozi had said as he took off on one of his walks in the drizzling rain. "Why explain yourself to yourself? Just do it."

She scoffed at buying a hairbrush after all, and her new daring elated her. She would surprise herself.

Renata pushed the button to the second floor. Apartment 2B faced the elevator. She rang the doorbell with the persistence of a delivery man, afraid she might change her mind.

The man she'd met downstairs opened the door.

"Oh, good evening!" He seemed surprised. He stepped aside and gestured for her to enter with a sweep of one arm.

"Good evening," she said, walking briskly into the apartment, as if she were leaping into cold water.

"Thank you for coming," he stammered.

She imagined Papoozi, taking off his coat in this room, filling the space with his voice. Men owned rooms, she thought.

The room before her was the overly tidy space of an invalid, where nobody pushes a chair aside or hurries to open drawers for a fresh tie. Everything appeared to be in exactly the right place, like an apartment after a death.

Signor Davide, a shriveled man in a wheelchair, sat in the corner, playing Solitaire at a small table, his lips moving without making a sound. He did not look up. He was absorbed in his game. The chair across from him had been pushed under the table—the chair Papoozi had used for their chess games. She saw that Signor Davide was focused on a game of Napoleon solitaire, Papoozi's favorite. Renata felt both fascinated and apprehensive at how Signor Davide was keeping Papoozi in his life a little longer. What could possibly happen next? Nothing. She felt sorry for Signor Davide but even sorrier for herself, who had given up wanting the impossible.

As a child she'd opened and closed her mother's compact, one she'd miraculously saved after her death. At night she'd put the compact under her pillow and lie awake, listening, waiting. She could remember how, years back, she used to fall asleep immediately, her eyes closing to the distant whispers of her parents; it was as if she were gently drowning.

Opening and closing the compact, she'd thought, was a way to call her mother back.

"Put that compact away," Papoozi used to urge her. "What good does it do? It's dangerous like a knife. It only gives pain. Move on." In the end she hid the compact away and did not take it out again.

Signor Davide, however, was not moving on. He continued to play the Solitaire Papoozi had favored.

She held her breath as if Signor Davide's determination could actually summon Papoozi. The room felt as if it existed in suspended time, where anything seemed possible.

"Signor Davide," she called out after a while, when he did not look up from his game. *You survived a war, a concentration camp,* she wanted to tell him. *You cannot crumble over an old man being gone.*

"Look! You have a visitor," the son said.

Signor Davide still did not look up. Renata became absorbed by the rhythm of the game, by the gentle slap-slap of cards, by the breathing of Signor Davide. How could she possibly encourage this man to move on?

"Signor Davide, I've come to see you." He looked up for a moment at the sound of her voice. Renata felt trapped. They were each stuck in a separate loneliness.

"Tell him! Tell him who you are," the son coaxed her. Hearing his voice startled her. Renata had forgotten his presence. *Signor Davide, let Papoozi be dead. Let him be done with this crappy life.*

"I am Renata," she said, leaning down so he could see her face. "I am Cesare's daughter." Signor Davide blinked, trying to focus on her features in the dim yellow light of the room.

"She is his daughter," the son repeated, so loudly he was almost shouting. "She came to see you."

The old man stared at Renata, his lips twitching slightly in what might have been a smile.

"I am Renata. I am the daughter of Cesare," she repeated.

Animated now, the old man looked her over meticulously, with the diffidence of someone who is hoping too hard. A trembling diffused through his body.

"Tell him why you are here," the son said, beaming.

Renata had no clue why she was there. Signor Davide was now looking at her with a tremulous expectation in his eyes.

"Signor Davide," she said, "it's Saturday. My father taught me to play a mean game of chess." She pulled Papoozi's chair out. "Beat me."

21

The fourth floor of the Ospedale Sant'Erasmo hospice seemed empty. It had a quiet grace in the afternoon light. Renata resisted peeking into the empty room that had been Papoozi's. "Time to move on," he'd always demanded, and today she did.

Domenico, hair gathered in a ponytail, a leather jacket hooked on a finger over his shoulder, leaned against the kitchen door, talking to someone inside. He waved when he saw her. "Hey," he called.

"Domenico, hey," she said.

Renata felt disturbed by the lunch carts lined up against the wall, muffled TVs that played in every room, and the ripple of death that permeated the ward.

"Okay, well, I just came to thank you." Renata turned to go. The real reason for her visit now seemed too complicated to even begin to express.

"Wait, wait," Domenico said. "Coffee somewhere?"

There was a refreshing directness between them, and amid the babbling of TVs and the steam from the radiators, she agreed that a bit of fresh air sounded like a good idea.

"I want to thank you for helping me the other night," she said.

"I'm glad if I could. We sent a brochure to your mother— you might want to look at it too."

Your mother. For an astonishing instant, Renata saw her mother sitting at the table in Via Saverio, reading the brochure. Then she realized he was speaking of Flavia, of course. She found her breath again.

"Thank you."

"Maybe it's too simple, but we hope that it helps a bit. We do the little we can, and it's close to nothing. A loss is a sorrow that cannot be truly shared, and it cannot be put in a box to be taken out and put away at will. You can't say, the pain is here or here," he said, pointing at different parts of his chest.

Renata had given up smoking for herself as much as for Steve. She'd wanted the pain of withdrawal, she realized, a pain she could pinpoint precisely on her body, not like the mess of her relationship with Steve that seemed to ache everywhere. A cigarette she refused herself caused a stabbing in her lungs, throat, and head. *Here is the pain,* she would tell herself, as if she could touch it. Being able to locate and define the pain gave it a time to last and then a time to cease.

"Tell me again," she'd asked Tessa. "How long is it before you feel okay after you stop smoking?"

"Six weeks," Tessa had replied.

"And with the acupuncture detox treatments?" Renata had asked.

"Six weeks, but an easier six weeks."

Renata and Domenico walked out into the sunshine together. He grinned happily, as if the sight of Vespas and bikes negotiating the busy road were a treat he had orchestrated just for her. The sidewalk was empty, which made the conversation with Domenico feel more intimate than she'd intended it to be.

"We have meetings for families who experience a loss," Domenico said.

She felt his eyes return to her, restlessly, and she wondered about what he expected from her. He seemed aware that there was something she needed to tell.

"I go back to Minnesota soon," she said.

"Ah, you are lucky to be leaving." His easy tone reminded her of the night at Ospedale Sant'Erasmo, but more a closeness achieved over a casual cup of coffee than the death of a father. "They say in the paper that this February is going to be the worst."

They walked around two kids kicking a ball to each other on the sidewalk. The cold wind clung to Renata's clothes, and the sound of their footsteps now seemed incessant. She wanted to get to the point of her visit.

"It's cold in Minneapolis too. That's where I live," she said. "It can be dangerous for the elderly, and my patients don't like it." *My patients.* There, she'd said it.

"You are a doctor?" he asked, surprised.

"I'm an acupuncturist," she said. "In America, it is a profession, not just for MDs like in Italy. But I'm not used to death."

"Nobody is," he said.

She looked at him with a new interest. What of him was scarred and vulnerable, she wondered. He had chosen to work with those who were drifting off to death.

They arrived at a small coffee shop wedged between a toy store and a video rental shop. The place seemed smoky even if nobody smoked. The colorful bottles of aperitifs behind the cash register, the modest array of sandwiches displayed on the counter, along with several empty coffee cups—all felt vaguely disturbing, like a persistent noise one cannot pinpoint. A silent TV flickered on the shelf.

"Maybe we just walk?" she said.

"That's good. I'm inside too much," he said, turning to leave.

The TV, Renata noticed, showed footage of a flood, debris floating over dirty water, a car spinning, then sinking. Then, for a moment, Obama gestured at a microphone, flashing his distinct smile.

She told Domenico how much she appreciated Obama's position against the war. She felt a surge of happiness that she had decided to vote for him.

"My father was at Mauthausen, and almost died there," she told Domenico.

"Was he Jewish?" he asked.

"No. He'd barely made it back from the front, and he was captured. He refused to cooperate. He did not want to talk about it, and that's how he was. He missed Naples, but he didn't say much about that either."

"I sang 'I' Te Vurria Vasa' to your father while we were waiting for you to arrive," Domenico said. "But I have to say that I am an awful singer."

"My father used to sing that song every evening," she told him. "It was a favorite of his, and I am sure you were a comfort to him, regardless of how it was sung."

"Yeah. I did what I could, and so did you. That's all we can do. I'm glad you came back to see me," he said. "I don't talk about things easily, but I wanted to tell you how sorry I am that I pushed you to let him go. I think it hurt, and that was not the way I am. I made things worse. I was worried afterward; you seemed alone."

The words *you seemed alone* were surprising in their bluntness, and Renata felt the twitch of tears under her eyelids.

"Thank you. I'm really grateful." She felt relieved that he had seen her discomfort but did not pretend he had not.

"If I can do anything—" he said.

"Well, yes, you could," she said. "You can. That's why I'm here." She opened her fist to reveal Papoozi's bronze medal.

"My father asked that we throw his war medal in the Navigli after his death," she said. She imagined the ravaged stones, sluggish water, carrying discarded plastic bottles. She felt the strange hope that the medal at the very last moment would disobey the laws of physics, so admired by Papoozi, and not sink. "I must do it, even if I don't want to. I would like you to come with me."

"What would you like me to do?"

"You can stand by me. You can tell me to let him go, just like you did in the room at Sant'Erasmo. And this time, I will let go." *And then I'll be truly alone.*

Afterward, she called Tito and asked him to pick her up at the house in Via Saverio. She wanted to talk to him there, not at the hotel or in the car.

"Of course," he said, perplexed.

She walked home from the subway stop in Piazzale Loreto, a large expanse surrounded by tall buildings, most seemingly still under construction. Anti-fascist demonstrators always used to march through it, holding signs and chanting, "*In Piazzale*

Loreto c'e' ancora tanto posto." The corpse of Mussolini had hung there, together with that of his lover, Claretta Petacci, and other well-known Fascists. Mussolini's son, Romano, was a famous jazz pianist, but she presumed he never performed in Milan. Supposedly he recorded at Studio 7, and she imagined a lonely stroll he might have wanted to take to Piazzale Loreto.

Renata barely made it upstairs before Tito arrived. She'd stopped to buy a birthday card for Loredana at the Bar & Ta-bacchi—an enormous card with rapturous sentiments printed in gold, the only one without a creepy attempt at humor. She'd added her own words, which seemed to communicate a desper-ate cheerfulness, and placed the card by the flowers and Flavia's small package.

Tito opened the front door with his old key and stepped into the kitchen. His shirt, beneath a smoky-gray herringbone coat, was a blinding white. He brought the crisp smell of winter with him. In his eyes she saw the melancholy of a martyr and was heartened to think that the dinner might be something he dreaded too.

"You look great. I didn't really have time to change," she said.

He glanced at her pants and a sweater, clearly unimpressed, but he said nothing.

"We should go soon," he said. "Loredana is at Il Tarocco already; Gianni gave her a ride."

"Sit for a moment," she said to Tito. "I want to talk about the house." They sat facing each other in the small kitchen, like survivors caught by a flood in their good clothes; loved ones, memories, family, a life—all gone in one sweep.

"You are sure you want to talk now?" Tito said. "It's a complicated matter. Later would be best. Now it all feels too rushed."

"Open the card," she said. "You read it first, here in the old house." He looked at her, baffled.

"Why now? Loredana does not like to wait."

"How are you holding up?" she asked.

"Fine, I guess. A bit nervous." he said, smiling. "I will be fine. I can't be happy. It's too difficult."

The weight of the marriage, the baby, finding a home—his face already seemed marked by the future conversation with Zia Marta and Zio Emanuele.

"We should go now, Reni. We can discuss what to do with the house another time. It's a celebration tonight, so no business talk, please. Oh, and listen, last thing. I got a call from the crematorium. Tomorrow I get back the ashes. I'll take the urn to Naples and spread them in the sea. It's not the cleanest sea, and it's rocky. He asked and I'll do it." *What a Milanese*, she thought, with a little smile. *Not the cleanest sea.*

She imagined Tito sitting alone in the Freccia D'oro, the fast train Papoozi had fantasized about taking back to Napoli. She could see him leafing through *Il Corriere della Sera*, the copper urn in a satchel on his lap. The train would pass crowded platforms at each station, bustling with arms waving handkerchiefs and the noisy sorrow of separations. Papoozi used to walk to Stazione Centrale just for the excitement, she remembered.

"I'm sorry I can't come," she said.

"It's fine," he said. He gave a dismissive shrug. His thoughts were clearly somewhere else. He thought of dispersing the ashes as a simple errand. He was now a man getting married and having a child.

Then she saw him in his elegant herringbone coat, with his *fresco lana* trousers carefully rolled up, lurching on the rocks and sand of Margellina, gripping his Bruno Magli shoes in one hand and the urn in the other.

He stood up, inviting her to do the same, and started to go.

"Tito, I want the ashes," she said to his back, her voice cracking. "You don't have to take them to Naples." He turned, his expression impatient. "His ashes in the sea of Naples is an old wish. It changed. Papoozi always changed his mind. Cosimo said—ask him. Papoozi told him that he wanted to see America, the Mississippi."

"In theory."

"Just think about it, Tito."

"Okay, I will." His eyes drifted again to the door.

"Open the card now," she insisted.

A wave of hope came over her as he picked up the card and looked at the large envelope.

"It's for Loredana, no?" he asked, pocketing it. Picking up the flowers and the package from Flavia, he said again, "Shall we go? What is it, Reni? What do you want?"

"I want to take Papoozi to the Mississippi."

"You want this so bad?"

"Yes." I am the firstborn, she thought, the one who carries out the father's wishes. She didn't allow the sentence to form itself in full: *if male*. But she wasn't so sure that being the first-born was the real reason for her desire. She imagined Papoozi studying maps under a yellow lamplight. Alone at a table with his books, with his pipe dreams. It was frightening to think that death washed away all desire. "We can split the ashes if you want."

"Okay," said Tito. "Let's go now. We're done, aren't we?"

"We are." She felt light, happy. "I'm sorry I didn't bring something nicer to wear."

"You look fine. I like it," he said, clearly relieved that they could leave at last. "Perfect choice, in fact," he said, with a twinkle in his eyes. "In these clothes, they'll kidnap me, and you'll be safe. For once, I'd be your protector."

"Remember?" she said. "We always wondered who they would pick. We could not figure it out."

"And guess what? Loredana and I are planning to go to Sardinia on our honeymoon. I hear it's fantastic." They cracked up.

She followed Tito out. The door to Via Saverio clicked shut behind her.

22

Il Tarocco spelled ambition from its doorway, where they were greeted by chandeliers, large mirrors, a vague art deco installation, and a resolute hostess in high heels. The main room was a warm buzz of voices—sleek women chatting in pairs going to and from the restroom and young waiters murmuring to customers as they moved through the tables in a tightly choreographed flow. Renata spotted Loredana, Gianni, and two young girls at a table, perusing the leather-bound menus with the apprehension of examining a manual for military maneuvers.

Seeing them, Gianni quickly rose to his feet and came to welcome them. He greeted Renata breathlessly, as if they'd miraculously bumped into each other by chance on the street.

"Renata!" he said, radiating happiness as he drew her into a hug, his lips brushing against her temple.

"You smell good, like a doctor," she said into his shoulder.

"That nice?" he said with a laugh.

The waiters made a slight detour around them as she stood in his embrace. She didn't look at them, afraid it would end the moment.

"Hey," called Tito from the table. "What wine?"

They both found the question hilarious.

"It's winter. Red?" Gianni asked, drawing back to look tentatively at Renata. It seemed the kind of question people ask when they already know the answer—but to hear the response as an act of love. She smiled in assent.

Gianni and Renata sat close together. He looked at her shyly, as if she'd responded to an intimate question. They read in each other the wish to be alone together, talking side by side, sipping from the same glass, letting desire grow. She imagined his arm draped over the back of her chair, and the pleasure of leaning back, feeling the warmth of his fingers against the nape of her neck.

The two young women sitting by Loredana gazed at Renata with expectant eyes. They introduced themselves as Annalisa and Rita. "You are from America?" Rita asked Renata. She had the chiseled features of a model.

"Yes, from America," Renata replied, moving around the table to hug Loredana, to avoid more questions on the subject. "Happy Birthday, Loredana!" she said.

"For God's sake! Stop getting old!" Gianni teased Loredana, giving her a big kiss on the cheek.

"Sorry!" She laughed.

Renata felt a pang of nostalgia for their playfulness, wishing she and Tito hadn't lost their own. In truth, she thought, perhaps we never had it.

They ordered the most uncomplicated dishes they could find. Rita insisted on helping Renata with her order, as if she were truly a foreigner. She didn't mind the help and followed Rita's finger along the writing as if memorizing a poem. Rita mispronounced all the ingredients and laughed at herself, shaking her curls with a playfulness Renata found utterly charming.

The waiter was good-natured about waiting. He was smiling, while his eyes rested unhurriedly on Rita's long hands, on her luminous face. He looked happy to simply stand there, ready with his pencil, included in a beautiful girl's joke. Gianni's shirt was a light blue, which heightened his features. His excitement made him look disheveled. His curls, chaotic. His hands drifted casually to the hollow of his neck while he talked, a gesture that took her breath away. His jaw displayed a fresh shaving cut, which gave her pleasure, suggesting he'd been nervous getting ready.

"Tito!" he called out in jest. "Can we start with dessert? It's a birthday."

"Yeah." Tito smiled.

Renata noticed that the two of them exhibited a new ease with each other, as she watched them choose the wine. They showed an affectionate camaraderie as they talked. She felt even more affection for Gianni knowing that he would be a powerful ally in the war with Zia Marta.

When Gianni turned to her, she said softly, "Do you know about Tito and Loredana?" He whispered *yes* in a way that felt directed toward her, as if he were referring instead to the two of them.

The waiter poured the wine, then lingered, seemingly bemused. Renata realized they were the youngest group in the restaurant.

"Is the wine good?" Gianni asked her, his hand brushing her knee to catch her attention. She took a sip and nodded.

Renata's cell phone vibrated, and after a moment, she slid it across the table to Tito. "Come on, take this back. I'm done," she said.

"You don't want to answer?" Tito asked. "It's someone for you."

"Maybe an American boyfriend!" Rita teased, then blushed, catching Gianni's gaze.

"Aren't you going to answer it?" Loredana seemed baffled.

"I can't blame you if you don't want to," Rita scoffed. "We're having dinner. It's so irritating."

"Of course it is," said Annalisa, exasperated. "These phones run our lives." Renata envisioned a young man talking animatedly on the phone, pacing, gesticulating, paying no attention whatsoever to Annalisa. Steve, similarly, had often given her cause to regret the invention of the phone. "Yes, my dear, we buy them. And we are idiots for buying them."

An uneasy silence fell among them.

"Annalisa," Loredana ventured. "Is Fabio joining us later?"

Annalisa shrugged and frowned. Phones, men—both were clearly a curse. Her demeanor suggested she was done with both.

"What about Stefano?" Loredana asked Rita. "Is he coming?"

"Oh, I don't see him anymore." Rita shrugged, sipping her wine. She made a face. "So long, he'll survive."

An image of Steve getting dressed flashed through Renata's mind—a white shirt twirling high, then his arms slipping through the sleeves in one swift move. *Voilà!* She heard her own laughter. *Do it again.* It was her favorite stupid trick. He slipped off his shirt. Again he did the trick. *Voilà. Magic.*

Gianni sensed her shift in mood. She detected timidity in his eyes.

"I'm switching off mine too! Here!" Tito theatrically raised his hand for everybody to see. He switched off the phone and slipped it into his pocket.

"Me too!" Rita said, after a moment's hesitation.

Laughing, everyone followed suit, fumbling under the table. Loredana shook her head but giggled too.

The appetizers arrived—tiny squares with goat cheese with a hint of citrus and lavender and thinly sliced carpaccio with capers. The band played tunes from Broadway shows.

"Are you from Turin?" Renata asked Annalisa. She had the fine features of the Piedmontese and their serene friendliness.

"Nearby. Moncalvo, in the hills," she replied. Moncalvo was a very small town in Piedmont. Renata knew of the squat, thick-walled buildings with tiny windows. During the war, in Piedmont they'd made cakes with acorns. Papoozi had spoken of it with fondness. "And you? Where do you live in America?"

"It's not New York, Los Angeles, or San Francisco," Renata said. She got a soft laughter in response. She had guessed the cities in Annalisa's mind.

"I'm in Minneapolis." Renata thought of telling her stories about winter in Minneapolis, about friends skiing to parties after a snowstorm when streets were impassable. Annalisa, from Piedmont, would like that, she thought.

"Renata, how come you went to America?" asked Rita abruptly, loud enough to attract attention from diners at other tables.

"Well—" She took her time to reply. "Let's see," she began.

She felt Gianni's eyes on her. In the mirror on the wall opposite, he looked like an eccentric poet, sipping wine, staring at her with a radiant intensity.

"It's a long story," said Tito, coming to her rescue. "Let's eat now."

"I like long stories," Rita said.

"No, it's short," Renata said. "I went on a student visa." She could imagine her patients' protest. *Why not say everything?* In the intimacy of small rooms, on the narrow treatment beds, they told her everything—stories of rain, lousy apartments, complicated loves, and no money. They told her of war in foreign lands, of lost friends and unexpected passion. They told the truth, and they expected the same from her.

"Ah," Rita said, already uninterested. Annalisa was asking Gianni where to take her car for a checkup. Tito knew a good place, he said.

Renata, relieved, leaned back in her chair.

"But you stayed seven years," Loredana said. She seemed determined to get to the bottom of the matter. Renata regretted coming to the dinner and going to America in equal measure.

"Yes," she breathed, wishing another diner might cause a distraction. "Seven years."

"With a student visa?" *Porca miseria ladra assassina.* She imagined a punctilious Loredana, keeping Tito to a precise schedule in their married life. *You said you'd be back at 5:05.*

"My mother says you are married," Loredana said. "Tito, didn't you tell her that?"

"Yes," Tito said.

Renata stared at her brother as the rest of the table—with the exception of Gianni, who was intent on pushing the food around on his plate—all stared at her.

At that moment the waiter brought their main courses, setting plates down in front of each of them with a flourish.

"Yes, I am married."

"Oh? To an American?" Annalisa asked.

"I am married to an American, in America." Renata's gaze floated upward to the shimmering chandeliers, the dark figures of the black-coated waiters moving in the light. "I'm leaving him."

Tito locked eyes with her, a heightened energy in their silent exchange.

"It was a brief marriage," Tito said, "and now it's over."

Everybody was quiet now.

Renata reached for the *baccalá* on Gianni's plate, spearing the soft fish with her fork a few times. Gianni looked up, surprised.

"I'm just trying to seduce you," she said, pushing her fork away. "How am I doing?"

She felt awkward; she had been alone too long, and he was young and utterly beautiful.

"You are dead on," he replied, leaning close to her and whispering something the buzz of the restaurant carried away.

23

Assholes, *figli di puttana*!" Cosimo's raging voice startled them. He strode toward their table, bumping into waiters and knocking against chairs. "None of you *cornuti bastardi* picks up the *maledetto* phone *di merda*? Not one picks up?" He pulled a chair over and sat next to Renata. "I had to use paid parking and didn't even know if you were still here." He glanced at Gianni and gave Renata a quick nod, whispering, "*Figo*, hot." The intensity of his gaze shocked her.

"Here I am," he declared, looking around at everyone. He had the toughness of a man who works all day with people and eats dinner in restaurants late at night, alone.

"Who's this?" Gianni asked.

Cosimo stood up briefly and gave a little bow.

"Oh. Where are my manners? I'm Cosimo." He sat back down, locking eyes with Renata. "Happy to see me?"

"What the hell are you doing here?" Tito asked.

"Saying goodbye to your sister."

Tito glanced from Cosimo to Renata but made no further comment.

"Your departing sister. Who is leaving Milan, and who has not mentioned returning. She clearly prefers other amenities to the ones we can offer." Then, abruptly, breezily, he turned to her to ask, "How's the snow in Minneapolis?"

"You would love it."

"Thank you, I wouldn't. I wouldn't like anything there," he said.

"The snow comes down fine, like salt at first, then slow and soft like the wings of moths."

Their eyes met. Renata looked down, playing with her fork. "You should see it," she said.

She felt a wave of solitude, envisioning watching the falling snow as she walked inside the glass skyway of the Minneapolis airport parking ramp, alone like a night watchman, listening to the sound of her steps.

"Oh God, this is going to be unbearably moving," Cosimo said. "Since you ask—no, I should not see it. *Che Diavolo dici?* What the hell are you saying? How would I do that? My English is crap. I fear airplanes. On my desk there's a pile of travel books I bought in multiple copies because I forgot I owned them, and they are covered in dust." His gaze moved restlessly about the room, seemingly scouring the impossible unknown of Minneapolis, the TV blasting news in English, the butcher shops neatly packaging meat rather than hanging bleeding carcasses as they did in Milan, the thousand lakes. "For fuck's sake, don't you understand?"

It would be evening in Minneapolis when she landed, Renata knew. The buildings would begin to lose definition at that hour. She could almost hear the *click-click-click* of street signs battered by wind. She sat up in her chair.

"You prefer the sea?" Loredana asked Cosimo.

"No," Cosimo said. "Fish do all sorts of things in the sea. Think of it. That's where they mate, where they shit—"

"Cosimo," Renata said sharply.

"Yes, I do. I love the sea. I'm just kidding." Cosimo turned to Renata. "Glad to see me, *principessa?*"

"Don't do this," she said, worried. This was the Cosimo who'd violently toppled his chair at Bar Noventa one night long ago, making a scene.

"Do what?"

"This."

She was filled with grief that she would not see him anymore—his melancholy air, the glint in his eyes when he teased her, the way he spoke when telling the truth.

Loredana was chatting intently with Gianni about wanting to buy a Vespa or the Milanese version, the Lambretta. Gianni offered to lend her his Vespa for a few days to try it out. "I could take you for a test drive first, if you like," he said.

Renata imagined Loredana zipping around Milan on his

scooter. *Il traffico.* The veering around buses and cars, their muffled laughter carried away by the wind. Renata brought her glass
of wine to her lips and drained it.

Cosimo noticed Rita and Annalisa staring at him, and he
suddenly composed himself. Annalisa smiled. Renata saw her
beauty bloom again, now that her prickly moodiness was gone.

"I thought we were saying goodbye tomorrow?" Renata
asked Cosimo, pouring him wine. "Hungry? Shall we order for
you?"

He dismissed the offer with a gesture.

"I cannot meet you tomorrow. I have to leave for a business trip," he said, taking a gulp of wine. *Business trip,* was pronounced with importance, and seemed to be directed to Rita
and Annalisa. "I have eaten already."

Renata could see that Cosimo was attracted to Rita. His eyes
narrowed, looking at her, his expression something between
confusion and excitement.

"So—what did everybody do today?" he asked jovially. Nobody answered, so he turned to Renata. "You?"

"A ninety-two-year-old man beat me at chess."

"You?" Cosimo's eyes sparkled with mirth. "You let him
win, you softie."

"That was the plan," she said, glancing uneasily at the blank
stares around the table. "I was going to let him win and feel
good about myself." Chess and old men were clearly unglamorous topics.

"Then?" Cosimo's interest acquired the comfort of a refuge.

Cosimo seemed entranced by the story, while the others listened as if to someone's meandering narrative, waiting dutifully
for the punch line.

"I could not read him. So I lost," she said.

After a brief silence, a conversation started abruptly about a
just-released movie, like a radio switched to full volume during
a tedious car ride.

"Gianni," Loredana called. "What did the guy say in that
movie? When we laughed, remember?"

"Lori, I told you twenty times!" Gianni said, with a chuckle, rolling his eyes at Renata. "Loredana is very distracted," he said in English. "I am too."

"Do you like being distracted?" Renata asked. "I'm delighted that you are." She, too, spoke in English.

"Thank you."

Renata liked that he pronounced it *tank yoo*, just as she used to, and her earlier sadness evaporated.

"Say it one more time," she asked.

"Thank you!" He obliged her with a grin, then moved toward Loredana, who was beckoning to him. Renata felt light and silly—a happily soon-to-be-unmarried woman.

Sensing Cosimo's eyes on her, she turned to him.

"What happened to your date?" she asked. "You had a date, yes?"

"It was good."

He stared at her, a fluctuating force in his eyes unsettling her.

"Why such a short date then?" she asked.

"I wanted to say goodbye to you." He took small thoughtful sips from his glass. "You did not brush your hair after all, *principessa*."

She liked the way Cosimo dressed, like a dissolute dandy. The way he held his glass, the deep clarity of his voice, all seemed to radiate confidence. He was a man at ease with wasting an evening.

"I guess not," she said, lingering a moment on his elegant features that many women had explored intimately, but which were a mystery to the map of her imagination.

"We established you had a date also, and therefore you were going to brush your hair or something." He crumpled his napkin. "Is it a date or not for you, then? Just asking,"

She laughed, glancing down to see an ink stain on one of his fingers that rested on the table. She liked this casual detail.

"I know," she said.

"What do you know?"

"That you are teasing me."

"I see." His eyes were so vivid that suddenly she didn't feel sure of anything.

Rita repeated the punch line of a joke in a movie, and their laughter sounded raucous in the elegant Il Tarocco. Beautiful young women breaking into peals of laughter, they took turns reminding each other of more jokes. Gianni jumped up and did a fast turn, enacting something of which they were all speaking.

"Gangster! Liar!" Rita and Annalisa cried out in unison, repeating lines from the movie.

"Have you seen this movie?" Renata asked Cosimo.

"It's crap," he replied, pouring her more wine.

"Just a little," she said, indicating a half inch.

They felt close, invisible to others. He filled her glass well beyond the half inch she had requested.

"I'm trying to get you drunk to take you to bed," he said playfully, but as was usual with Cosimo, she had no idea what he really meant. "It's getting too difficult to do it in any other way."

The waiter brought an elegant chocolate cake, with swirls of cream forming a Fabergé-like design, topped by long, thin candles.

"I'm very gentle in bed, you know," Cosimo murmured, eyes half closed. He rested one cheek on his palm, elbow propped on the table.

"Why? Are we going to bed?" she asked with a laugh. But she felt lonely when he looked away.

"Just saying."

Loredana made a wish and blew out the candles, holding her long hair back. Her neck was beautiful and her gestures suggested an old-fashioned grace. Tito opened the champagne, in an elaborate sequence as ancient as the ritual of birthdays. Papoozi used to make a disaster of it, spilling and spraying the champagne, sending the children into irrepressible giggles. Gianni poured, his thin wrist tilted with military precision, his lips soft and smiling. He poured a full glass for Renata.

"Men are of one mind, see?" Cosimo pointed at her glass with one finger.

"I know," she said with a smile. "I was a little boy once, remember?"

The murmur of conversation picked up around them.

"He's handsome," Cosimo said of Gianni. "There is a nice quality about him. Unspoiled, yes?" he said in English.

"Yes."

Suddenly Gianni seemed to stand alone, and he turned toward Renata, pushing his curls away from his face, a question in his eyes.

"He has no clue of what he possesses," Cosimo said. "You must get older to know what you have and what you could lose, drink a few too many, be a lonely ass who speaks too much at dinner, and remembers everything. He's great. You should like him."

Tito brought them two slices of cake. Clean shaven, striking in his white shirt, Tito seemed thrilled at celebrating at Il Tarocco, even though he preferred a *tavola calda*. "Men sit wearing jackets in restaurants, and must talk and talk," Tito used to scoff. Tonight his face seemed weary, but his smile was jubilant, which made her happy.

"Great evening, Tito!" Renata said, squeezing his arm gently.

"You want a kiss, I see." Tito bent to give her a quick peck on the cheek. She felt a little catch in her throat. In its informality, so unlike Tito, the kiss felt like goodbye.

"Hey, and what about me?" said Cosimo.

"Jerk." Tito obliged, then set the plates with cake in front of them. "Cosimo, I'm glad you are here," he said, with a casual affection Renata envied.

The music picked up, with a catchy tune Renata didn't recognize. Tito sat by Loredana, an arm around her shoulders. Couples started gathering to dance. Rita stood up, cheeks flushed, and Annalisa followed her with a little shrug.

Loredana pulled Gianni by the hand. "Coming?"

From her seat at the table, Renata watched them all go.

24

Cosimo fumbled in his pocket, then set a pack of Muratti Ambassador cigarettes and matches by his plate. "Come back to Milan," he said.

The prospect of returning frightened her. It seemed so simple. Against the strength of his energy, her life in America seemed but a filigree. "Fuck's sake, Milan is your home. You have a house here and a brother." He didn't say *and me*, but the words were present in the wild hurt of his eyes. "C'mon. Do you ever wake up in Minneapolis and say *No, I can't. This isn't it?*"

"I said the same thing to myself waking up in Milan."

"But in Minneapolis you can decide you're going home."

"Ah, that."

"That."

One year, Papoozi had given her a dollhouse for Christmas, with no furniture or dolls. She'd liked the empty rooms and made-up stories that the inhabitants had all been killed. Nobody had survived to go up the stairs and in and out of the rooms alone. A train had run over them all at a crossing. They saw it coming and held hands as they waited for it to arrive.

"Sure, why not?" Renata said recklessly, flinging her hair back. "Of course I could come home. I mentioned it, remember?"

"I take the question back." Cosimo was, as usual, quick to notice her mood shift.

"It's a good question."

"Too sentimental." He grinned. "How's life in Minneapolis?"

"Very good. It wasn't a big mistake or anything."

Renata saw the old shopping lists and photographs stuck to her refrigerator, the dark bedroom lit by streetlights. *Dear God.*

"It's not bad at all." Her voice sounded lively in an anxious way.

"I'm glad to hear that," Cosimo said. "It's not home, but it's something then." He leaned back, unbuttoned his left shirt cuff, then buttoned it back up, his concentration intent upon the delicate job.

"Yes, it's something," she said.

She thought again of her life in Minneapolis. Her mind seemed curiously unwilling to finish the images she started to draw. It occurred to her that she had liked not knowing what lay ahead. There was a bravery and foolishness to it that seemed, suddenly, immensely appealing. Papoozi had told her that when you moved away from a place you knew, you listened and watched with greater attention, as if you were a spy. You'd try to guess the lives of people next to you on the bus; you'd make them up. Everything was fluid, even you, he'd told her.

She glanced around the restaurant. The waiters moved among the tables like shadows underwater, lighting candles. The dance floor was crowded. Tito was dancing too, moving his arms around like a kid in gym class.

"No lighter for you tonight?" Renata took the matchbox from Cosimo and shook a match out—a stubby roll of paper and wax, just as she'd remembered. The paper could be opened into a cone, and when you lit the sulfur top, a ballerina in a white skirt twirled, burning, in the air.

"Want a last dance?" she asked, pulling a second match out to light the first to make it dance.

"Do I look like a man who wants a last dance?"

She could feel the question go to her head like a shot of grappa. "I don't know what a man wants."

"I want you to come back." He took the matches from her. "To Milan. Why not? Mind you, I don't play chess, my game of *briscola* is lousy, and I would take you skiing."

"I know you would."

They shared a light chuckle.

"What's holding you back?" he asked. "Anything else? Eventually, I'd need reading glasses. Do you have a problem with that?"

She imagined Cosimo's hair streaked with gray, the lines radiating from the corners of his eyes when he smiled.

"I'd keep an immaculate handkerchief in my purse, and I'd clean them for you," she said.

"I'm afraid I wouldn't clean your reading glasses."

"I know. I'd never be the one you do little things for."

"This is the big issue?"

"You'd sleep with beautiful women and ugly women and so-so women," she said.

"Why would I do that?"

"You always did, that's why," she said.

"Is that so?"

"I'm being polite. It's your adventure. Your India and America. No planes to fear, bags to pack."

"You are ruining the mood. Why? I don't understand you."

"You do. Perfectly."

They avoided each other's eyes by looking around, at the flowers that seemed made of wax, at the bottles of San Pellegrino in the middle of the tables.

It was the end of the song and everyone returned to their table. As Gianni walked back to his seat, he shot her an indecipherable look, which felt like a buzz, a high-pitched noise that only she could hear.

"So. It's a date, then?" Cosimo broke the silence.

Their eyes locked.

"It's a date," she agreed, pulling her hair away from her face.

"By the way, your hair looks great as it is. Always has."

Tito stopped Gianni to share an amusing anecdote, but Gianni, distracted, glanced toward her.

"What the hell is going on for you in Minneapolis?" Cosimo asked, rearranging a glass, then a spoon on the tablecloth.

"It's confusing."

"What's the confusion?" he asked.

"The kind I like."

The waiter came by to take away the dessert plates.

"Have you spoken of the American election with what's-his-name yet?" Cosimo inquired. "Don't. If I remember correctly, the other night it sank our ship altogether."

"I won't speak of the election," she said.

"We were also quite drunk, I believe."

"I won't speak of the election, and I won't get drunk," she said with a laugh.

"You are determined to have your way tonight with this attractive sexy specimen?" Cosimo asked with a pointed glance at Gianni. "I can't see why. Ah, women."

"Women."

The waiter brought coffee. Tables were emptying around them, and Renata could detect a faint sound of traffic outside.

"Time for presents!" Rita declared cheerfully.

"Give us a moment," said Tito. "Let's take a breath."

Annalisa proposed that they tell ghost stories or love stories. She had plenty of both, but they were best around a fireplace.

Renata caught Gianni's look over his glass.

"Do you have a gift for Loredana?" Cosimo asked.

"Yes. You?"

"No." He rustled in his pocket. "But I have one for you."

It was a pen, the kind tourists buy, with a transparent bubble along the shaft, where the miniature reproduction of famous tourist spots slide up and down when the pen is tilted. This pen displayed in miniature the Milan Duomo. Renata felt strangely touched. The pen was a small delicate thing, a reminder of her messy days in Milan when she was young.

"Thank you," she said in a whisper, touched by his tender gesture.

"It's nothing," he scoffed. "You always carried twenty like this in your backpack."

"I like it," she said with a shaky voice. "I really like it, Cosimo."

"You would."

He stood up abruptly.

"I must go," he said.

"I'm sorry you have to," she breathed.

"Good, because you won't see me again any time soon." He gave her a quick peck.

"You really have to go? Now?" she asked.

"Yes."

He went around, shaking hands briskly and efficiently, like a political candidate seeking office, then he walked out quickly without looking back. The things Renata had meant to say blurred and faded with each step he took. *He's leaving*, she thought, taking it in. She visualized him going into the night as snow began to fall, the floating flakes illuminated by the light of the lampposts. Then it was Steve she envisioned walking alone under the lampposts, dipping in and out of the light and into the darkness in between, his collar up against the cold.

Tito was across the room alone. She quietly joined him. They stood in silence like passengers on the deck of a ship.

"I need the phone back for a moment," she said. "Can I have it?"

"Sure," Tito said handing her the phone.

"Did you have a fight, you and Cosimo?" he asked her. "Or was that Cosimo being Cosimo?"

She agreed that it was just Cosimo being Cosimo, but she felt it wasn't so. She went to the patio, watching Tito from afar with a new curiosity. He massaged his neck, standing at a distance from the group. She liked to think of the comfort of his future domestic life.

She called Tessa.

"Hello," Tessa said after the fourth ring. "Hello. Renata? Is that you? What's up?"

Tessa's voice was filled with a contagious vitality.

"I'm here at a restaurant in Milan full of middle-aged couples. One is starting a sing-along in a whisper, and I am thinking of you and the clinic. I feel I have been gone for so long."

There was a little silence.

"Not that long," Tessa said. "Are you going to tell me you are not coming back? Is that it?"

"Why do you say this?"

"Diagnosis. You sound tipsy. Don't make decisions."

Renata wanted nothing more than to crash on her bed in Minneapolis at that very moment. She missed the sound of the radio from the apartment upstairs, the sight of coyotes limping through the snow on Excelsior Boulevard, the narrow second-hand bookstores filled with tattered books, like one might find in a grandparent's attic. On Tuesday, Raynard—the patient who read her Tarot cards in payment—would fling his long legs off the treatment bed. *How did my last Tarot reading turn out?* he would ask.

"I'm busy working here," Tessa said. "We have a new paying patient. I have to go. You know, I had a strange dream that you called me in the middle of the night and told me you decided to leave Steve. Hey, listen. Is it the thought of returning home to Steve that makes you think of staying in Milan? Hello? And what about me?"

"No, I'm not staying. I did call you in the middle of the night; you could barely stay awake." Someone in the restaurant was playing the piano now, and she imagined Steve, in one silly night at a bar, playing piano with great precision, leaning into the music and away. "I decided that I am leaving Steve. We'll talk when I'm back. But I need a place to stay."

"Jesus, okay. My couch works?"

They shared a light laugh. That couch, smelling of Tessa's dog, had always been a cozy island when things got complicat-ed, and it had followed Tessa from one apartment to another with its implacable old springs. Thinking of that couch, Renata felt that she would have no difficulty speaking to Steve. The two of them had talked and talked in her head, but even her imagined conversations turned moody and raw. They had badly wanted to be each other's big love forever. They'd left secret notes in surprising places. Once Steve had left quite a few inside an umbrella, creating a snowstorm of love when she'd opened it in the rain.

"Okay, make sure you're heading back. I can't vote for Hil-lary twice."

"Oh. Hm. We should talk about that."

"Oh God. What now?"

"In person. Let's chat in Minneapolis."

Renata returned to the table. Gianni sat by her, hands bur-
rowed in his pockets, his face turned to her. The intensity of
his gaze made her a little dizzy. The chatter around them felt as
irritating as a TV left on for days.

"Want to go to the patio?" he asked.

He followed the direction of her eyes. The restaurant entrance was empty. In that moment, it seemed that a lot more
passed between them. They were both thinking of Cosimo, she
thought.

"It's going to be cold," she said, as if this were her primary
concern. "But I'm used to it in Minnesota."

"We can go anywhere you wish. But I'd like you to ask me,"
he said, looking ruffled and spirited, like a little bird. "Don't say
all right or *I guess*. You ask me to go somewhere together, if you
want to."

"Well, this takes the prize for the most awkward first-date
conversation, doesn't it?" she said, with a laugh.

"This can also take care of the first date altogether. If you
wish." He rubbed the shaving cut on his cheek. It was clear that
any graceful stalling would be of little use.

They sat, as if seeking closeness in a foreign country. She
savored the silence.

"Why all this?" she said.

"Because you must want it exactly like I do."

The muted noise in the restaurant was broken by the clatter
of cutlery being dropped and chairs pushed back.

"I want a date with you," she said. "But I am leaving tomorrow. I am going home. I want you to know I truly am leaving.
I am doing it. I have been with one man for years. I have never
done something like this with another man."

"I know. I do know that. We could take a little break and talk
more? Shall we go to the patio? Do you mind if I smoke?"

"I don't mind." She actually wanted him to smoke. When

he exhaled the smoke would touch her skin, warm from his breath; it would cling to her clothes, and she would smell it in the morning. "You smoke Marlboro? Muratti?"

"Anything. If nothing else is left, I smoke Gauloises like a legionnaire or Virginia Slims like a girl."

Gianni's casual playfulness had returned. She wanted to ruffle his hair, tell him how happy he made her. Il Tarocco seemed austere against his lithe figure. The tables, now empty, were strewn with napkins, abandoned as if by schoolchildren rushing off to recess. Friends and lovers had spent hours in those chairs, at those tables, Renata thought, wanting and telling stories.

"Hey, Gianni," Tito called. "Reni. Hey! It's time for the presents. Loredana is getting tired."

Renata glanced at Loredana, noticing the heavy abandon in her posture, her joints drained as if by a magnetic force. "Of course," Renata agreed, and Tito looked at her with such gratitude that she flushed.

"Renata," Rita proclaimed, "America goes first! You're the super guest."

"No. I'd like to go last," Renata said to a murmur of protest. Everyone seemed impatient to have it their own way. Renata tried to explain, but no clear words came.

"Don't you speak in a whisper," Papoozi had told her as a child. "Never."

"I'm going last," she said loudly, resolute. Papoozi had demanded courage in facing the future; he'd read to her about blind bats that were guided by their senses, living in complete darkness without fear.

In the fairy tales she'd discovered as a grown-up, the first two wishes were fulfilled; the third brought the chaos of the unexpected. Her third wish had been to understand where her home was.

"What present shall we open, then?" Rita asked.

Loredana opened Gianni's first. From the wrapping paper, she pulled a gray backpack that made her squeal with joy.

"You remembered that I liked it!"

"Hey, Gianni! My birthday is coming up," Annalisa said, inspecting the backpack. "This is one fantastic cousin you have!"

Next came Annalisa and Rita's gift—Guerlain perfume in a golden box and a gift certificate for a spa treatment. "We could go to the spa together if you lived here. There is a new one, in Piazza San Babila," Loredana said to Renata with a smile.

Renata didn't care about the new spa in Piazza San Babila, but she returned Loredana's smile, attempting to look interested.

"Last gift!" Loredana called out, pointing at the small bag. She pulled out the gloves and scarf. "Oh! These are so beautiful! Thank you!"

"They are from Flavia. My present is the card with the images of cats," Renata told her.

A silence followed as the crappy card was passed around for all to admire. Rita and Annalisa tried valiantly to say something nice about it, the way one comforts a friend after getting a terrible haircut.

"Open it!" Tito urged, enthusiastically.

Loredana ripped the card open, prompting a forced cheer from everyone but Renata. She stared at the wineglass in front of her, which Cosimo had filled to the brim.

Loredana read the card to herself in a whisper, gesturing wildly with one hand.

"What?" Tito asked. "What is it?"

"Read it." Loredana passed it to him. "The apartment in Via Saverio goes to us. She is giving it to us! We have a place to live. With best wishes and great happiness for a happy marriage from your older sister."

"Wait." Tito looked at Renata. "You're giving us the apartment?" Renata grinned, a little surprised at herself too.

"It's not from me, it's from Papoozi. That's what he wanted," she said softly.

The waiters seemed interested too, smiling with nods of congratulations, without knowing exactly why.

"It's like winning the lottery!" Rita cheered. "You lovebirds won the lottery!"

"Reni, the lottery!" Tito laughed. "Remember?"

"Someone in the family had to win the lottery eventually," she said.

Every Friday evening when Papoozi brought home the lottery ticket, Renata recalled overhearing her parents' ferocious arguments late into the night about how they would spend their winnings.

"A *scialatella* first—a lush, leisurely dinner. Then a new refrigerator and a car," Papoozi had insisted.

"A car! A new house with two bathrooms, balconies, and a garden for my roses," her mother had interjected.

"Too showy, everybody will know. The children might be kidnapped."

And on and on they went.

Every Sunday Papoozi used to slowly rip the ticket up over the garbage pail, with a look of disdain.

Tito drew Renata and Loredana into a hug. The others cheered with excited outbursts and a frenzy of congratulations.

"It's from Papoozi," Renata repeated.

More champagne was passed around, and they all sat down for a last toast.

"To Tito and Loredana!" cheered Annalisa, Rita, and Gianni.

They raised their full glasses. Renata raised hers, silently, to Papoozi. I have done my duty as the firstborn, the one who fulfills the father's wish, she thought. They all emptied their glasses in unison. Tito's eyes teared up, whereas hers were dry. She held his stare. *Make me cry.*

25

The street was empty, the air crisp. Renata and Gianni walked out of Il Tarocco, their collars turned up. A thin layer of ice cracked under their feet. Headlights cut across their bodies in a dense amber color that pierced the light fog.

"In Minneapolis they don't believe me. They think I'm kidding about the use of yellow headlights in winter."

"What else don't they believe?" Gianni asked, stopping at the corner. His cream Vespa was parked under a stone archway that led to an enclosed courtyard.

"That I have a small family, and I don't come to visit every summer."

"Why don't they believe it?"

"Italians are supposed to have big families. Money to fly back, I guess."

Past the archway a typical tenement building rose with a sequence of identical doors along a shared balcony. Bicycles, visible in the dark, leaned against a wall by a pile of wood. It all gave out a musty, spicy fragrance she loved. The wondrous hidden courtyards of Milan.

"Vespa okay with this cold?"

"Yes, sure. It's not that cold." Renata felt talkative, as if she were meeting someone after traveling alone for days. "You want to smoke here now?"

"Yes."

She was happy that he agreed. His hair was rumpled, his eyes red-rimmed. She tried to imagine what his first love had looked like, what she'd said when he was with her. She wondered if she'd blushed as easily as he did, and if they'd laughed about it together.

"Let's go under the archway. It's warmer there," he said.

Shutters and doors were closed all around, which gave the appearance of a neighborhood quarantine. A dirty white dog limped along the sidewalk, stopped, watched them for a moment, then crossed the street.

"He doesn't like us," Renata said, with a laugh, her voice echoing imperceptibly under the archway. "Are you cold?"

"No." He unbuttoned his coat, fumbling for cigarettes and lighter. "I like you." He lit a Marlboro. "I hope you come back. I'm sure the dog wants that too; he is just shy with American women."

"I just live there."

"No." He let out little puffs of smoke while he spoke. "You are who you are where you live."

"I don't think so."

"Well, you should."

She pulled her hair back against a gust of wind.

"How many rings of smoke can you make?" Renata asked.

"Not sure." He inhaled, then exhaled three perfect rings. "Three. If you lean against me, I can go up to five. Possibly six, if you put your arm around my waist. The sky's the limit if you put your hand under my coat."

"You'd have to open your coat in the cold."

"It's open." He leaned back against the archway and turned his head to her. She put her hand under his coat, feeling the warmth of his body. *Do something you want to do that you cannot take back*, Tito had said.

"What's the strangest thing you have ever seen in Minneapolis?" he asked.

"Coyotes. And a white squirrel."

"You didn't dream it?" he asked, his voice husky against her hair.

"I'm not sure." She put her hand back inside his coat.

"Cool." He smiled.

She imagined herself in his life. This smile would be in the mirror when she looked up, brushing her teeth.

"Tell me something about you I won't believe," he said.

"I don't lie."

His fingers quivered slightly holding the cigarette. "Is that right?"

"So, I am American?" She could not see his eyes clearly in the dim light.

He brought the cigarette to his lips and took a slow drag.

"To me. It makes me a bit shy. Not you being American, but the fact that you stayed long enough to be considered one. I would have returned at the first glitch. I'm the only son of a widow; I'm too soft."

"What would you like to be?" she asked.

"Old."

"Do you really want to?"

"Yes. I would have nothing to lose. I'd do anything I want. Travel. Talk to strangers in a language I barely speak. Do everything I'm afraid of doing in places I'm scared to go."

"Truly?"

"Yes," he said. "I'd like to be able to do that."

"Marry rich then," she said softly, unable to take her eyes off his skin, admiring its luminous, fragile quality in the dark. He turned his head away as he shifted his back against the brick wall.

"Is your husband a rich American?" he asked.

"No."

"American?"

"Yes, not rich."

She didn't like to have the American husband there with them. She decided it was time to start letting him go. She took a deep breath.

"Can I have a cigarette?" she asked.

He took one out, unhurried, placed it between her lips, then leaned in to light it. The first hit of smoke triggered a hiccup of pain in her throat. She inhaled more deeply and teared up. Gianni dropped his cigarette, crushing it beneath his heel without breaking eye contact.

Renata smiled at him, tears trickling down her cheeks as she inhaled again. She took another drag, wiping her cheeks with her fingertips.

"Perhaps you would like to stop?"

She nodded, dropped the cigarette, and stepped on it.

"We should go somewhere warm," he said.

"Yes."

"Want to go to my house?"

"Yes."

She found a Kleenex in her pocket and dabbed her tears, as she remembered her mother doing after kneeling in prayer.

"Have you ever driven a Vespa?"

"No."

"This one is solid. Gets you through anything. It's terribly fast." He talked, holding her gaze. "Want to take us home?"

"Me?" She had a nervous smile.

"Say yes. I want to be in a memory you can't forget."

"I will remember you."

"I want to make sure. Will you drive us home?"

She looked up at a flight of birds crossing the sky over the courtyard.

"Yes," she said.

"Can you do it?"

"I want to."

"Okay then."

"Okay." Her hand reached for his hair, let it slide between her fingers. He let out a breath of release at her touch.

"I might come to America," he said.

She traced his jaw with her fingertips, sensing the pulse of his throat when he swallowed. She passed her thumb over his lips, touched the warmth of a sigh.

"How's your English?"

"Just okay." She slid both hands under his coat, and he glanced down to where her hands had disappeared. "But I play piano. I'm a computer wiz."

She tugged his shirt up. "This is not a job interview."

"I know. You're running your fingers over my bare skin."

They fell on his bed, still dressed, and lay there, floating on a faint smell of rosewood incense, sinking together into the silence. It was her first time in this home, in this bed, with this man, a man she'd just met a few days before. He reached for her hand. His was thin and delicate, pale like the hand of an impoverished pianist. She turned to look at his head on the pillow, at the thick tangle of his hair. Their eyes met. I don't know who you are and what this is, she thought. She felt unspeakably happy.

ACKNOWLEDGMENTS

I am beyond grateful to Peter Geye for his invaluable time, attention, and insight. He has been an extraordinary ally. I also thank the Loft Literary Center for creating a welcoming space where writers can meet and work in a consistent way.

I am indebted to Sena Jeter Naslund and Karen Mann for establishing The Naslund-Mann School of Writing, a creative community where writers flourish. I thank Sena for inspiring me with her passion and writing.

I am privileged to have such an extraordinary mentor and now friend in my life as Robin Lippincott, who is always challenging me to do better and believing I can. My gratitude goes to Eleanor Morse, who made my writer's journey feel less lonely and always meaningful, to Rachel Harper for her generosity and wisdom when my enthusiasm did not match my skills, and to Roy Hoffman, who sustained my writing with expert guidance and great clarity. I will always remember Phil Deaver for his warmth and support.

I would also like to give a warm thank you to Elliott Foster, Jon Pipkin, Sandra Scofield, and Sarah Stonich for their part in this journey.

Deena Metzger filled my life with hope and magic in my first steps in my writing and still does. My most heartfelt thank you.

Jacob Bennett, Katie Boyer, Cindy Brady, Julia Brown, Rick Brown, David Domine, Jean Faraca, Kelly Hill, and Teddy Jones have encouraged me by offering advice and companionship in our exchanges about each other's work.

For their generous feedback, I am grateful to my colleagues and friends Debra Blake, Paula Granquist, Coralee Grebe, Amber James, Kurt Johnson, Christopher Johnston, Todd Kortemeier, Brookelynn Espegard, Rachel MacDonald, and Lisa Larson.

A special thank you to Holly Watson.

I am deeply grateful to Jaynie Royal for her fabulous work and to the entire team at Regal House Publishing for their commitment to *The War Ends at Four.*

Grazie mille to my family. My husband Peter, my daughter Daria, and my son Gabriel are so marvelous and supportive that I occasionally question if I made them up. Finally, I am thankful for my beloved golden retriever, without whose faithful presence this novel would have been written in half the time and with none of the pleasure.